"Are you ready for an edge-of-your-seat thriller featuring an awkward ten-year-old hero with a bum ticker and other medical problems on the run from sinister government agents who will stop at nothing to retrieve the McGuffin (spoiler alert: it's a medallion with supernormal powers) in his possession? Yes? Then *Hollis Whittaker* is the story for you! . . . A gripping, thrill-filled yarn with clearly delineated characters, both good and bad, the story unfolds as the chase races through the States. . . . CB Shanahan has a marvelous knack of storytelling, and a wonderful way of describing, action, scenery, and the thoughts and feelings of young people. This book would be a great gift for the young teen in your life. Or the young-at-heart adult. Action thriller, mystery story, adventure yarn, friendship and bonding, science/supernatural fiction? You decide. It's all there. In fact, it would make a heckuva movie or mini-series! My highest recommendation!"
—**Seamus Kennedy**, Co-Author of *Clean Cabbage in the Bucket*

"The present-day and World War II–era are cleverly combined in the suspenseful novel, *Hollis Whittaker* by CB Shanahan. Adventure and science merge with a hint of the paranormal in creating this fabulous story. Even though the plot moves between parallel time and space, the continuity of the storyline remains intact. It has a superb story arc that builds to a climactic and intriguing finale. The anticipation of what is going to happen next and the anxiety of how the characters are going to outwit their predators keeps the intensity of the story alive. This is an exciting novel that will appeal to those who love out of the ordinary adventures with ordinary heroes. As there are some mature threads within the story, it is probably most suitable for twelve-year-olds and older."
—**Susan Sewell** for **Readers' Favorite, 5-Star Review!**

"*Hollis Whittaker* is one of my favorite books of the year. Like the year, it is surprising, with a fair bit of tension to the journey and much uncertainty ~~ ~ ~ ~ ~ ~ ~
Add the virus of some governn

know it, and it is the perfect, timely escape. *Hollis Whittaker* is a five-star fun book, highly recommended for the excellent writing, drama and education, too."
—**John O'Brien**, *Ohio Irish American News*

"This first novel by CB Shanahan is a triumph of artistry, energy, and inspiration. The author's treatment of the tactile and the metaphysical are deftly brewed into a rollicking, time-bending escapade that pulls one headfirst through every space and corner. As someone who has taught this genre for fifty years, I highly recommend *Hollis Whittaker* to anyone who enjoys a well-crafted, compelling adventure tale."
—**Steve Romanoff**, Professor Emeritus and singer-songwriter

HOLLIS WHITTAKER

Book design, cover design and digital imaging by Deirdre Wait, High Pines Creative
Cover images: tree by CB Shanahan; others © Getty Images

Published by: Encircle Publications, LLC
P.O. Box 187
Farmington, ME 04938

Visit: http://encirclepub.com

Sign up for Encircle Publications newsletter and specials
http://eepurl.com/cs8taP

Printed in U.S.A.

HOLLIS WHITTAKER
by CB Shanahan

I

5:27 p.m., Wednesday, August 22, 1945

Winded and trembling from fleeing through the woods for most of the afternoon, Eleanor Cole finally felt safe enough to pause. She rested an arm on a maple tree and ripped off her shoe. A heel had snapped off her pump a ways back.

The air felt good across the sole of her foot, but she was in no position to wallow. She slipped the shoe back on and removed the other, pounding it against the tree until that heel broke off. It was better to have flats anyway. Her ankles had twisted several times when her heels had met with soft earth in the scramble of the past few hours.

She replaced the second shoe and squatted at the base of the tree, head in her hands, the bark grating into her back. She was trying to keep quiet, but the sobbing became uncontrollable in a moment where she finally felt alone. The dried leaves crunched into her tartan skirt as she dropped onto her butt.

She desperately wanted a drink of water. After so much running, her mouth was as dry as day old toast and a metallic taste of blood in the back of her throat extended all the way down to her lungs. The exertion from the afternoon must have robbed her of every ounce of spare moisture in her body.

There was a water bubbler two rooms down from her office, but that was a room she wasn't likely to be seeing again. There was no fan to cool her, no air conditioning or ice cold soda pop.

The forest threatened to collapse around her under the weight of humid boughs and sagging leaves. The vines strangled the tree trunks and dangled down branches, nearly brushing her shoulders as another feeble wind cut through the area. The touch of muggy air offered inadequate relief from the heat steaming off of her body. The temperature was still in the upper 80s and a potent smell of baking leaves rose from the ground. Normally she loved the outdoors, but she was beginning to feel nauseous. Her untucked blouse was soaked through with sweat and had gone from pure white to a translucent dust rag gray.

This morning she had spent an hour fashioning her hair like Rita Hayworth's, a new start, she figured, to motivate her out of her comfort zone and onto something beyond drone work. That had fallen to hell, too. People always said she resembled the movie star, so she tried to play it up, add a spark to things, but Rita wouldn't look this disheveled after a month in the Amazon.

They were going to get her and she was frantic with thoughts of what they'd do. This morning she was nobody, a 25-year old country girl still living with her parents, tending to the chickens and struggling through a joyless job to save up for her own house in D.C. This afternoon, she was public enemy number one. The whole state—no, the whole country—would be looking for her. And there was no doubt the search had begun.

But they wouldn't find the tom-tom. It was gone. She'd tossed the medallion into a stream earlier just in case they caught up with her. Col. Clay's career would be ruined.

She tried to calm down, controlling the tears and raising her head. She needed to get her bearings. Her breathing slowed. The sobbing spasm in her diaphragm eased. Except for the occasional blustering of the forest floor, it was silent. There was no one else. Any approaching footsteps would be apparent across the leaf-strewn ground and she couldn't hear anything, even when she strained to focus. She leaned around the tree and caught a glimpse of the lowering sun through the canopy. That meant she was still heading east. Good.

Twice a second her head throbbed with the beat of her heart. She rose to her feet and took a long, deep breath, trying to clear her mind. Even with the relative calm of the moment, she couldn't stay put. Losing the heels would help. Pulling off her slip was a possibility. It would free up her movement, but she couldn't risk leaving something that obvious lying on the ground. It would be far too blatant a clue and would make it easy to assess the direction she was heading. Tugging the blasted thing off anyway, she tucked it under her arm. It could be used to wipe sweat off her forehead.

She kicked some leaves over the discarded heel, then charged forward. She didn't need to run anymore, but she couldn't dawdle.

It dawned on her that she didn't have her pocketbook, so no ID, no money. It seemed like such a minor detail when she thought about what was at stake, but her head was clearer now and she knew she needed a longer-term plan than just getting away. Home was out of the question. It was the first place anyone would look for her. Would they think to monitor her grandparents? Probably.

Who did she know in Amberton? That was in this general direction. No one. No one, besides Nellie. But they hadn't spoken since Nellie's family had moved fifteen years ago. The last she'd heard, Nellie was working in a shoe factory and had moved out of her parents' home. A woman on her own might understand her predicament, particularly since they'd been inseparable when they were younger. All right, she'd try for her old childhood friend. She might not even recognize the woman if she ran smack dab into her and she certainly didn't have an address for her. At this point, it didn't matter. It was a destination and that was better than nothing. She'd make for Amberton and look up Nellie in the telephone book. And if she had married, well bad luck to her. The plan would have to change.

She marched to the east and after a long while, she could make out the sound of running water to the north—the Passaconic River. She couldn't be that far from Route 36. It wasn't a well-traveled road, but it led to Amberton. She could stick to the tree line and if a car approached, she'd try to determine if it was friendly. If it didn't seem safe, she'd duck back into the woods before the driver could see her.

It took an hour and a half before she reached the road, a much longer hike than she had figured. And by now, the bugs had begun biting with abandon, attracted as they were to clammy skin. Swatting only seemed to attract more of them.

The blacktop cut through the thick of woods, a single sliver of civilization dividing miles and miles of forest. The pine trees had left layers of needles along the roadside, blown clear of the tar by the speeding motorists. Behind her, the sun was sinking into the horizon. She couldn't see it through the trees, but the sky had gone a bluish gray with a thick cloud cover and the light was vanishing from the day. The air was muggy and still, the smell of cooking asphalt rising up from the tarmac. Like an oven, the road would continue to give off heat for hours. She could feel it from two feet away.

She considered a passing motorist's perception, that she might be seen as a vagrant. Nobody in their right mind would pick her up. She straightened out her blouse and tucked it in, running her fingers through her hair in an attempt to rein it in. Then she set out north on the no-man's land between the woods and the road. Every few minutes, when she heard a car or truck approaching, she would bound to the left and duck behind a tree, scrutinizing the vehicle and its occupants. If anything looked too military-like, she stayed hidden. Several cars in a row had been driven and occupied by young men with crew cuts. It might have been safe to try to stop them, but this wasn't an instance where she could take a chance, so she let them pass.

She heard the telltale hum of another approaching car from the south. She was just past a bend in the road. It would be fifteen to twenty seconds before it was upon her, but because of the bend, she wouldn't have much time to examine the car or its driver. And on top of that, the light had mostly faded, making an accurate appraisal harder.

She hopped over a marshy bit of ground and hid herself behind a pine tree, her feet squishing into the waterlogged soil. The car was just on the other side of the corner.

It puttered into view. The interior was dark, but Eleanor could make out the silhouette of a hat. At least she thought it was a hat. She squinted. Yes, it was a hat, a lady's hat. The chances of spotting a woman driving on her own at this time of day were low, but it was the opportunity Eleanor was hoping for. She stepped into the road and waved an arm over her head. The headlights rose up to meet her and about ten yards away, the car crept to a stop, its engine idling. Eleanor was on display for the driver, the full power of the headlights shining directly on her, blinding her. She held up a hand to shade her eyes, fully aware that her grubby clothes, messy hair and the slip tucked under her left arm might scare the woman away.

For a few seconds nothing happened. She was like a deer in the light. Then she slogged to the driver's side. The scarlet red Ford Deluxe seemed fairly new or was perhaps just well maintained, its exhaust billowing out from the tailpipe. The window was half-rolled down and as she approached, the older woman in the car discreetly locked the door. The woman was in her early- to mid-sixties wearing a small-brimmed hat with a large ribbon. She looked guarded.

"I'm so sorry," Eleanor said. "My car's broken down at our cabin and I've had to trudge through the woods on my own. I'm so sorry."

The woman paused for a moment before easing up a bit. "Oh my dear, that's all right. I'll just let you in." She stretched across the passenger seat and unlocked the door.

Eleanor smiled and circled around the nose of the car. "Thank you so much," she said as she hopped in, her skirt gliding easily over the bench seat. She pulled her slip onto her lap breathing in the car's new leather scent.

The woman slowly accelerated the car, the breeze through the windows refreshing Eleanor's spirits, making her feel somewhat normal again, and helping to clear the feeling of mosquitoes on her skin.

"Were you heading into Amberton?" the woman asked, seeming feebler than Eleanor expected.

"Yes, that would be wonderful." She stowed the slip between her hip and the door after catching the woman eyeing it. Then she checked herself and noticed the top buttons of her blouse had come undone. Trying not to draw attention, she buttoned them back up.

"Is your cabin close?" the woman asked. "I'm sorry, what did you say your name was?"

Eleanor couldn't leave a trail that anyone could follow. From this point forward she needed to become someone else. "I'm Evelyn, and no, we aren't close at all. I must have walked through seven or eight miles of countryside."

"Oh my! Is your husband not around? Did he leave you to find help on your own?"

Eleanor realized she had instinctively used "we," and the woman must have picked up on it. There was a generally accepted rule that a woman would have found a husband by her mid-twenties. It should have been an outdated notion, but she fought the urge to stand up on her soapbox. This wasn't the place for that. In fact she wondered if she'd ever be free enough to stand out in a crowd again. Blending in was the name of the game now.

"He's in France. Been stationed there for the past eight months. I spruce up the cabin every month while he's away. It keeps me busy and, honestly, I like to stay on top of things, otherwise the cabin will look abandoned. Sometimes I wonder where all of the dust comes from."

The woman nodded her head in commiseration. "By my age you'll have cleaned enough dust to make another house."

Eleanor's new life took shape over the next twenty minutes as it was created from sentence to sentence. Her fabrication included a husband in the army and a Labrador retriever named Chester. And though the thought infuriated her, she had cast herself as a stay-at-home wife. She wouldn't live anymore acquiescing to egotistical men. She couldn't. But for the time being, it was best not to raise too many red flags. The older generation expected women in their mid-twenties to have a husband and she needed to avoid ruffling any feathers, especially with an older woman, who was likely to hold conservative views on marriage. Her right hand remained cupped over her left to hide her naked ring finger.

The woman at the car's helm was named Margaret, her hair curled in starchy ringlets. She'd been married for forty years to a gentle stick of a man named Simon who managed a Sears and Roebuck Department Store. They had three grown daughters, and she was just returning from visiting her eldest, Carol, who had a husband serving in Japan.

The full darkness of evening had descended upon the women as they drove. A flaxen quarter moon occasionally made itself known, but it was mainly irradiating the cloud cover from above. Every few minutes a car or truck passed in the opposite direction, its lights causing temporary blindness for the women. The woods on either side of the road were black. Eleanor could only make out the first row of trees as the headlights of the Deluxe overexposed them, then they quickly disappeared into the darkness, flitting by the passenger window.

As they approached a hill, Eleanor noticed an increasing amount of light coming over its crest, more than just an oncoming vehicle. Something hit her as wrong. They had passed a sign for Amberton not long before and it said the town was still five miles away.

"Is that Amberton already?" she asked.

The car slowed a bit on the hill as the engine struggled. Margaret stayed silent for a few seconds longer than Eleanor would have liked. "Well, that *shouldn't* be. Amberton's still a couple miles from here. That's someone's headlights, dear."

Eleanor instinctively braced herself as they neared the apex, clutching the side of the door. There was too much light. "Let me out," she said.

Margaret turned toward her passenger. "What's that?"

"Let me out. I need to get out!" Eleanor grabbed the door handle as the car climbed the hill at forty miles per hour. She placed her shoulder against the door. "Margaret please, stop the car!"

Margaret slowed a bit. "What's the matter Evelyn? It's just another car. Are you okay?"

"No, I need to get out now!" The Ford was still moving at a good clip. Eleanor wondered if she should chance leaping out.

"Oh my gosh Evelyn, what is it?"

The car crested the hill and a roadblock became evident fifty yards away, forest on both sides of the pavement. There were two cars, barricades, several very imposing men and a harsh light on a stand beating down on the road. One of the men was holding up a hand signaling for Margaret to stop.

Eleanor was trapped. If she jumped out now, the men would definitely give chase. This had been set up for her. She knew it. She'd managed to escape through the woods before, but she'd had a much more advantageous start earlier. Perhaps Margaret would convince the men she was a friend. Her vision narrowed, the fight or flight instinct fully engaged.

She froze.

As the Ford rolled to a stop next to the lead man, Margaret lowered the window fully. The man was easily over six feet tall, a dark unbuttoned suit jacket and fedora pulled low to his eyebrows. "Good evening ma'am," he said, glancing at Margaret and then at her passenger. But his eyes stayed a fraction of a second too long on Eleanor.

She yanked the handle and flung the door open, leaping out of the car and dropping her slip as she broke into a sprint for the woods.

The men at the roadblock straightened up and focused on the fleeing woman, the leader pulling a sidearm from beneath his jacket. He took aim at Eleanor and pulled the trigger. She went down face first just feet from the trees. The light was weaker where she had fallen, but there was enough bleeding over from the checkpoint to partially illuminate the spot where she'd fallen. The men all converged on her, the back of her dirty blouse steeped in blood, pumping from a wound in the center of the shirt, a hole blown right through the fabric. She moved her head to the right and her fingers twitched.

The lead man reached down and frisked her thoroughly. Then he wrenched her onto her back, her body limp, and he continued patting her down head to toe, without a thought for modesty. Eleanor's eyes stared blankly at the sky, her lips parted. She was gurgling as much as breathing. There was no exit wound on her chest. The bullet was still inside her.

The man straightened himself and looked down at her. "It's not here," he said.

"What do you mean, 'it's not here?'" The voice was Margaret's, who was standing by the car in the crook of the driver's door. Her tenderness had disappeared. This was the voice of authority.

The man didn't pull his gaze from Eleanor. "I mean it's not here."

Margaret stomped around the car, a tight gray skirt restricting her gait. She hooked around the passenger door and lifted Eleanor's slip from the pavement. "Here," she said, rifling through it before dropping it. "Goddammit!" She peered into the Deluxe's passenger seat. Her hat had slipped down a little and she snatched it off her head and threw it into the car, her stiff locks barely shifting. "Goddammit!" Her hair was gray, high and tight, her suit conservative. She spun around.

"Why the hell did you shoot her?"

The man didn't respond.

Margaret stepped toward them, stopping inches away from Eleanor's feet and leered down at the bloody body beneath her. "Where is it?" she snarled.

Eleanor's eyes didn't move.

"I thought I shot her in the side," said the man.

Margaret grabbed Eleanor's shoulder and pulled, exposing a back caked in dried leaves and a bullet hole directly in its center spurting out blood. Then she let go and the injured woman flopped back onto the ground. Margaret shot the man an angry scowl. "Well, you missed."

They glared at Eleanor. "Double check," Margaret said.

The man bent over Eleanor and ripped open her blouse, buttons popping off with the force. Enraged, he reached down to the bottom of her skirt and yanked it up. Eleanor let out moans of pain as he pulled her torso off the ground and continued jerking at the garment until it was bunched up around her waist. "Look for yourself!" he bawled.

Margaret kicked Eleanor's leg, which didn't even get a reaction from the incapacitated woman. "What did you do with it?"

Eleanor's breathing was short; her eyes had begun to glaze over. Margaret hovered over her for a few seconds, then leaned over and slapped Eleanor's face, knocking it to the side. It didn't rouse her. "Where is it?" Margaret seethed.

Nothing.

Margaret stood up straight, eyes widening, reached her arm out and took hold of the pistol the lead man had in his holster. The man relinquished the weapon without a word.

Margaret placed her foot in the center of Eleanor's bra and shifted her weight onto it, causing groans of pain and increased gurgling.

Eleanor rolled her head toward Margaret. The added weight on her chest made it impossible to breath.

"Goddammit!" Margaret screamed, her eyes wild and piercing, dragging Eleanor out of her listlessness. The two women glared at each other. Margaret pointed the gun at Eleanor's head, and put more of her weight on the dying woman's chest. The pain was unbearable for Eleanor. Her eyes rolled up in her skull. And Margaret pulled the trigger.

II

Present Day

"What are you watching?"

Hollis rolled his eyes. He'd hoped that by holing himself up in his room, his parents would leave him alone, but his father Graham had just broken the seal. Next he'd be telling the boy what a beautiful day it was outside and how there was a whole new neighborhood to explore.

"It's about the pyramids," he answered, clinging to the hopes that an educational show would supersede the requirement to "get some fresh air." He aimed the remote and turned up the volume, settling himself deeper into the pillow against his headboard. Maybe his father would accept that he was fully ensconced, and shouldn't be disturbed.

Hollis had bought several books on ancient Egypt and spent hours watching YouTube documentaries about it. Mummies and pyramids were of particular interest to him. His plan was to become an archeologist when he grew up... or a comic book writer.

"Well, Ramsses can wait," his father said. "I thought your mother told you to clean up your room."

The fifth grader surveilled his new room. It was half the size of his old bedroom, a dull gray box that would be his home for the foreseeable future. The same tiny television sat atop the same bureau, which he watched from the same bed. There wasn't even enough wall space to put up all of his posters.

But he'd thrown his dirty clothes in the hamper and shoved a bunch of toys under his bed. Was he supposed to do a spit shine or something? It looked clean to him. "I did," he said.

"Okay, we'll let your mother deal with that." His father, a heavyset man, lay down on the bed next to Hollis, creating a sinkhole that threatened to pull the boy in. Hollis had never met anyone who managed to breath at such a monstrous volume as his father, like the natural act took effort. They watched the show for a few seconds, the scent of Graham's aftershave still heavy despite the fact that it was the middle of the afternoon.

Graham wore tan shorts and a blue Polo shirt, his weekend attire, year round.

"Who's that dude?" the old man asked. His father sometimes feigned interest in something before getting around to his true objective. It was a transparent tactic and the boy had no choice but to play along with it. In this case, his father wasn't referring to the show, but the poster next to the TV.

"That's Kaos, King of the Orcs."

Kaos was an olive green beast covered in scars, whose muscles had their own muscles. The raging hulk had yellow eyes and strands of ashen hair wisping off his head. The Crag of Fire loomed behind Kaos, spewing forth magma and rock, an inferno that burst into the sky, fusing into ominous black clouds.

"Kaos, huh? He looks like a tough hombre. Doesn't that keep you up at night?"

"No."

They watched another few seconds of programming and then his father finally got to the point. He grabbed the remote between them and shut off the TV. "What say we go enjoy a bit of the day?"

"I was watching that," said Hollis.

"I know, but you can watch that anytime," Graham countered. "The ancient Egyptians are always on, but you don't get too many days like this, believe me."

Rolling his head back on the pillow, the ten-year-old released an extended groan.

"Come on, sport. Do your mother a solid."

Hollis hated being called sport. He wasn't any good at sports and, in fact, didn't even like them. And he wondered if his father just threw the term at him to deflect from his weight problem. Hollis knew he had a few extra pounds, but he wasn't fat like his old man, or like "Lumpy" Dobratz.

He rolled himself over and dangled his legs over the edge of the bed, resigned to his fate. Go out and play. It will do you good. He wasn't sure why it was so important. What was he going to do anyway? He didn't even know anyone in the neighborhood yet. It was a matter of going outside for the sake of going outside.

Then he thought back to Mike Trammel at his old school, who on several occasions had tried to convince Hollis that he'd been adopted. The first couple of times, Hollis didn't pay the boy's words any heed, but Mike had always spoken with such assuredness that Hollis began to wonder if he was right. He wasn't doing it to tease Hollis. It was always mentioned in a matter-of-fact way. Plus, Mike's parents had grown up with Hollis' parents, so they would have known.

Hollis cast a glance at his father. Other than being heavy, Hollis didn't overly resemble him... nor his mother for that matter. He didn't have any brothers or sisters. It just seemed impossible to know without his parents coming clean.

On the other hand, his parents were all he'd ever known. They cared for him. That much was obvious. Should it matter, even if they weren't his real parents?

Graham patted him on the back, groaning as he raised himself up from the bed. "Thanks pal," he said. "It might not be as terrible as you think." He made his way out the bedroom door, assuredly to relay to Hollis' mother that he'd roused the young boy.

Hollis strapped on a pair of sneakers from under the bed and trudged downstairs to the kitchen, sliding the glass door to the back yard open, a gentle wind wafting past him. His mother, Lonnie, was seated on a stool at the granite-topped island, a Scrabble board, half-played, laid out before her. She was mid-game with a friend over the phone. The fifth grader had tried to explain that she could just use her phone to play, but for some reason she liked to have the cardboard in front of her. He was beginning to suspect she used the game as an excuse to gossip.

His father, also loitering around the island, paid him no heed. The order had been given and the generals were in repose. From underneath the kitchen table, the family's bulldog regarded Hollis with indifference. Even Risley didn't want to go outside.

Hollis peered at the back lawn in need of a good mow and the line of trees on the outskirts of the property. A few cotton ball clouds flecked the sky, an admittedly beautiful day with little humidity and a slight breeze, just as his father had promised. The boy's eyes adjusted to the glare of a fully lit morning.

He stepped out, closing the glass door behind him and sauntered to the center of the yard, pausing to take in the surroundings, the pleasant scent from the fir and pine trees and the wind tousling his thin chestnut hair.

He cut around to the side of the house to the end of the wooden fence that separated their yard from their neighbor's and peeked out into the neighborhood. They were located halfway through a circular cul-de-sac, a newly constructed prefabricated set of homes, each just different enough from the previous to make the homeowners feel a sense of uniqueness. To Hollis, they all looked the same.

He liked their previous home. It was musty and creaky, and you could feel the wind blowing through the windows on blustery days, but it had character. An old wooden farmhouse with lots of land to explore.

He waited for signs of other kids, but there were none. In the week since they'd moved in, he'd spied a few outside playing, but right now the street was empty. He'd never lived in a neighborhood with other families and he didn't know if he'd fit in here.

Hollis sized up his house. This was it, the place he'd grow up. His father had a new job and that's the way it was. He and his best friend, Edgar used to stay up on weekends playing video games and eating Doritos. They still texted via their parents' phones, but it wasn't the same. No one else really liked the same games or TV shows as Hollis, or music or movies for that matter and chances were that none of the kids would.

With no siblings and no friends, he had to make an afternoon for himself now. He plodded out back again, kicking the occasional pinecone as far as he could. In a burst of inspiration, he decided to see how quickly he could make it to the back of the yard and exploded into a full-on sprint, stopping just beside a pine tree as he tagged it.

Due to a heart defect he'd been diagnosed with at birth, it took a few seconds to catch his breath. The doctors told him his heart pumped about 35-40 percent, which didn't mean much to him, but apparently it was a little worse than average.

He studied the distance he'd run. Pretty fast, he thought. "I'm a sprinter, not a marathoner."

Past the first few trees, the woods were dark, practically black, and he wondered what secrets they hid. Maybe there'd be a cave that no one had ever discovered or a Native American burial site. He set a sharp eye back toward his new house before marching into the great wooded unknown.

The shade inside the canopy of trees delivered a cool bite to the breeze and the air, steeped in wild earth, permeated everything. High up in the branches, two crows were keeping an eye on him. This wasn't human domain. It was the world of animals. One of the crows leapt from the branch, its wings cutting through the wind with a flutter.

Hollis figured the other kids in the area were probably playing video games or checking out Snapchat or YouTube. A couple of them had waved to him when they'd seen each other, but it didn't matter now. He'd just probed the neighborhood and there was no one else around. *One thing at a time*, he said to himself.

He delved deeper in, every once in awhile looking back at his house fading farther into the distance. He noticed a mound a short jog up on the left, perhaps the carcass of a water buffalo or a secret entrance to a long forgotten lair. He hiked to it, hoping to discover something no one had seen in hundreds or thousands of years, but it was only a lump of earth, stiff and unyielding.

He was making his own path, sometimes having to climb over fallen trees or duck beneath branches, forcing twigs out of his way with his hands and closing his eyes in case anything snapped back unexpectedly. Every step was met by the crunching of leaves underfoot. This was the heart of the woods with no hint of civilization.

In the distance, a gently graded hill showed promise. He fixed on it, reaching its apex in good speed. Atop the mound he examined the earth around him, stooping over to grab what looked like an

Indian arrowhead. It was black and one edge was quite sharp. Closer examination revealed it to be just a rock. He tossed it with the full might of his arm, but his aim was off and the rock hit a tree deflecting it off to the ground.

The far side of the hill dropped off much more abruptly than the way he'd come, strewn over with rocks and sticks all the way to the valley floor below. There was something in it that reminded him of Kaos, reigning over his vast kingdom. He raised his arms in triumph and roared at the top of his lungs just like the Orc King. Then he listened for a reply without getting one.

He knew he was nothing like the great Orc. Lucas Sherman, from his old school, used to call him Jonah after the Superbad actor and Hollis hated to admit that he could see the resemblance, especially in that they were both fat. The worst part of being teased was when there was truth to the digs. But he couldn't bring himself to enjoy basketball or football, or anything physical other than riding his bike. Comics were more enjoyable than any of it, and so the weight was likely to be staying on.

There was water up ahead, whispering through the rustle of the trees. It was faint, but unmistakable. His internal compass had rarely led him astray and he soldiered on toward the sound. In great strides, he leapt from rock to rock down the hillside, almost losing his footing at one point on some loose stones. The valley floor, covered in decaying leaves, was closer than it had seemed. He started the ascent of the next hill, which took a little more effort. Maybe he *should* work a little harder at dropping a few pounds; he was breathing more heavily than he wanted.

In a few spots he needed to grab hold of large rocks to steady himself on the steep climb, his sneakers slipping off stones because of slimy moss. At the top of the second hill he glimpsed the water, coursing slowly across the forest floor. It was too small to be a river. More like a stream.

When he reached it, he squatted along its edge among the entanglements of an enormous beech tree, whose trunk split five ways, each as large as another tree. It was easily the most massive tree in the forest, more like a dinosaur. His feet rested unevenly on its exposed roots, which had, over years or decades, worked their way inexorably to the stream. He studied the flowing water, as clear as glass, and underneath it, a mix of stones, slime and earth. It didn't seem all that deep. Hollis lowered his fingers into the stream. It was liquid ice. "No swimming in that," he said.

He dropped onto his haunches and leaned his elbows on his knees, fixed on the sunlight wandering though the leaves, touching the water and splitting into thousands of shimmering paparazzi flashes. This would do. This spot. It would be his fortress of solitude, the kingdom he would rule, a place of his own. Shuffling his way back, he sat against the giant tree. He hugged his knees closer, resting his chin on them.

There was something soothing about the sound of the water running, seeking its way across the countryside to a lake somewhere. Maybe he'd bring some supplies out here—a bug-out kit. If a meteorite came crashing to earth or Yellowstone Park erupted, he could be safe out here. Of course, he'd bring his parents out here too, but he'd need the basics to be able to survive: a canteen, a blanket, a knife, a compass, trail mix, a pot and utensils, a lighter.

This was as good as watching a show about the Egyptians.

An odd looking stone embedded in the upper reaches of the stream-bed caught his eye. It was just on the far side of the water, covered in muck. Was it metal? He stood up and made his way to the stream's edge, leaping as far as he could and landing with one foot in the water on the other side.

"Aww!" he cried, pulling his waterlogged foot out and squishing the sneaker down on the dirt edge lining the stream. He leaned into the crumbling bank and reached down toward the stone, except it wasn't a stone; it looked manmade.

He pried the item from the muddy bank and held it up to examine it, wiping away as much muck as he could before dipping it into the running water to clean it off better. It was heavy for its size, flat and circular like a medallion. The object resembled a rough stone, but glinted as if its raised edges were polished metal. It seemed to be a mix of silver and stone depending on how the light hit it. There were no etchings on it, just ridges, like it was cut directly from the earth. Along its rim, a thin metal band—rusted away to nearly nothing—

clasped the object, and attached to the band was a ribbon of fabric that was almost completely rotted. It looked like an olympic medal from another era.

Hollis tried to think of a logical explanation: an Indian artifact, maybe some sort of commemorative award? It seemed old, but whatever it was, he liked it. He stuffed it in the back pocket of his shorts and bound back over the stream heading for home, his left shoe squishing as he tromped.

III

The cinderblock halls inside Jeremiah Wilson Elementary School were painted a shiny turquoise, reminiscent of the post World War II years when kids were taught just how protective a school desk could be against atomic bombs.

The color on the walls wasn't due to the school board's aesthetic preferences, but because there were always leftover cans of semi-gloss at the end of a painting year that were preserved for the next time. The sock hop came and went, the Summer of Love, Disco, Reagan, Brangelina and as the definition of risqué intensified from Elvis' gyrating hips to Lady Gaga's meat suit, the school's interior remained comfortably consistent. It never struck anyone to ask why they didn't just try another color.

Until recently, the philosophy fit the curriculum, too. It worked in 1950, so it ought to work now. Reneé Denoncourt made attempts to sway the school department toward a new educational ideology in her first few years at the school in the late 1990s, and several younger teachers had tried since, but the old guard put the brakes on reform each time, preferring the "sit down, shut up, and open your mouth, so we can shove it down your gob" method.

Teachers fresh out of college rarely stuck around for more than a year or two, frustrated that mindless memorization wouldn't sink in so readily on kids who were plugged in and entertained 24/7, and who were years beyond giving a second thought to a dress made of meat.

But a chink in the armor showed the previous year when the school board passed new guidelines for fifth graders in an attempt to prepare them for middle school. "Team teaching" shifted the ten-year-olds from a solitary homeroom to a set of teachers specializing in subjects.

Where they used to rely on one adult for all of their educational needs, they now visited different classrooms just like the big kids.

Hollis was enrolled in the mid-sized facility, having started fresh with the new school year just a few weeks prior. JW Elementary wasn't all that socially disparate from where he'd come in New York State. Kids in fifth grade already had their friends. No one needed another.

His grades were already matching those he'd earned at his previous school, average or even a little below, his scholastic tendencies leaning toward indifference and distraction.

Seated in the middle of the class, he creaked open the lid of his homeroom desk and removed science and math textbooks and a three-subject notebook, closed the desk and laid them on top. The tan notebook, spiral bound, was already well worn around the edges, with the words math, science and computers written in all caps across the top and underlined. The rest of the cover was crowded with doodles, including a centerpiece of a skull and crossbones, its jaw dripping blood.

The bell ending class clanged, a piercing metal monstrosity bolted onto the upper wall in the hallway. It didn't mean that the students were free to move.

Standing behind her desk at the head of the fifth-grade classroom, Janelle Miller raised a piece of paper and flapped it back and forth. She had been teaching at JW Elementary for thirty-seven years, her first job out of college. A set of mom jeans fit loosely around her portly frame and her shoulder-length brunette locks covered the neck of a red V-necked shirt. Her flowery fragrance had permeated into her classroom walls over the decades and left a sustained and unambiguous scent that would, for the rest of the children's lives, spring them back to fifth grade.

The kids joked that she didn't shower, bathing herself in perfume to cover the strong body odor she put off. The myth had a half-life of the rest of her career, as do all yarns spun about teachers in grade school. It stemmed from a day in 2004 when she had forgotten to wear deodorant.

"If your parents haven't gotten back to me about conference night, tell them to shoot me an email by tomorrow," she said. "I'm looking at you Sarah, Zachary and Tyler. Got me?"

The offending parties nodded their heads.

"Okay," Mrs. Miller said, taking a seat at the desk.

The students filed out of the class, yammering and pairing up into their cliques. Hollis was among the silent stragglers at the end, head low, books clutched to his side.

He made his way along the edge of the hallway to Mrs. Bennett's room, just four doors away. A few teachers stood watch in an attempt to keep the chaos in between classes to a minimum and for the most part, it worked. Kids scurried around like a nest of ants, an Amazon jungle's worth of racket, but at least it was orderly.

A rail of a woman, Mrs. Bennett was seated at her desk, swiping away at her phone, a blank stare on her face and an occasional glance up to see how many of the children had come in. Sporting an oxford blue blouse, she was one of the well-liked teachers among the students.

Posters and drawings lined the walls of the rectangular room, the chemical makeup of the sun, the parts of an atom and cells. A model of the solar system spanned the entire room, dangling by fishing line from the tiled drop ceiling. The sun, like a bright yellow beach ball, was in the corner near the room's entrance while the planets ranged out toward the back window and the poor, demoted dwarf planet Pluto. A large, colorful replica of an atom dominated the left side of Mrs. Bennett's desk with removable parts, a three-dimensional jigsaw puzzle, onto which additional protons, neutrons, and electrons could be placed.

The bell rang at 11:02 and Mrs. Bennett gave a last intimate smile at her phone before laying it down on the desk. "Good morning," she said as the conversations dwindled. "I asked you to read the chapter on atomic structures last night. Why don't we open to page 47 in our texts."

She stepped to the doorway, shoes clomping on the terrazzo floor, as little hands pried open their outdated textbooks. Grabbing the handle, she pulled the door inward, only to have a single, straggling student slip in at the last moment. The boy, scrawny even by fifth grade standards, had a mane of wavy black hair, spilling down like a willow tree over the shoulders of a Grateful Dead concert t-shirt. He marched to an empty seat in the front row, textbooks in the clutch of his right hand.

"It's nice of you to join us Kirby," Mrs. Bennett said to a chorus of classroom giggles.

The boy laid his books down and shot her a thumbs up. "I'm ready."

"Oh good," she replied. "You had me worried there for a bit." She closed the door and moved to the blackboard, grabbing a piece of chalk. "Who wants to try drawing a hydrogen atom?"

A few hands shot up, but Hollis' wasn't one of them. He hadn't cracked a book the night before, having spent the time in pursuit of a magic sword on the family's Xbox. He had no idea what a hydrogen atom looked like.

"Alexus," Mrs. Bennett said, holding out the chalk. A girl, with inky jet-black, straight-as-a-ruler hair, stepped up to the blackboard and drew a near-perfect circle with the letter P in it, then added a larger ring around that, on which she placed a small circle with the letter E above it. She looked at Mrs. Bennett, with a smile that indicated she was finished. "Very good. That's exactly right," Mrs. Bennett said, taking the chalk and patting her on the back as the girl returned to her seat.

Gesturing toward the drawing, Mrs. Bennett began explaining. "So this is hydrogen. It's the simplest atom with just one proton and one electron circling around it."

Hollis studied the illustration. He hadn't done his homework, but Alexus' drawing was scraping at his brain, like hearing two similar sounds phasing. He gazed down at the textbook, at the illustrations in its pages and the gnawing feeling of something not right bit at him.

He clenched his eyes shut for a moment and then re-examined the drawings. This was the textbook and it was obviously right. Mrs. Bennett had agreed with Alexus' drawing, and she was the science teacher. His safest move was to keep quiet, so he let it go and his mind conjured up memories of his sanctuary in the woods, far from school and teachers, his private kingdom. At his throne by the beech tree, he was the ruler of everything he saw.

Reaching into his back pocket, Hollis pulled out the weighty medallion he had found two weeks earlier. It had become his good luck charm, stripped of its deteriorated ribbon and scrubbed clean. He held it in his hands, the ridges along its front and back seeming familiar now, like frozen ripples of water, smooth and wavy. The classroom's fluorescent lighting reflected off the shiny parts, which were silky smooth, offering very little friction when he rubbed his hands over them. Mrs. Bennett's voice faded into the nether region of his mind, just background noise with nothing to interest him, but his name was enough to snap him out of it.

"Hollis," Mrs. Bennett said. "What is that you have?"

He stared at the teacher like he'd been caught committing a crime. "It's just a thing I found in the woods."

"Well, put it away and join us in science."

He stuffed the artifact back in his pocket.

"Could you come up and show us all what a helium atom looks like?" She held out the chalk for him to take.

He let out a long breath and lowered his head. It was inevitable now. He would once again look like a lunkhead in science class. He stepped to the board, taking the piece of chalk, and inspected the large empty space on which he was expected to draw. The hydrogen atom scribbled out by Alexus was glaring at him from the side in all its imperfections.

What was helium? It was the stuff they put into balloons to make them float. His best friend in New York, Edgar, once sucked in some helium from a balloon so his voice would shoot up a few octaves. It was like air. Hollis raised the chalk and without thinking started sketching. First he clumped together a series of dots, dozens of them, hitting the chalkboard like a machine gun. Then he repeated that clump three more times so there were four distinct, but complex spheres.

A glance at Mrs. Bennett assured him that he was doing it wrong, but it just seemed right to him. He was struck by a sense that the blackboard wasn't enough. Scanning its edges, he lowered his arm, looking back at the classroom walls and at the board again, then back at Mrs. Bennett. "I don't think I have enough room."

Mrs. Bennett cleared her throat. "Okay. Well why don't you just finish up the best you can."

Hitting his chin with the chalk several times, he shuffled to the far edge of the board—past Alexus' sketch—and using the side of the chalk rather than its point, he began shading in a curved column several inches thick from the bottom up as far as he could extend. "I can't reach any higher," he said.

Mrs. Bennett had her arms crossed. "That's okay." She held out her hand and he returned the chalk to her and slogged away from the front of the class.

"That's interesting Hollis, but not exactly what I'm looking for," she said. Giggles erupted from the class.

As Hollis reached his seat, Mrs. Bennett was finishing four tight circles on the blackboard. She placed a P inside two of them and an N into the other two, then drew a pair of orbits around that nucleus and placed two electrons on them, with corresponding Es. "This is a helium atom. There are two protons, two neutrons and two electrons," she said as she pointed to each of the atom's parts.

He examined the corrected version of the helium atom, which seemed as wrong as Alexus' hydrogen, and returned to something more enjoyable—doodling. It was a good way to keep his mind off of his humiliation. He never liked being called to the blackboard, but it was especially horrific when he hadn't done the homework.

His attention mostly on his notebook, he could feel the occasional set of eyes from his fellow classmates upon him. His only hope was that it would be forgotten and he wouldn't become known as a dunce. History was a much better subject for the boy anyway. He didn't have a head for science or math.

Hollis glanced down at his absent-minded doodling. It was unlike anything he'd drawn before, a series of interconnected hexagons. They made for a cool design. There was no rhyme nor reason to his placing of each next hexagon, he just continued drawing them where they belonged.

When the class ended, Hollis gathered up his books and clumped in with the rest of the kids leaving. Alexus glanced back at him with a condescending, wrinkling sneer. He wanted to tell the girl that her diagram was awful, but evidently it wasn't. She whipped her head around lashing him across the face with her ebony tresses, causing him to brake mid-step.

Outside the classroom, the students split in different directions, Alexus and her friend Jayden to the left. That was good; Hollis was going right.

"It's not you," came a voice from behind. "She's a bitch to everyone." The student who'd shown up tardy for class pulled around to Hollis' side. He was half Hollis' size and known for being "an instigator."

"I don't mind," Hollis said, without an ounce of truth.

"I'm Kirby Cooper-Quinn," the boy replied, reaching for Hollis' hand. His palm was clammy and dwarfed by Hollis' and he locked on for an extended period, shaking with the vigorous power of a kid triple his size.

"Hey, I saw you riding your bike yesterday. I live on Raleigh Street," Kirby said.

"Where's that?" Hollis asked, finally able to withdraw from the handshake.

"It's a couple blocks over from you. You should hang out with Milo. He lives across the street from you. That's who I was hanging with."

"Oh yeah," Hollis replied. "I've seen him."

Kirby and Hollis shared a few classes, including math, where they were heading. "So how come you're never outside?" Kirby asked.

"I'm outside, like, all the time."

"Oh yeah? I never see you."

Hollis shrugged. He hadn't remembered seeing Kirby. Maybe it was just bad timing.

They arrived at their next class and hung out back for a bit chatting about the other folks in Hollis' area. Terrell, a few houses down, had a PlayStation in his bedroom with an epic surround sound system that his older brother had bequeathed to him when he joined the Marines. Brandon, who was at the house on the corner, had an older sister nobody liked and a younger brother who was hit by a car when he was young. The kid had made a full recovery within a few weeks. Everyone on the block avoided Mrs. Donovan's house, most of the others referring to her as creepy, but Kirby wasn't sure why. She was old, but always seemed nice to him.

By the time the bell rang and the kids had to take their seats, Hollis was wondering if he had found his first friend. They'd agreed to ride their bikes back home together after school so Kirby could show Hollis where he lived.

Mr. West entered the room, leaving the door ajar. Perhaps the most fashionable teacher in the school, he had a set of thick red-rimmed glasses affixed to his head at all times, mahogany curls that were touched up by a stylist at least every other week and flawlessly fitted attire. He looked more like a TV host than a teacher. Retrieving a stack of papers from his desk, he held them aloft. "Good news. We're starting the day with a pop quiz."

Hollis felt his stomach drop as the classroom let out a collective groan. Not only was math his worst subject, but he hadn't done the homework. He swore that tonight he would start doing what was required more regularly, especially for math and science. It was a promise he'd failed to keep on a great many occasions, but not any more.

Mr. West dropped off the quizzes at the front desk of every row and the students passed them backward.

Hollis laid the sheet of paper on his desk and glanced it over, an inexplicable feeling of calm coursing through him, as if he'd done this quiz a thousand times and knew all the answers without even looking at the questions. So with barely a glance at each line, he started writing. He knew it was a mistake to trust instincts on a math quiz, but what else could he do? He had no idea how to figure out the problems.

He hastened through the quiz with no regard for the math involved, barely skimming over the problems. Before he could even comprehend what the question asked, he was scribbling an answer. What is ¾ minus ½? ¼. If Annabelle has 1½ cups of ice cream and eats half, how much is left? ¾ cup. What is 918 x 642? 589,356. Within 20 seconds, he had completed the quiz, part of him worried he was about to receive a zero and another part confident in his intuition. He scanned the sheet one more time and figured there was nothing else he could do.

His chair scraped along the floor as he rose, and the eyes of the entire class were on him, including Mr. West's. He stepped to the front holding the quiz in both hands at his chest.

"What is it Hollis?" asked Mr. West.

There was a battle waging inside Hollis' gray matter. Should he head back to his seat and give it another go? How bad would it look to get a zero? Nobody else was done yet. He stood mute for a moment.

"Hollis, did you have a question?"

It was now or never. In nearly a whisper, he replied. "Done." Then he offered up the paper.

Mr. West cast a look of utter disappointment at Hollis. "Are you sure you don't want to take a little more time with it?"

Hollis shook his head and Mr. West let out a sigh, taking the sheet from the boy. Kirby was the only one to remark. "You da man, Hollis!" he said without a hint of self-awareness. As the class laughed, Hollis made a beeline for his seat and buried his head in his desk.

For the next couple minutes, the room fell into a hush, the other students chewing on pencils and erasing parts of their work. Hollis had taken to surveying the others as they scribbled their answers. They were all so intent, even Kirby, who didn't seem to care about grades.

"Hollis," said Mr. West, a serious focus in his eyes. "How did you do this?" The heads began to raise up one after another, attention focused on the teacher before turning back at the boy. Hollis' jaw fell an inch, unsure how he had done or how to respond.

"Hollis?" This time, Mr. West seemed less stern and more stumped.

"How did I do what?"

"How did you do this test so fast? You didn't show any of your work."

"I don't know."

"These are all right. You got a hundred."

Hollis felt the class focusing on him, silent. His heart was pounding fast. Mr. West was waiting for an answer, but the boy didn't have one to give him. He shrugged his shoulders.

IV

The neon lime BMX Hollis had received for Christmas lay upside down on the driveway, balanced on its handlebars and seat, its rear wheel loosened. The boy's hands were smeared with blackened grease from the chain, which he was rethreading around the sprockets, a pair of pliers sticking out of his back pocket. He pulled the back wheel taut and tightened the bolts with the pliers.

Maybe a marathon wasn't in his future, but he could still repair his bike as well as any adult. He leapt to his feet and flipped it back over, yanking it up by its seat with his right hand, his left turning the pedals half a crank to ensure the chain was working. The wheel spun freely with the rhythmic clicks of a perfectly calibrated machine.

The stubby blacktop driveway couldn't hold a candle to the windy quarter mile of gravel that led up to his last house. Before they moved, he used to be able to reach car speeds just coasting down the old bumpy dirt road, but on this one, all you could do was ride in circles. And if you tempted fate and tried to get up any speed heading into the neighborhood, you might just run into oncoming traffic.

Hollis' faded orange t-shirt emblazoned with the bold-type words "get er done" was streaked with grease around the bottom. He lowered the bike and the tire screeched to a halt against the driveway. Holding it at arms length, Hollis gave the bike a final inspection, leaned the frame against his hip and wiped his hands on his jeans—which already had the stink of metal and oil.

The clouds had been threatening to spit since school let out, and Hollis had felt an occasional drop while repairing the bike, but he wasn't going to let a little rain ruin his fun. Despite the shorter days, the weather was still warm enough for t-shirts.

"Looking for your training wheels?" a voice howled from the end of the driveway. It was Kirby Cooper-Quinn on his own bike, closing the distance fast. He skidded to a stop next to Hollis.

"The chain fell off," Hollis said, ignoring his friend's ribbing. "I had to get my dad's tools to fix it." Hollis had become pretty adept with real tools over the last couple of years, and he hoped it might impress Kirby. But if his friend was impressed, it didn't show.

"Sweet. Hey, you want to go riding?"

"All right," Hollis replied, straddling the seat and using his right leg as a kickstand. Kirby had become Hollis' best friend in the past few weeks and his connection to the other kids in the area. Most of the streets weren't too heavily traveled so his parents let him ride his bike almost wherever he wanted. There was a shop named Youssef's a few blocks down that was crammed with candy and comic books and it had become his favorite hangout, especially when he had a little allowance money burning a hole in his pocket. Maybe it was worth trading in the old driveway. In his old home, the nearest cool shop was in the mall and his parents had to drive him there because it was too far by bicycle. "Where do you want to go, Youssef's?" he asked.

"There's a trail in the woods behind Terrell's house with an awesome jump." His friend said. Hollis preferred a trip to Youssef's, but whatever. Bike jumping in the woods was good too.

"Okay, cool."

Kirby swung his bike around and beat a path for the street and Hollis put all his weight on the right pedal and was quickly on his tail.

"Hollis!"

The two boys stopped at the end of the driveway and spun around to face the Whittaker house. Hollis' mother was calling to him. "We need to go somewhere, honey."

"Okay," Hollis hollered back.

"You're coming with us," she replied.

Hollis emptied his lungs and let out a disappointed *tsk*, countering with a futile alternative. "We were going riding!"

"You can go riding later. Come on."

"Aw man!" Hollis faced his new friend. The decision had been taken out of his hands.

"Whatever," Kirby said. "I'll show you tomorrow." He took off once again for the road. "Smell you later!"

Hollis slogged the bike back to the house, leaning it against the wall just inside the garage. He pulled the pliers from his back pocket, inadvertently dragging the medallion he'd found in the woods with them. The item tumbled loose clanging on the concrete floor. He shoved the pliers onto a shelf and snatched up his good luck charm. Placing it back in his rear pocket, he stepped in through a door that opened from the garage to the kitchen. His mother was filling a glass at the sink by the far wall. Behind her, white granite capped off a mahogany stained wooden island, cluttered with mail and various groceries that had never been put away: dish soap, paper towels, a carton of rice, a bottle of wine and a bunch of lemons. Two cushioned stools were tucked neatly under the island's overhang.

Complementing the newly painted bright-white cabinetry and stainless steel appliances was a backsplash of glossy gray tiles.

His father was at the kitchen table, closer to the garage entrance, gliding his fingers along his phone, the gray sky casting a dim light on him through the set of sliding glass doors.

"What do you say pal?" his father asked without looking up.

"Where are we going?"

His mother took a few steps toward the table. "We have a meeting with one of your teachers."

Hollis' shoulders hunched over. He trudged to the table and slumped into a chair, accidentally kicking Risley underneath. The animal shifted his stubby spotted torso with a groan. "Sorry Riz," Hollis said in a despondent voice.

His mother Lonnie sat next to the fifth grader and put her arm around his shoulders with a comforting smile, laying the glass of water on the table. "My poor little trooper."

His parents were a bit of an odd couple. His father Graham bore an uncanny resemblance to a silverback gorilla, solid enough to sprout acorns and with thick fur covering his whole body. He was also several inches shorter than Lonnie, who could have passed for a middle-aged Susan Sarandon if only the actress did her wardrobe shopping at Target.

Hollis didn't want her mock support. If she really felt bad, she wouldn't drag him back to school when he'd only been home a couple hours. She had it in her power to set him free for the rest of the day to check out the jump behind Terrell's house and hang out with Kirby, but she made it seem like she had no choice.

"I don't want to go back to school."

"I know you don't," she said. "But Mr. West said it was important."

Hollis buried his head in his arms on the table, his words muffled. "I didn't do anything."

His father replied. "Nobody said you did anything, buddy. Mr. West said he was impressed with you."

"Hmpph!" Hollis wasn't putting in any effort in math class; the answers just rolled out of his mind as easily as if he were breathing them. "So why do we have to go in if I'm doing good?"

"Tell you what," his father said. "How about some ice cream afterwards?"

Hollis raised his head. He wanted to make it seem as if he was considering the options, knowing he didn't have a choice. He was silent for a moment. "Can I get a large?"

Both of his parents glanced at each other and smiled. "If you think you can finish it this time," said his father.

~ ~ ~ ~ ~ ~ ~ ~ ~ ~

Graham parked on the curb just outside the front doors of JW Elementary, a spot usually reserved for buses. Spits of rain were falling every once in a while as breaks in the clouds cast light in splotches across the metallic green Subaru. The water beading off of the car gave the illusion of a polished gemstone. Hollis had learned to care for his bike from watching the old man, who vacuumed his car every Saturday and waxed it four or five times a year.

The boy undid his seat belt and hopped out of the car, his hand almost sliding off the silky smooth door as he closed it. Maybe he should wax his bike... make it more aerodynamic.

He followed his parents in through JWE's front doors. Having parked in the bus lane, Hollis couldn't shake the feeling that they'd committed a transgression, but there was something odder still about an empty school. It didn't just look unnatural, it sounded dead, like an old ghost town with echoes of its vanished inhabitants. The cinderblock walls had a way of amplifying the footsteps of three people in a way it didn't do with hundreds. It felt to Hollis like he was in trouble, a condemned man walking to his doom with a guard by each arm. He glanced at his parents' faces. Blank. Was it because they didn't spend time in the school during the day that they didn't sense its awkward empty energy or did adults just grow accustomed to weird situations?

JW Elementary was laid out like a giant H, the front office and nurse's station located in A Wing, next to the school's entrance at its lower left side. Classrooms lined all of the walls, with the gymnasium and cafeteria taking up the majority of the connecting hallway. Student artwork was displayed on the free space on the walls, but newspaper articles about the school and its students were also framed at various intervals. Features from the local paper, *The Delacroix Post*, were accompanied by pictures of smiling students and staff members and were always community-oriented, which is to say, they were heartwarming.

From B Wing, the sound of a muted conversation echoed down the hallway. It was Mr. West and another man. As Hollis and his parents approached the math room, the voices became more distinct. The smell of chalk dust greeted them as they entered through the open door.

Mr. West, clad in his red spectacles, was in his usual wooden chair that creaked whenever he swiveled or leaned back. Behind him, the blackboard was wiped clean in preparation for tomorrow's school day. With a great ham hock of a leg resting on the corner of the desk, an unknown behemoth, the same age as Hollis' grandparents, was breathing heavily and grinning. The stranger, of unknown Hispanic origin, was endowed with a rotund face and broad nose to match his body, a full head of salt-and-pepper hair parted to the side and a snowy beard. He had a gentle smile, dark eyebrows, and wrinkles around his eyes that hinted at a lifetime of laughing.

The men halted their conversation when the Whittakers entered. "Hi there," Mr. West said, rising to his feet and moving to receive them. "You must be Hollis' parents. I'm Dan. Thanks for coming in."

"I'm Lonnie, and this is my husband Graham," Hollis' mother said as they shook hands with Mr. West.

"Hi Hollis," Mr. West said, mussing the boy's hair with his hand before turning to the odd man out. "I'd like to introduce you all to a friend of mine, Teo Ayala. Teo's a neighbor of mine and a retired scientist."

The stranger in the oatmeal Polo shirt and chocolate corduroys struggled to his feet, giving reprieve to the desk. He didn't look like much of a scientist, more like a retired wrestler. The man shook hands with Hollis' parents and then all attention turned to the ten-year-old.

Mr. West opened up the dialogue. "I asked Teo to come in so he could meet Hollis. A couple of us have noticed some things that are way out of the ordinary for someone his age. I don't know if you've been helping him with his homework, but I've never seen anyone like him."

"I don't help him much," Graham said, looking at Lonnie. "Do you?"

"No," she answered. "So he's, what, doing good in math?"

"And science," said Mr. West. "Mrs. Bennett and I started realizing that he was way beyond what we were teaching. I mean *way* beyond. To be honest, I didn't know what to think and then she said he was so far off the charts that she mistook his genius for goofing off. It took her a week before she realized he was answering fifth grade questions with doctorate answers."

"Atta boy," Graham said, rubbing his son's back. The force of his father's hand made Hollis stumble forward a step. He didn't know what to say. He hadn't even been doing the homework.

"So anyway," Mr. West added, "I was wondering if his last school noted any special aptitude on Hollis' part."

Lonnie and Graham shook their heads.

"I tell you what," Mr. West said, stepping toward the blackboard and scribbling an equation: 984 x 363. "Hollis, what's the answer to this?"

"Its 357,192," the boy replied.

"Oh my god," Lonnie said. "Is that right?"

Dan grabbed a calculator from his desk. "Nine hundred and eighty-four," he said, punching the buttons, "times three hundred and sixty-three." He turned the calculator toward Graham and Lonnie. It was the number Hollis had given, which left the two parents staring at each other.

"Let's try another," Mr. West said as he wrote another problem on the board. "Hollis, go ahead."

The boy answered without hesitation, "nine period fifty-seven."

Mr. West punched the numbers into the calculator, "Five thousand eight hundred and nine divided by six hundred and seven." The calculator once again showed Hollis to be right. "The thing is, not only have we not started long division yet, but we certainly haven't gotten to decimals. Did he go over these things in his last school?"

"No," Lonnie said. "I think they ended on long addition."

Hollis wondered if it had gotten warmer in the room. Eyes were upon him, all seeming to want to prod something from him, but he had taken to staring at his sneakers, doing his best to avert everyone's gaze. He stuffed his hands in his pockets.

"Hey buddy," his father said softly, as if he might hurt Hollis with his voice. "Do you want to tell us how you know how to do this stuff?"

Hollis shrugged his shoulders. What was the big deal? He was starting to think it would have been better to just play dumb all along. He could have gotten a few wrong and then he'd be out riding his BMX with Kirby. Maybe that's what he should start doing.

"Did you learn it on TV or something?" his mother asked.

"I don't know. I was just guessing," the boy replied. He plodded over to an empty seat and collapsed into it. There was no getting out of this. Moving a few feet away wasn't going to stop their focus. He glanced up and they were all staring at him, as if they pitied him. It wasn't his fault. He hadn't done anything. "I don't want to do this anymore," he said.

The adults grew quiet as a soft glow of gold and rust warmed the room from the twilight outside, the sun still partially visible on the horizon. The earlier clouds had parted and the shadows from the nearby buildings and trees were stretching farther across a damp ground.

His mother sat in front of him and leaned on his desk. "Are you okay, honey?" she whispered.

"This is boring." His eye shot to the blackboard and the posters of math equations lining the upper walls. He looked at his father, who was standing silent with the other two men.

"Can you do me a favor?" his mother asked.

He gave her his attention.

"Can you help us for a little while longer? We're just trying to figure some things out."

He nodded his head in resignation. *Get 'er done*, he figured.

"Hollis," Mr. West said. "Would you mind if Teo asked you a few questions?"

"I guess," the boy replied.

The scientist grabbed a textbook from the top of Mr. West's desk and lowered himself onto the floor next to Hollis, bending one leg up and wrapping an elbow around it. The man's head was level with Hollis' elbow, as he flipped through the book and placed it on Hollis' desk splayed open to an illustration of the solar system. From his crouched position, the stranger could just get an angle on the image himself and Hollis had a bird's eye view of the top of the man's gray hair.

"Mrs. Bennett said you seem to know all about the subatomic world," said Mr. Ayala. "But what do you think of this picture?"

Hollis inspected the drawing. He recognized the sun and the planets, but there didn't seem to be much else right about it. "I don't know. It's good."

"It's good?" the man asked.

Hollis took a deep breath. The depiction of the solar system was like a pebble in his shoe. He glanced at the poker-faced Mr. Ayala and judged that the man was on-the-level.

"It doesn't look right," the boy said.

"It doesn't? What's wrong with it?"

"I don't know. Everything."

A genuine smile broke through Mr. Ayala's beard. And then the man turned to Mr. West. "Hey Dan, do you have a pen?"

Mr. West delivered a pen to the scientist, who had raised himself up onto his knees, giving him a better angle of the textbook.

"Why don't you draw in how you think it should look?" said Mr. Ayala, handing the pen to Hollis.

"We're not supposed to write in the books," Hollis countered.

"It's all right," said Mr. West. "It'll be fine this time."

Hollis moved the pen toward the page, but stopped. "There's not enough room."

"What do you mean?" asked Mr. Ayala.

"Everything's too close together."

"Mmm hmm. Well, you're exactly right Hollis. Why don't you pretend that the distance doesn't matter."

That was fine with Hollis. He redrew the planets in different orbital positions. He moved Jupiter to the other side of the sun and earth down a few centimeters, each of the planets on their same orbital path, but in alternate spots.

Leaning his elbow on the desk, Mr. Ayala asked, "So why did you move all the planets?"

Hollis shrugged his shoulders. "I don't know. That's where they should be."

"I see. Okay."

Hollis continued drawing without any prodding. He added a small planet in an orbit between Mars and Jupiter, then two more on the outer edges of the illustration, past Pluto. Finally he sketched in a tilted orbit on the outskirts of the solar system where he placed a large planet.

"Interesting," said Mr. Ayala, pointing to the last planet Hollis had drawn, and interrupting the boy's illustrating. "What's that one there?"

"I don't know."

"You just thought there should be a planet there?"

Hollis shrugged and nodded.

Mr. Ayala pulled his phone from a clip on his belt and typed. In a moment, he held the phone next to Hollis' depiction of the solar system.

"Wow!" the scientist roared with a bellowing laugh. "Hollis, that is... most interesting."

Hollis' parents and Mr. West crowded around the phone and compared the image on display with Hollis' drawing. It matched.

"I don't get it," said Graham. "Why is that better? What is this an old textbook or something?"

Mr. Ayala was shaking his head and still smiling. "You see this?" he asked, indicating the image on the phone, "I'm using an app. This is what the solar system looks like right now, I mean at this very minute. The book just has the planets in random positions because... well, what does it matter in a textbook? But your son here corrected the positions for how they're aligned now. And it looks like he's adding the dwarf planets, which the book doesn't seem to tackle."

The adults were silent for a moment before Mr. West spoke. "So... Hollis, did you memorize this or something?"

Hollis shook his head. "It just seemed right."

"That's not even what got me," said Mr. Ayala. "You see this planet here?" He indicated the final shape Hollis had drawn. "We think there's another planet out past Pluto because its gravity affects the orbits of objects around it. They call it Planet X. We don't know where it is or if it even really exists. It's only hypothesized, but Hollis here thinks he knows where it is."

Graham bit his lip, his right eyebrow creasing ever upward. "But... you don't think... he couldn't possibly know..."

"No," Mr. Ayala replied. "But I have a friend working with one of the biggest telescopes on the planet. It might be fun to see if he'd check it out."

V

Hollis was overlooking the stream in the wooded spot he'd claimed as his own. He sat among overgrown roots resting his back on the massive beech tree, the latest issue of *Lurkin's Realm* in his grasp, fresh from Youssef's. It was the series that introduced Kaos, King of the Orcs, to the world. The boy figured the comic books would be sought after by collectors in the future, so when he wasn't reading them, he stowed them in plastic sheaths in the upper drawer of his bureau. The first read-through was always the most exciting and he used his secluded domain to fully immerse himself in the comic. He'd already read through it twice to make sure he absorbed everything.

Hollis surveyed his kingdom, scrunching his knees up, *Lurkin's Realm* nestled between his chest and his corduroys. Dusk was nearing and the autumn air was cool and moist from the rainfall the night before. His spot was dry, but the wet leaves throughout the forest gave off a pungent odor.

He explored new sections of the woods whenever he came out, but this area had become a second home to him. Despite the benefits of some of the other spots—like better vantage points and natural defenses—his initial instinct to make the beech by the stream his seat of power was a good one. The energy was right.

A rustling in the soggy leaves caught his attention and he shot an eye to the right a few yards away. It was a gray squirrel foraging around the ground. The creature stopped and started in short bursts, sticking its head under the leaves before scurrying another few feet, its tail twitching sporadically. Every once in a while, it sat on its haunches and scrutinized its surroundings, but didn't seem to notice Hollis. That was fine with the boy; he'd been taught about the interplay between wildlife and the environment and he wanted his kingdom to be healthy. This animal was simply one of his subjects. The squirrel entertained Hollis for a few minutes, eventually running too far away to care about.

The boy rose to his feet, stretching his arms above his head. He pulled a crumpled up piece of plastic wrapping from his front pocket, shook it out and slotted the comic into it, then he withdrew from his sanctuary, trodding the pathless route home.

The backyard was speckled in dead leaves, and more of them slipping off the trees as the boy made his way to the kitchen door. His mother was marching back and forth between the island and the table, talking on her cell phone. His father sat at the counter, listening to the conversation.

"He just walked in," she said, her eyes bright and wide. "I'll put him on."

It couldn't have been any of his friends, because his mother was far too animated. Same for grandparents.

She brought the phone down to her chest and spoke softly to her son. "Do you remember going to Mr. West's room with us, honey? Remember the man we met there, Mr. Ayala?"

He nodded.

"He has something he wants to tell you." She held out the phone and Hollis took it without thinking. "Hello?"

"Hello there Hollis. I don't know if you remember me. I'm Mr. West's friend, Teo. We met last week after school."

"I remember."

"Let me tell you, my friend, you've made some people very happy. Do you remember the corrections you made in that science book, when you put in some planets that weren't in the illustration?"

"Yeah?"

"Well I had a friend point some very powerful instruments where you thought our missing planet was, and do you know what?"

"What?"

"It's there, Hollis. I don't know how you did it, but it's there."

Hollis' response was more automatic than anything. "Cool."

"Would you like to see a picture of it?"

"Okay."

"I tell you what, I'm going to bring it over right now, if that's all right."

The boy pulled the phone from his ear and spoke to his mother. "He wants to bring a picture over."

"That's fine, dear."

"Okay," Hollis said to Mr. Ayala.

After handing the phone back to his mother, Hollis brought the comic book upstairs to his room, pulling the bureau drawer open and placing it inside. He had the entire series there, each wrapped in cellophane. He fanned through the six other issues, going back chronologically toward the bottom of the drawer, where the original was. He removed the first issue from its plastic and sat on his bed, thumbing through the pages. The illustrations seemed so different from the rest of the series and Kaos wasn't even in the publications back then. He hadn't appeared until the third. But it was still worth having the early editions for their historical value.

Hollis tumbled back and read through half the comic, his legs hanging over the edge of the mattress, kicking one at a time into the air before letting it plop back down onto the side of the bed frame with a satisfying thud.

His eyes were glued to the Crag of Fire, but his mind was back at school. How did everyone else instinctively know just what to say to continue a conversation? He could never think of anything to add, at the time anyway. Just yesterday Kirby told Josh and Melody about an episode of Star Wars Rebels. "Hollis saw it," his friend had said.

Words escaping him, Hollis could only bring himself to nod. If it were just Kirby, he would have been fine. He would have gone on about how much the Sith Lords controlled the fate of the galaxy, or that the cartoon was far better than any of the movies, but with two extra sets of ears, he'd just frozen up. It's the same way he was in his old school. He could always think of something to say after the fact.

And this whole genius thing was only making it worse. He was offering answers less and less in Math and Science classes. The other kids were getting sick of him always being right and it was destroying his chances of fitting in. He noticed the eyes rolling every time he raised his hand.

Maybe he should leave all this kid stuff behind and start watching sports. He closed the comic book and dropped it on the bed. For a moment, he just stared at the ceiling trying to focus on what was important. Football season was in full swing. Most of the other guys were Redskins fans. He could look up the basic rules online, learn a few names and positions and start watching games. Maybe he'd enjoy sports if he knew more about them. Even if he couldn't be a star athlete, he could be the kid who knew all the stats, every player, every move.

He shot up from the bed and looked at the television on top of his bureau. Was there a game on now? He could flip around and find out. But he glanced outside one of the windows and ambled over to it. The colors of the woods were deeper at this time of afternoon, especially after rain. Leaves were falling off the maple trees in the back yard like the ashes from a volcano, covering the ground in shades of brown and yellow.

Screw football. This was better. Why should he have to give up his fantasies for something he didn't care about. What did everyone else see in a bunch of grown men grumbling and tackling one another in pursuit of a ball?

Hollis cranked the window open and a strong gust of wind tousled his hair. Closing his eyes, he took a deep breath. Autumn. Nothing ever stayed the same, did it? The sights and smells of the season were unique to themselves. Trees ebbed and flowed in the wind, they shed their summer leaves in the colder months and that was how it was meant to be. It's what they needed to do to thrive. There was something profoundly perfect about the notion. Every living organism had its own coping mechanisms, enabling it to carry on. Perhaps, he thought, sports was what some people needed to cope. And maybe it was all right that he needed something different.

His mother knocked on his door and peeked her head in. "Honey, Mr. Ayala's here."

"That was quick," he responded. The boy followed his mother to the kitchen where his father was seated with the scientist, looking at the print-up the man had brought. Hollis and his mother took seats at the table and his father handed the picture to him.

"Do you like it?" Mr. Ayala asked.

Hollis shrugged his shoulders. "It's okay." The planet appeared to be little more than a pinprick. The only reason it stood out from the countless stars around it was a circle around it drawn with a metallic marker.

"I know it doesn't look like much," Teo said as the photo made the rounds, "but this is a big discovery. Do you know how many people have discovered planets in our solar system?"

The boy shook his head.

"Three. That's it. You're about to get your name added to a very short list. What do you think of that?"

"Good, I guess."

"Honey," his mother said, "that's more than good, that's amazing!"

Mr. Ayala turned to Lonnie and Graham. "Listen, I'd like to call the friend who found the planet and have him come talk to Hollis. He's the one who should be writing up the discovery. I'm a little out of my element with astronomy."

"Yes, of course," Lonnie said, both parents nodding.

"Great," Mr. Ayala replied. "His name's Niels Odden. He works near Cape Town in South Africa at the SALT. That's the South African Large Telescope. So it's going to take him a few days to get here."

"You hear that champ?" Graham asked his son. "There's a man coming from South Africa to meet you."

"How far's that?"

Mr. Ayala let out a belly laugh and leaned back in his chair, eyeing the boy.

"It's on a whole other continent," Lonnie said.

"I was down there once," said Mr. Ayala. "It's close to twenty-four hours for the flight alone. I'll call him when I get home. My guess is he'll be here in a couple days."

~ ~ ~ ~ ~ ~ ~ ~ ~ ~

Every once in awhile, Hollis could hear Mr. Ayala's booming laugh. The boy had been listening to the mumbles from the kitchen for the better part of a half hour, wondering when he would be forced from his solitude. And the moment had arrived. He could hear his mother's footsteps on the stairs.

When he finally entered the kitchen, the weight of expectation was heavy upon him. It was time to explain the sudden onset of his scientific and mathematical abilities to the scientists.

A batch of chocolate cupcakes, fresh out of the oven, cooled on the granite-topped island, filling the room with sweet, comforting bakery goodness. They were compensation for the task at hand, a way for his mother to make up for what would be a truly dull experience for the boy.

His mother took a seat at the table next to his father and opposite Teo Ayala and his friend. It had been two days since Mr. Ayala had visited and he'd brought the man from South Africa. Each of the adults had a cup of coffee and there was a laptop opened in front of the stranger.

Niels Odden was a diminutive man with a beard, wire-rimmed glasses and chaotic chestnut hair. For some reason, Hollis kept expecting scientists to come wrapped in lab coats and ties, but like Mr. Ayala, Niels didn't fit the bill. He wore faded blue jeans, a frumpy sweatshirt and dirty, shredded sneakers. About the age of Hollis' parents and soft spoken, he lacked the presence of Mr. Ayala.

"There he is," Teo said as he shook hands with the boy, Hollis' arm flopping like a wet towel. "This is Niels Odden."

The stranger shook hands with Hollis, rising to his feet and stretching in front of Mr. Ayala. "Hello Hollis, I'm thrilled to be meeting you." The new scientist had a thick Scandinavian accent that took the boy a second to process. "You want to check this out?" Niels turned his computer toward Hollis. It showed several photos one after another with a small dot of light moving across the image. "That's your planet, Hollis. And it's traveling along the orbit you predicted."

"Cool," Hollis replied.

"That is cool, isn't it?" Mr. Odden turned the screen back toward himself again and studied it. "Hollis, I came here to talk to you about this planet. I'd like to know how you knew it was there."

The fifth grader didn't have an answer for him. He studied the looks on the scientists' faces, animated and enthusiastic. Maybe he should be a scientist when he grew up. You could dress like you wanted and live in exotic lands. And apparently he had a knack for it.

Hollis sat down at the head of the table. "I don't know. It just felt like there should be one there."

"And you've never studied the planets, the solar system?" Niels asked in his barely recognizable English.

"I guess I studied them in school."

"Where do you think you've gotten your ideas from, mostly the textbooks in class, or maybe on the Internet?"

"Just in school. I don't really care about the planets or anything."

"You've never stopped on a television show about them, maybe?"

"I don't know, maybe."

"I catch him watching educational shows once in awhile," Graham said.

"Okay, okay, that's something. Now tell me," Niels said, "you don't have a telescope of any kind?"

Hollis shook his head and Niels turned to Graham and Lonnie for confirmation.

"No," Lonnie said. "Well, he's never shown any interest, so it didn't even dawn on us."

"Mm hmm," said Niels. "I'm going to tell you that I've been scratching my head ever since I saw the planet and I want to..." he looked at Mr. Ayala, "attribute?"

Teo nodded.

"I want to attribute Hollis' discovery to luck, but there is just no way he predicted the planet's location and trajectory based on a guess. The orbit is far too abnormal. And so I continue to scratch my head." Niels fell silent for a moment, inspecting the laptop's screen before focusing again on Hollis' parents. "Now, Teo says that Hollis has been doing well in school, perhaps better than he has before."

Graham and Lonnie nodded. "Yes, but only in math and science," Lonnie said.

"Interesting," Niels replied. "The rest of his studies, he's... you would say normal?"

"Normal for what he's always been," Graham said. "He's about average in the rest of his classes."

"Mm hmm. And when did his sudden burst of creativity start?"

"Three or four weeks ago," said Graham. "Then a week or so after that, Dan West asked us to come in."

"And was there anything preceding this, some sort of trauma or injury... um... an emotional jolt or... I don't know... anything?"

"Well, we only moved into the area in August," said Lonnie. "And that's been a big adjustment for him."

"And for the two of you as well."

Graham and Lonnie nodded.

"You know what?" said Niels leaning back in his chair with a smile of resignation. "I am not a psychologist. Maybe I could take a look in his room to see if he has any books or materials that may have given him some insight. Would that be okay?"

"Sure," Lonnie responded.

"And then Hollis, you and I can just talk for a little while at the table here to see if I can pry any more out of you. Does that sound all right?"

"Okay," Hollis answered.

"Yes? It's not bad, Hollis, trust me. You could be the youngest person to ever have his name on an article in *The Astronomical Journal*. And you can help to pick out a name for the planet. That might be more fun for you. In a few years people will be talking about this planet and you can tell them that you discovered and named it."

Hollis shrugged. "Okay."

"And after we publish it, people will want you to be on television. You will become famous."

The boy sat up in his chair. "Really?"

"Oh yes."

A smile spread across Hollis' face. "Cool."

VI

"You should call it Corvo," Kirby insisted.

"What's *that*?"

"*Corvo*, you numbass. Corvo Attano, from Dishonored. You played the frickin' game two days ago."

"Oh yeah, he was cool," Hollis replied.

The boys were discussing possible names for the planet that Hollis had discovered as a bubbling pall of dark clouds threatened rain, and a cool breeze swept dried leaves along the concrete sidewalk. Hollis made sure not to step on the cracks between the cement slabs, though he didn't let his friend in on his custom. He'd gotten in the habit when he was in first grade because of the old rhyme, "step on a crack, break your mother's back." It might have been childish, but it was habit now.

Afternoons had a way of slipping by whenever they walked home together, which was essentially every day. They had been walking their bikes instead of riding them, their backpacks slung over their shoulders.

"I don't know about Corvo," said Hollis. "Think I could use 'Hollis?'"

"Don't name it after yourself. Everybody will think you're stuck up."

The boy released a lungful of air. "Okay, what about Lonnie?"

"Lonnie? Isn't that your mother's name? Lonnie the Planet? Are you frickin' kidding me?"

"Well, I don't know."

They turned the corner onto Hollis' street and crossed over to the other side, popping their bikes over the curbing. Kirby straddled his bike's seat, his toes barely reaching the ground as he glided along beside his friend. "You know what you should call it?"

"Kirby?"

"No man, cut it out," Kirby replied. "Gator."

"You mean like an alligator?"

"No, it's my lucky charm." Kirby stopped the bike and reached into his front pocket, pulling out a rabbit's foot keychain. He handed it to Hollis. "That would be awesome sauce to have a planet called Gator."

"You call a rabbit's foot Gator?" Hollis rubbed it between his fingers. It was filthy and missing bits of fur, but it was soft as silk.

"I don't know. My father gave it to me. He had it since he was a kid and that's what he used to call it."

Hollis handed the item back. "Well, why would I call it after *your* lucky charm?"

"I don't give a crap. Do *you* got one?"

Hollis pulled the medallion out of his back pocket and handed it to his friend.

"This is your lucky charm?" Kirby examined both sides.

"Yeah."

"It's cool. What is it, metal or stone or something? Where'd you get it?"

"I found it in the woods."

"Awesome. What do you call it?"

"I don't call it anything."

"So what is it?" Kirby handed the object back to Hollis.

"I don't know. A medal?"

"It looks cool. You should have it checked out."

"Checked out for what?"

"To see if it's a five dollar shake, Dipshit Magee. What if it's worth like a thousand bucks?"

Hollis nodded, shrugging his backpack higher onto his shoulders and marching forward again. It was possible that his medallion was worth something, but that didn't matter. Even if an expert said it was worth a thousand dollars, he wouldn't sell it. But it couldn't hurt to have it looked at. "Okay, maybe."

Hollis knew most of the neighbors by now, or at least their names. An African-American couple, Mr. and Mrs. Owens, maybe his parents' age, owned the bungalow they were in front of. The white paint on the picket fence was chipping off, but otherwise the front yard was impeccably kept.

The same couldn't be said for the ranch on the right that the boys were approaching, with its towering raggedy hedgerows and overgrown lawn. A divorced computer guy lived there, a man who didn't bother too much with the yard work, which irritated some of the neighbors. Hollis ran his hands through the shrubs as he passed.

"So you don't like Corvo?" Kirby asked.

Hollis grimaced.

"What's wrong with it?"

"I don't even own the game."

"Yeah, but I do and he's awesome."

"What do you think about Kaos?" asked Hollis. "He's pretty bad."

"Kaos, from *Lurkin's Realm*?"

"Yeah."

"I don't know. He's pretty cool, I guess." Kirby held out his hand to swat the hedges as the fifth graders made their way by. "Hey, you want to sleep over?"

"I slept over last time," said Hollis.

"Okay, I'll sleep over your house."

~ ~ ~ ~ ~ ~ ~ ~ ~

The television was attached to the main living room wall with a swiveling arm, a wide flatscreen with a spaghetti factory of wires dangling down to electronics on a wooden media console: router, cable box, DVD player, earphones, speaker unit. Sitting on the floor in front of the sofa, Hollis and Kirby were playing an online third-person shooter video game with a satellite team that was depending on them. The rumble of explosions shook the media console, an undoubted annoyance to Mrs. Whittaker and Hollis could sense her watching from the room's entrance. He knew what was coming. His mother never cared about her poor timing.

"Boys, it's time for bed."

Hollis' shoulders drooped, but he kept playing.

"Hollis and Kirby."

"What?" Hollis grumbled.

"You know what, mister. It's time for bed."

"We're almost done."

"You were almost done a half hour ago. It's *past* your bedtime. Now come on, let's go."

"We just have to clear this one section."

The boys continued playing and within seconds Lonnie was lumbering two feet away, just inside their peripheral vision. "I'm going to just turn it off," she said. "I don't know if it saves it when you do that."

"No!" Hollis cried.

Kirby sensed the impending doom. "Aw man!"

"Five seconds," she said.

Hollis paused the game and the boys looked up at her. "You can play again tomorrow," she said. "But I need you both in bed now."

Lonnie retreated as the boys struggled to their feet. They had been playing the game since before the sun went down and their bodies had solidified. When Hollis shut off the television, the only illumination shone in from the adjacent kitchen, its yellow rays soaking into the living room carpet and making both boys squint when they stepped out of their cavern.

Lonnie was washing dishes, and from a stool at the granite island, Graham chuckled at Comedy Central on the small flat screen under the cupboards. The boys handed Lonnie their cereal bowls, Graham clapping his hands once in triumph. "Does this mean we get to sit on the sofa?" he asked.

"We could always put the Xbox in *my* room," said Hollis.

"Not a chance," Lonnie replied without glancing up from the sink. "You two wouldn't get *any* sleep."

Hollis looked to his father for support, but an apologetic look had washed across the man's face. "Whatever your mother says."

~ ~ ~ ~ ~ ~ ~ ~ ~

In Hollis' room, the boys emptied their pockets, preparing for the nighttime clothing change. The medallion clunked with a thud as it struck the cedar bureau. Kirby snatched up the silvery object and ran his thumb along the lines and bumps on both sides. There was a wavelike smoothness, slippery as teflon. Then he examined the rusted metal band around its rim.

"You oughta turn this into a necklace," Kirby said.

Hollis already had his t-shirt off. "What do you mean, like a girl?"

"No man, like Wolverine. You gonna call him a girl?"

"Oh. Oh yeah," Hollis replied.

"All you gotta do is run a string through this little loop here. Looks like that's what it used to be anyway."

Hollis took the pendant from Kirby and checked out the rim. "Yeah, I thought about that, but I figured my mother wears necklaces. I didn't think about Wolverine."

"That's cause you're an oxymoron. You got any string around here?"

Hollis handed the item back to Kirby and snuck out to the living room again where one of the family's many junk drawers was sure to have a ball of twine. He returned with a black shoelace, which he handed to Kirby.

"Cool," said Kirby, looping the lace through the slot on the metal band. He tied the ends up and handed the medallion to Hollis, who hung it around his shirtless neck.

"What do you think?" asked Hollis.

"I think you look a little less like an ass potato."

Hollis checked himself out in the reflection from his TV on top of the bureau and nodded his approval. Then he threw on a sweatshirt, pulling the pendant out so it was on display.

Kirby ran into the hallway and grabbed a couple blankets from the closet, throwing them on the ground. "Toss me a pillow," he said.

Hollis leapt onto the bed and threw a pillow down to his friend lying on the floor. Then he buried himself under the blankets, pulling the top over his head. He closed his eyes and breathed in the fabric softener off the freshly cleaned sheets.

"These blankets smell awesome," Kirby said from inside his cocoon at the foot of Hollis' bed.

"I was just thinking that my mom washes them too much."

"You're numb."

For a moment, it seemed that Kirby might fade into slumber, but

Hollis' eyelids hadn't grown heavy at all. "I don't even know if she's my real mom."

"Your mother's not your mother?"

"I don't know. I might be adopted."

"How come you think that?"

"There's this kid at my old school that said I was."

"So what does he know?"

"His parents grew up with my parents, so they knew each other. Maybe they told him the truth."

"And what, you think your parents are lying to you?"

"I don't know. I've never asked them or anything. Do you think grown-ups tell their kids when they're adopted?"

"How the hell should *I* know?"

After a moment's silence, Hollis closed his eyes, ready to try to force himself to sleep. It's just that Mike Trammel's arguments kept replaying in his head. They weren't going to allow him any peace. He cracked his eyes open, the blanket resting on his forehead, his arms at his sides. He took in a deep breath and noticed a faint metallic blue glow that he'd never seen before. He lifted the covers around his chest. The glow was emanating from his medallion. It was faint enough that if his eyes hadn't grown used to the lack of light, he probably wouldn't even have noticed. But with his more sensitive vision, it was clear. "Hey, come check this out," he said.

"Check what out?" replied Kirby.

"This thing is glowing."

Kirby emerged from his blankets and climbed under the covers with his friend.

"Can you see that?" Hollis asked.

It took a second for Kirby to notice. "Oh yeah. Cool."

"What do you think, it's radioactive or something?"

"No," said Kirby. "I've seen watches and all sorts of stuff glow in the dark. That doesn't mean it's radioactive."

"So what does it mean?"

"I don't know, but it makes my rabbit's foot look lame."

VII

6:00 a.m., Wednesday, August 22, 1945

The twin bells on Eleanor Cole's brass alarm clock clanged in dissonance, an unholy end to an inadequate night of sleep. Lying on her side with her head snuggled in the embrace of a down pillow, her eyelids unzipped just enough to note the time. The sun hadn't even woken up yet. She reached her arm behind the clock and pressed in the switch, turning the infernal noisemaker off.

There was a cool draft whispering in through the linen curtains, the window having been left open the night before with hopes that it would help her rest. Despite her best efforts, sleep hadn't come until somewhere between 2 and 3 a.m. She rolled over onto her back, closed her eyes and nuzzled into the blanket, the allure of sleep clutching hold of her. If there'd even been a hint of light, this would be easier. The coziest of all times was the moment after waking in a cold room and a warm blanket, but she could only allow herself a few seconds of indulgence. Any more and sleep would win out. Her head was swimming in a half woken state, with the remnants of a dream still echoing around her gray matter. She forced her eyes open and stared at the wall beyond her feet.

Though there wasn't enough light to distinguish it, Eleanor knew the wallpaper design because she'd chosen it—milky white with yellow roses and lime green stripes. She had helped her father hang the paper over a few warm days the previous autumn after the crops had been harvested. He had taught her about matching the patterns and squeegeeing out the bubbles.

He was undoubtedly in the fields already pulling weeds, the never-ending struggle with Mother Nature. Or maybe feeding the hogs. Most of the year he worked from well before sunrise through early evening. He said he'd learned the importance of diligence while fighting on the Western Front in the Great War, though he never really opened up about his time there.

Her father started every morning with a hot cup of tea with milk and sugar, and a couple slices of homemade soda bread smothered in butter and honey, then he'd get an hour or so of work done and allow Eleanor's mother time to rise. The aroma of bacon and eggs was his signal to head back in for a full feed.

Eleanor lifted her head and eyed her bathrobe hanging by the door on a hook. The nip in the air made the distance seem farther than it actually was and she dropped her head back down again. Was this all that life had to offer her? One day followed the next in increasing tedium. She had gone as far as she could in her career as a secretary for a male chauvinist, and the thought of following in her mother's footsteps didn't appeal to her in the least. She wanted to lead her own life, not follow the dreams of a future husband.

If the war had taught her anything, it was that women had been undervalued throughout history. Rosie the Riveter had affected her more than she ever imagined an illustration could, as had newspaper stories of millions of women joining the workforce at jobs traditionally held by men. But as the men were returning from the war, the jobs were defaulting back to them and women were expected to take their places in the home again. She loved her mother, but she would no longer settle for a conventional life.

She considered the cold trek to the robe again; it wasn't going to get any easier. On the count of three, she thought. But she only counted to one before casting the blanket to the side and sliding into her slippers. She shuffled to the door and threw on the robe with a shiver.

The smell of a hot breakfast hit her immediately upon entering the hallway. Downstairs, she shuffled into the kitchen where her mother was cracking eggs into a frying pan. The kitchen was the only source of real warmth in the morning with the wood burning stove going full blast. Normally it wouldn't be a problem in August, but the temperature had dropped dramatically overnight. Within a few hours she'd be longing for the frigid air, but for now all she wanted was a steaming cup of coffee and a seat by the stove.

Two thick candles on the table gave off enough light to see.

Without a word to her mother, she grabbed a mug from the cupboard and poured some of the coffee that was keeping warm on the end of the stove, then pulled up a chair next to the heat.

"They're supposed to be running an electrical line up this way," Eleanor said before sipping from the mug.

Her mother answered absent-mindedly. "Mm-hmm."

Neither of her parents cared about getting electricity. In fact, Eleanor had a theory that it somewhat scared them. "Do you think we'll be getting it?"

"I don't know. Why would we even want it?" Her mother flipped an egg with the spatula and sprinkled on some black pepper, the grease from the bacon splattering all over the pan. "It's just another bill."

Her mother was clad in a beige bathrobe and a full floral apron strapped on to protect it. Her cheeks had begun to sag and her hair was graying, but a picture in the family room taken at her wedding showed that she was energetic and beautiful when she was Eleanor's age. Eleanor envisioned a life of dull routine leading to inevitable dotage. Something had to change.

The outside door creaked open and Eleanor's father, a lanky man with thin white hair, button up shirt and suspenders dominated the entrance. "Make no mistake, the humidity's coming back today," he said. Her father pulled out a seat from the table and perched himself onto it, sitting with his legs splayed wide open, brown slacks with stained patches covering the knees. "What's the scuttlebutt this morning?"

Eleanor's mother scooped sausages, bacon and eggs onto three plates, handing one to Eleanor. "Your daughter wants to know if we're getting electricity." She brought the other plates to the table and returned to the stove.

"Yeah, I heard they was running a line up here," her father said as her mother returned to the table with the pot of coffee and mugs. "I'm not sure we *need* it, do we?"

Eleanor knew the conversation wasn't going anywhere, but she figured she'd lay out her arguments. "We could get a radio and a fan and we could turn on lights with the flip of a switch. What's not to like?"

Her father snickered and caught eyes with his wife. "Allow me to translate that, mother. We could buy a radio and buy a fan and buy some electric lamps and then pay someone for electricity so we can use them or we can keep on doing like we always done without any problems."

Mother nodded her head and slid open the metal bread box on the table, pulling out half a loaf of hearty brown bread and a serrated knife. She cut a slice of bread and lifted the lid of the ceramic butter dish. The butter had melted a bit the day before, but was solid again.

Eleanor brought her plate to the table where the silverware was set up for her. "I could buy some of it. I have a job," she said.

"But after you get married, you'll move out of the house and we'll still have a bill we didn't ask for," her mother said, spreading butter onto her bread.

"When I get married?" Eleanor replied exasperated. "I went out with a man once last year. At this rate I think the dowry's safe to invest."

Her parents laughed.

"And anyway," she said, "I'm not sure I'll ever want to get married." She stuffed a load of sausage and egg into her mouth waiting for the inevitable blowback.

"That's fine by me," her father said, tucking in.

"That's, what? No..." Her mother swiped at her father's arm as he chuckled. "Dear, you can't talk like that. You'll settle down when the time is right. That base of yours is full of men, isn't it?"

Eleanor didn't want to answer. She worked at an army facility, but the thought of being a military wife only depressed her. She took another bite. It was hard to believe they'd let the matter drop, but that's exactly what happened. After breakfast, with no other mention of electricity or marriage, Eleanor washed her face in the bathroom and brushed her teeth, then headed back upstairs. She closed the window and sat at the alder vanity she'd had since she was a child, staring at herself in the mirror. It was still cold in her room, but the heat of the kitchen and a warm breakfast had helped. The sun on the horizon was brightening things as well.

The beauty essentials were neatly organized around the edges of the vanity, brushes, pins, curlers, scissors, tweezers, makeup canisters, perfume bottles and her special mix of sugar water and lavender that she used to style her hair. She grabbed a copy of *Movie Stars Parade* magazine from the top drawer. She needed inspiration for a new look, something carefree. And she found it after only a few pages—Rita Hayworth. They could have been sisters, or so she'd been told. Copying the starlet's hairstyle wouldn't make her life any more interesting, but it couldn't hurt, could it? She propped the magazine up against the side of the mirror and reached for a brush.

By the time she rose from her chair to take in her new look, a full hour had passed. She scrutinized herself from every angle and doubted a Hollywood stylist could have done a better job, but a glance at the clock warned her that she needed to get moving. Darting to the closet, she picked out an outfit, throwing on the ensemble as hastily as she could. She snatched her purse off the bureau and scurried out the door, spinning back around and returning for a couple squirts of perfume before finally heading downstairs.

Her mother was reading a book at the table, but did a double take when Eleanor entered the kitchen. "What on earth have you done to your hair?"

"It's the new me, mother. What do you think?" Eleanor spun around.

Her mother shook her head and lifted herself up from her chair, reaching for another log for the stove.

"Where's Pop? I need to go!"

"Down at the chickens, last I saw," her mother replied, closing the stove door with an iron pole and taking one more gander at her daughter.

Eleanor threw open the outside door and barked to her father. "Pops! Pops, I gotta go!"

Her father poked his head out from inside the chicken shed and nodded, disappearing once more as Eleanor felt the time ticking away. It was seven or eight minutes before he made it back to the kitchen and Eleanor was pacing between the stove and the table entertaining her mother in the process.

"Okay," her father said, composed as always, "let's get you into work... What in the name of all that is holy happened to your head?"

Eleanor stormed toward the front door with her father shuffling behind her grinning at the misses.

VIII

Present Day

As an only child, Hollis had found friendship in Risley, the family's lumbering bulldog, but it wasn't so cut and dry with other kids. The boys his age—consumed with sports—discussed college football games and basketball players; they used terms like "pick and roll" and "blitzing the quarterback," and he realized he needed another way to fit in.

He wasn't interested in sports and was dreadful at them. Maybe if he'd been a natural, the other guys would seek out his participation, but with ailing heart muscles and little to no physical coordination, that wasn't in the cards.

Hollis only had one real friend from his last school, Edgar, and they'd stuck together as much out of necessity as anything else, both of them socially awkward around their peers. They overthought situations; possible reactions were gauged before anything was uttered.

Kirby was different. Everybody liked him. Except Alexus and a couple of her friends. It wasn't that Kirby had amazing insights, rather that he lacked self-awareness. He never felt awkward, no matter the company or the subject. Hollis knew what an advantage that was, but it wasn't a trait he could copy.

Just weeks before, he'd flipped over his bike's handle bars landing on one of the scrawny juniper bushes lining his driveway and splitting one of the main branches. It was a risky stunt intended to impress the kids across the street, but they hadn't even noticed. Since then, the shrub had turned brown along its side. Now, he only hoped his parents didn't recognize the dying bush, or in the least, that they wouldn't connect the dots and hold him responsible.

The accident was one of the rare times he'd been wearing his helmet. Hollis, like many of the other kids in the area, tried to get away without one when he could. His mother had seen him messing around and told him to put one on minutes before the big accident. Maybe she was psychic.

However, once again, helmets were safely stowed next to the garage door where they were sure not to get scratched, while Hollis and Kirby circled the driveway on their BMXs, each pulling his entire bike up with full ferocity, trying to lift the contraptions off the ground whilst riding them. Kirby was making strides, but Hollis was only able to lift the front wheel a few inches. He knew a "bunny hop" was cooler than a "wheelie," but he had a lot more to lift than Kirby.

In the distance, a dog was incessantly yelping. Otherwise the neighborhood was dormant. An occasional vehicle whooshed by, usually too fast for the residential area, and at one point, an SUV narrowly avoided flattening a squirrel that was scuttering across the road.

The conversation in the Whittaker driveway had passed squarely away from bicycle tricks to the best kind of pet to own, with Hollis fixed on dogs. "I don't know," said Kirby. "I'm stuck between a boa constrictor and a bearded dragon."

"What the heck's that?" asked Hollis.

Kirby's mind was still spinning. "Or a falcon."

"Nobody has falcons as pets."

"Yes they do, you seedless grape. That's how come they have hoods for them and arm protection."

"What's a bearded dragon?"

"It's a lizard."

"What are you gonna do with a lizard?" Hollis stopped his bike, clapped his hands and whistled toward a non-existent lizard in the middle of the driveway. "Come on, Lenny!" He whistled again. "Come on boy! I got you a bag of flies."

Kirby started to chuckle.

"Come on you big dumb lizard," Hollis continued. "Roll over. That's a good boy."

"That's totally what I'd do, dude," said Kirby, which made Hollis break out in laughter. "And I'd call him Lenny too. Lenny the lizard."

An old green Volkswagen, which had been chugging down the road, pulled into the driveway, black exhaust spewing from its rear and a voice on the radio too muffled to discern coming from behind the windows. The sides of the car were rusted along the bottom and the antenna on its roof was snapped off to a nub. The jalopy groaned to a halt well short of the boys, ticking as its engine cooled down. The radio fell silent and Teo Ayala rolled out of the driver's seat with a padded envelope in hand.

"Hey Hollis," he said, holding up the envelope and moving toward the boys. "You know what I have here?"

"I don't know," Hollis replied.

"This, my friend, is the very first article on your planet. This journal won't even be published until tomorrow, but you get an advanced copy."

"Cool."

Teo handed the envelope to Hollis, who struggled a bit to tear it open. The boy pulled out the magazine, the cover of which was an illustration of the newly discovered planet, with inset photos of Hollis and Niels Odden. Across the middle were three words, "Planet 9 Found." The subtext read, "Fifth grader leads astronomer to missing planet."

Mr. Ayala towered over the boys as Hollis flipped through the journal, Kirby's head leaning up against Hollis' shoulder.

"Do you want to show your folks?" Mr. Ayala asked.

"Yeah," the boy answered before calling out and dashing for the front door. "Mom, Dad! The article's here!" Teo and Kirby followed him inside, where his mother was seated at the kitchen table thumbing through her phone and his father, at the island on the other side of the room, was cutting up vegetables for dinner. Risley waddled over to greet Hollis and his friends as quickly as his short legs would take him, taking the time to sniff Teo's ankles.

"Mom, Dad. Check it out," Hollis hollered, tossing the journal on the table. Lonnie lifted the magazine as the small crowd gathered behind her.

"Well, I'll be," she said.

Graham was bursting out of his already tight t-shirt. "Hey, hey! Look at that thing! And there he is on the cover. That's our boy!"

Lonnie located the article and started reading it aloud, but stopped after only a few sentences when it was clear that it was a journal for fellow scientists. It might as well have been written in lawyer-speak.

"I don't even know what to say," said Lonnie, looking at her son. "Honey, this is the most amazing thing I've ever seen. Are you happy with it?"

"Yeah," Hollis replied. "It's awesome."

"Hollis man," said Kirby, "that is totally sick. I'm going to tell people we were friends way back when you first got a brain."

"You know," said Mr. Ayala to Hollis' parents, "this is going to get out around the world pretty fast after it hits the streets, so to speak. What do you think about setting up an interview with the *Post*?"

"I guess so," said Lonnie, focusing on Hollis again. "Are you okay with that, pal?"

Hollis shrugged his shoulders, still focused on the journal. "Sure."

~ ~ ~ ~ ~ ~ ~ ~ ~ ~

Mrs. Bennett pointed to the blackboard, where that night's homework assignment was written. "Remember, read through all of chapter twelve. It's short. It won't kill you."

A communal groan escaped from the student body, the kids collecting their belongings and moving toward the door. Hollis worked his way into the middle of the herd, shuffling his feet a few inches at a time behind the kids in front of him. He felt a poke on the side of his shoulder. It was Alexus, and she didn't look smug.

"Hey," she said with what could best be interpreted as a genuine smile.

He turned to face her, the rest of the students flowing around them. "Hey."

"I saw your article in the paper this morning. It was really cool." She held her books up with both hands across her chest.

"Thanks," he replied.

"So like, my mom says you're like a genius or something." Her eyes diverted for a second just past Hollis as Kirby approached him from behind.

"I don't feel like one," he said.

"So like, how'd you know there was a planet out there?"

"I don't know. It just felt like there should be one there."

"That's weird," she said, with a laugh, "but like, I don't know, totally cool, you know what I mean?"

"Yeah, he's not so stupid now is he, *Alexus*?" Kirby said with a snarky inflection when he mentioned her name.

"Shut up, *Kirby*," she replied in the same tone. She smiled at Hollis, stuck out her tongue at Kirby and marched away, her jet-black hair bouncing in step.

"What a bitch," said Kirby.

"She was being nice," Hollis replied.

"That's only 'cause you're famous now. I guarantee it, if you weren't in the paper, she wouldn't be talking to you."

"I don't think she's *that* bad."

"What, do you want to date her now?"

"I didn't say that."

"Do you want to marry her?" Kirby's voice had grown more childlike.

"Shut up!" Hollis pushed his best friend who stumbled back a step, bending in two as he giggled.

"I now pronounce you Hollis and Alexus Whittaker," said Kirby, making a sign-of-the-cross with his right hand.

By now, Hollis had begun to smile as well. "You're a moron."

Mrs. Bennett's voice rose from behind her desk. "Gentlemen, don't you have anywhere else to be?" The class had cleared out and the two boys followed suit, pushing each other on the way. Mrs. Bennett shook her head and held her smile until Hollis and Kirby were out of the room.

~ ~ ~ ~ ~ ~ ~ ~ ~ ~

Mr. West leaned his shoulder on the blackboard with his arms crossed in front of his chest and a stick of chalk in his grasp. He removed his red-rimmed glasses and lowered his head into his hand, exaggerating a grimacing squint as he pinched the bridge of his nose.

"Anybody *besides* Hollis?"

It was a familiar scene. Mr. West had been hammering a mathematical rule into their heads for the past few days and after all of his efforts, the only student in class who seemed to fully grasp the concept was also the only one who understood it before he'd begun. He didn't know if the other kids were becoming humbled at Hollis' intellectual prowess or if they were just getting dumber. Whatever, he figured, it was starting to fray his nerves.

He'd suggested skipping Hollis up a grade or two to the front office staff, but the wheels of the educational system were old and rusty and weren't designed to cope with a student of Hollis' rare abilities. Plus the boy was only flourishing in math and science; he was still below average in the rest of his classes. So for now, Hollis would remain a fifth grader with vast potential stuck in an elementary cage, and Mr. West would continue as a mediocre mathematician humbled by a ten-year old and pulling his hair out wishing that some of Hollis' talent would transfer to his classmates.

Mr. West held his glasses between his fingers and surveyed the class. "Kirby, help us out, would you?"

Hollis lowered his hand.

Kirby, who was doing his best to stay invisible, sat up at attention. He extended his arms to their full length above his head, palms outward and interlocked, and cracked his knuckles. "Okay, let's see. You got the sixteen twenty-fifths, right?"

Mr. West tilted his head to the side, without responding.

"So sixteen twenty-fifths minus... fourteen fiftieths... is always going to get you..." Kirby glanced down at the textbook and flipped a few pages, but the answer wasn't there and he turned his eyes back to the blackboard. "Sixteen twenty-fifths..."

The vintage bell clamored, signaling the end of class, and the children stirred to life.

"Stop!" said Mr. West, freezing the students mid-rouse. He paused, looking at his star pupil. "Hollis?"

"Nine twenty-fifths," Hollis replied.

"Nine twenty-fifths," Mr. West repeated conclusively, turning to the chalkboard and erasing the problems he'd scribbled on it minutes before.

The class started their haphazard retreat to the exit like a shaken snow globe filtering out a hole in its bottom. The last two were Hollis and Kirby, the boy wonder characteristically quiet as his best friend plied him with whatever random topic was inside his head at the moment. As the pair passed in front of Mr. West's desk a jolting metallic clang shook the teacher from his thoughts. He turned to see Hollis retrieving an object, which had fallen on the ground.

"What's that?" Mr. West asked.

"That's his good luck charm," Kirby answered.

"It's my good luck charm," Hollis added. "String must have come undone." The boy fished a shoestring from underneath his shirt and looped it onto the medallion, retying the knot, his books a jumble under his elbow ready to fall to the ground.

Mr. West eyed the object from above the fifth graders. "Hey Hollis, do you mind if I take a look at that?"

Hollis handed it to Mr. West, who examined both sides, feeling the silvery stone-like surface between his fingers. "This is weird," he said. "This is your good luck charm? What, do you wear it like a necklace under your shirt?"

"Yeah."

"Where'd you get it?"

"I found it in the woods."

"It's pretty neat. Do you know anything about it? What's it made out of?"

Hollis shrugged. "I don't know."

Kirby leaned in for another glance at Hollis' medallion as Mr. West moved the object up and down feeling its weight.

"I told him he should have it checked out," Kirby said.

"That's not a bad idea, Kirby," said Mr. West. "I'd bring it to Relics and More. They might at least be able to tell you what it is. I'd be interested to hear what they say."

"Where's that?" asked Hollis.

"It's right near Oriental Gardens. Your folks ever bring you out for Chinese?"

"Oh yeah," said Kirby. "I know the place you're talking about. It's got a model train in the window and an old bike and everything."

"That's it," Mr. West replied. He handed the medallion back to Hollis. "Fern Mori, a really nice lady. Tell her I sent you."

IX

Cool November winds were blustering bits of trash in circles along the sidewalks, shreds of soiled napkins and iced coffee lids. The same gusts were blowing directly into Hollis' face as he and Kirby rode their bikes home from school. His eyes were tearing up from the chilly temperatures and he used his jacket sleeve to wipe his runny nose as he pedaled.

The sooty smell of oil burners enveloped the downtown, freshly heating up for the first time since spring. The breaks in the cement made a steady rhythm as Hollis rode over them, Kirby leading the way and pulling to a stop at the corner of Central and Second, Oriental Gardens straight across the one-way, two-lane road.

"That's it there," Kirby said, pointing two doors down from the Chinese restaurant. The display window was filled with bric-a-brac, a rusty model plane dangling from the ceiling, old comic books, furniture, and a penny farthing bicycle, just like Kirby had said.

Traffic on Central Street, the main thoroughfare in town, was at a standstill, flustered motorists waiting for the light two-hundred yards ahead to change. Kirby picked a gap between a muddy one-ton dump truck and an SUV and rode his bike between them, catching eyes with the truck's driver. Hollis followed. Stopping in front of the truck, both boys then made their way between two cars in the second lane and onto the far sidewalk.

Hollis examined the Relics and More display window contents up close. The toy train Kirby had mentioned was a 1950 Lionel Postwar set, an all black engine with various colored boxcars and tankers attached behind. Raggedy Ann and Andy dolls rested on an old oak desk with their red yarn hair and triangle noses. Oil lamps, vases and clocks lined a set of olive green metal shelves.

"That's a cool train," Hollis said.

"Yeah, it's probably like five hundred bucks," his friend replied.

Kirby leaned his bike against the building and shouldered his way through the spring-loaded glass door with Hollis on his tail. The cramped shop's interior was as aged as everything in it; ruts had formed in the wooden floor from more than a century of wear, the bare wood creaking with every footfall. The musty air had a hint of mildew perhaps left over from a flood the town had experienced a year earlier. A tinny voice crooned out an old song over a set of speakers to the accompaniment of brass and strings and the tonal quality of a soup can.

There were shelves reaching to the ceiling crammed with just about everything imaginable: albums, books, typewriters, board games, magazines, toys, plates, shoes, lamps, sewing machines. Various pieces of furniture blocked the passages between some exhibits. On the right side, glass display cases housed the more expensive items like jewelry and political memorabilia. And behind the display case, a set of suspicious eyes, not much higher than the case, kept watch over the fifth graders as they rummaged through the antiques.

When Hollis and Kirby finally made their way over to the counter, an older, stout Japanese woman with graying hair, rose off her stool. The woman, in a white t-shirt that read "Vintage 1956," wasn't much taller than Hollis.

"Hello boys," she said. "Looking for anything in particular?"

Kirby leaned on the glass case. "Dan West is our math teacher and he said you might be able to tell us about this thing we found."

Hollis pulled the medallion from around his neck and laid it on the counter.

"Oh Dan! How's he doing? He's such a lovely man," she said, picking up the object. Her voice had taken on a melodic, welcoming tone.

"He's good," said Hollis.

She placed on a pair of glasses that were dangling around her neck, causing her eyes to double in size, and examined both sides of the medallion. Then she reached beside the cash register on the back wall and retrieved a magnifying glass, studying the artifact more closely. "This is really neat," she said. "I don't know that I've ever seen anything made out of this material before. I don't even know what it is."

She laid the object back down on the case. "If I were to guess, I'd say it's a piece of folk art. Do you know what that is?"

The boys shook their heads.

"It's probably something that someone made in their home. Maybe they were an aspiring jeweler or something. Where did you get it?"

"Out in the woods by my house," Hollis said. "It was stuck in the mud by this stream."

"Yeah," she said. "I'd say someone wore it as a necklace, just like you're doing, and it must have just fallen off at one point." She picked the artifact up again and rubbed it between her fingers, then scraped it with her thumbnail. "But I'll tell you, that is a *bizarre* material. I can't tell if it's stone or metal or some sort of..." She shook her head. "I don't know... composite? You know what I'd like to do? I want to take a picture and upload it to a website I use once in a while to see if anyone has seen anything like it. Would that be okay?"

"Sure," said Hollis as Kirby nodded in agreement.

"These folks are good," she added, motioning for the boys to follow her into the back room past the main counter. "I'm sure somebody will be able to tell us at least what it's made out of."

The cramped back room was in more disarray than the store, except the majority of the flat spaces were occupied by reams of paper. A fluorescent overhead light cast an unhealthy hue across the office and an archaic desktop computer rested on the middle of a solid mahogany desk, a digital ball bouncing around on its beige 1990s display. She moved the mouse and the computer chugged to life, whirring and sputtering before finally displaying a spreadsheet. She closed the program and laid the medallion down on the desk.

"My name's Fern," she said as she reached into one of the desk drawers and pulled out a digital camera. "Fern Mori. What are yours?" She pushed piles of paperwork to one side of the desk.

"I'm Kirby Cooper-Quinn," said Kirby. "And this is Hollis."

Hollis waved, but Fern didn't notice. She was stacking papers on top of one another. "Well, Kirby Cooper-Quinn and Hollis, I'm glad you came in. This will be fun."

"It glows in the dark too," said Hollis.

Fern snatched the medallion off the desk and scrutinized it. "It glows in the dark, does it?" She cupped her hands around the object and brought it up close to her eyes, then relaxed. "Nothing here," she said. Fern laid the medallion back on the desk and stood up, stretching to reach a set of curtains and shutting them. "Do me a favor, Hollis. Would you shut off the light and close the door?" She pointed to the light switch next to the office entrance. Hollis took a couple steps toward the wall and did as requested. The computer screen still illuminated the room, but otherwise everything was in shadows. The old Japanese woman transferred a sweater from the back of the chair to the computer screen, covering it, lifted the medallion and raised it to her eyes again before shuffling to the corner of the room and repeating the process. "I don't see anything, boys."

She handed it to Hollis, who cupped his hands around the object and brought it up to his own eyes. "It's glowing. Can't you see that? It's blue." He moved next to her in the corner of the room and Kirby followed behind him. With his hands still cupped around the object, he raised it for Fern to see, and it emanated a faint blue glow, just as the boy had said.

"Oh yeah," she said. "Now I see it."

He handed it to her and swapped positions with Kirby, who was pushing to get a closer look.

"I don't see it," said Kirby.

Fern turned her back to the room and allowed Kirby to come along side her as she covered it with her hands. She flipped it around and agreed with Kirby. "You're right. It's not glowing anymore."

With that, Hollis moved in for a closer look and the glow from the medallion slowly reappeared. "Oh my god," said Fern, glancing at the boy. "Hollis, go stand against that far wall."

Hollis plodded to the other side of the room while Fern and Kirby regarded the object, whose glow faded to nothing.

"Now come back," said Fern.

Hollis retraced his steps and pulled up next to the other two, and once again, the medallion started glowing. Stumped, the woman offered the item to Hollis. "Here, take it."

As Hollis clutched it, the glow grew a little brighter.

"No way!" Kirby said. "That is messed up!"

Fern stood for a moment her mouth agape. "Now give it back to me and go back over there," she said. Hollis did as instructed and the medallion once again lost its inner light. "Oh my god," she said. "I've never seen anything like this." For a full minute, the room was silent except for the radiators ticking. Fern shook her head and reached for the curtains, opening them again and letting in the afternoon light. She looked at Hollis and motioned to the light switch. "Can you...?"

The boy turned the light back on and opened the office door.

Fern laid the medallion on the cleared space on the desk and snapped a photo of it, the flash like a bolt of lightning in the small room. Then she turned the medallion over and took another shot. Plugging the camera in to a cable attached to the rear of the computer, she sat down in a creaky wooden swivel chair. A barrage of pictures showed up on the computer screen, the most recent ones of the medallion. She opened a browser and clicked on a bookmark, which slowly opened a webpage called "Ant-eeks." She started a fresh post, noting that they were in the northern Virginia area, that the object had been found in the woods, and that it glowed a faint blue when near its owner. After a few sentences of description, she uploaded the images and posted the query.

"I have no idea if anyone will know why it glows near Hollis," she said, "but someone will know something about it. I'd say by tomorrow, we'll at least have somewhere to start."

~ ~ ~ ~ ~ ~ ~ ~ ~ ~

The school building hadn't changed the following morning, but to Hollis, it wasn't just walls and classrooms, windows and doors anymore. The angles were glaringly obvious, the ratios of hallways to rooms. He noticed patterns to how everyone moved. There was light and shadow, cacophony and silence and all of the innumerable differences in between. Laundry detergent was prominent. Everyone gave off a distinctive odor, from lemony bushes and floral undertones to bacon and sulfur and rotting eggs. He'd always rolled his eyes at the malodorous fumes in the past. They didn't bother him now.

There was a veritable technicolor of sights, sounds and actions, each combining with the other in some way. And they were all beautiful.

In the playground, Hollis had been trying to explain to Kirby that the chances of winning the lottery were essentially zero, but his friend wasn't having any of his logic.

"I'd totally buy a Ferrari," said Kirby, " a yellow one. Those are the ultimate."

"You're not even going to be able to drive for another six years," Hollis contended.

"That doesn't matter. It'd be there when I get my license. Plus anyone can drive on private property. That's a fact. And I'd definitely get a place with a racetrack if I won the lottery, so I could technically drive whenever as long as I stayed on my property."

"Are you even old enough to buy property?"

"Money greases the wheels, my friend. You have a lot to learn about the real world. What about you? What would you do with a ton of cheddar like that?"

"I guess I'd buy my old house. I loved it there. And I'd have a private jet so we could go back and forth."

"Why not just buy some mansion by the beach? That'd leave your old crap hole in the dust."

"I'd get one of them too, I guess."

"Man," said Kirby, "you don't even need to win the lottery. You're totally gonna be rich with this whole planet thing. I mean, you got an interview with CNN tonight, right?"

Hollis nodded. "Yeah, and a couple newspapers and a few other TV stations tomorrow."

"That's awesome! Can I come?"

"I don't see why not."

"Is that what you're wearing?"

Hollis glanced down at his school ensemble, a long sleeve red and white baseball shirt stretched around his gut and a pair of jeans. He shrugged. "I guess."

Kirby shook his head. "No. Uh-uh. That is not what you want to be wearing for your first interview."

"Why not?"

"Look, if you want to play the part, you have to look the part. We got to get you some real duds."

The boys had sought out a private corner, not far from the wire fence surrounding the playground. They were splayed out on the grass and an inflatable red rubber ball rolled a foot away from Kirby. He reached over and tossed it back to the kids playing soccer with it. The JW Elementary playground was a hive of activity, some of the students on the swing set and monkey bars, others playing war or skipping rope.

"Like what?" Hollis asked.

"Huh?"

"What kind of clothes should I be wearing tonight?"

"You gotta wear something fitting. You got any t-shirts with planets on them?"

Hollis considered his wardrobe. "No."

"What about a tie?"

"Nope."

"Oh man, well I'll loan you something. You can't go out there looking like that."

"Your shirts wouldn't fit me. You weigh like about as much as my arm."

"All right, well don't worry. We'll get you situated. This is an important one."

From straight on, Hollis caught Alexus and Jayden approaching. They were making a beeline for him, Alexus' silky black hair waving side to side like in a shampoo commercial.

"Aw crud," said Kirby. "Here comes Alexus and Jayden. Don't invite them tonight."

"How come?"

"Cause they're like... I don't know. Just trust me. They'd be a total drain."

"I don't know why you hate them so much. They're okay."

"Sometimes I hate it when I'm right," Kirby concluded.

The girls stopped at Hollis feet. "Hi Hollis," they said in unison, casting irritated glances at Kirby, who was more than happy to return the sentiment.

"Hi," Hollis replied.

Alexus handed Hollis a scrap of paper, which he took and examined.

"That's my email," she said. "In case you want to... I don't know, do homework together sometime or something."

"Okay," said Hollis.

The girls smiled, spun around without acknowledging Kirby and headed back toward the side of the school.

Hollis stuffed the scrap of paper in his front pocket.

"You're not keeping that, are you?" Kirby asked.

"Yeah, why?"

"What, are you like actually going to email her or something?"

"I don't know, I guess... Maybe."

Kirby glared straight up at the overcast sky and raised his palms toward them. "I'm trying," he said to the ether. "I'm trying. But you're not giving me much to work with."

X

H is new-found aptitude in math and science earned Hollis a bit of jeering from the boys in junior high, and the mocking, which had been building for the last couple days had made its way down to one or two fifth graders, ever-ready to emulate the older kids. Hollis had grown accustomed to low-level taunts in his last school, but it had always been because of his weight. He couldn't fathom why someone would ridicule another person for being smart. They wouldn't make fun of someone for being better at basketball, would they? Or for being richer? But for some reason intelligence brought a stigma. For once, he had an enviable talent and somehow it was being flipped around and used against him.

After school had let out, Hollis and Kirby joined the clusters of classmates on the concrete sidewalk for the daily mass exodus. A few of the kids from the adjacent junior high merged in among the elementary students, and there were always a few looking to make trouble. "Make the mathletes proud, kid," one tall noodle of a boy said to him, patting him on the back as he traipsed by. Another particularly muscular specimen shouted "Poindexter!" as he glanced back at Hollis from a few paces ahead, holding onto the last syllable so it must have lasted ten seconds. The group of similarly dressed hooligans flanking the piece of meat joined in a chorus of laughs.

"They're just jealous," Kirby said.

Hollis didn't believe his friend was right, but he didn't argue. "I know."

The two boys were walking their bikes. Normally, they'd be riding, but it was a lot harder to hold a conversation while peddling. Hollis considered hopping on his bike anyway to put some distance between himself and the junior high kids.

"They wish they had one millionth the brain you do," said Kirby. "Bunch of chucklebutts."

"Whatever."

Hollis was trying to put on a brave front, but he wondered if it would be like this for the rest of his life. Most of his classmates agreed that the older kids were cruel, but what would happen when they were all in junior high? Was he destined to be picked on then too? He realized he'd never even considered how his life would turn out. Being an adult seemed like it was so far away and yet junior high was already on the horizon. After that was high school, and then he'd be a grown-up. That was it. Was he destined to be a scientist, wearing corduroys and shredded sneakers and looking through telescopes every night?

Hollis and Kirby were heading straight to the antique store from school to see what Mrs. Mori had found out about the medallion. Someone on the internet would know what it was.

"What are you going to do if this thing's worth a lot of money?" Kirby asked, his flannel jersey unbuttoned and revealing a John Lennon t-shirt underneath.

"I already told you I'm keeping it."

"Yeah, but what if it's worth like a million bucks? Maybe it was George Washington's or Sacagawea's or something?"

"I'm still not selling it."

"Yeah, but some museum might want it."

"I guess we'll cross that bridge when we get to it," said Hollis.

"Twenty-five bucks."

"What, you want to buy it?"

"No, that'd be my cutoff. If someone offered me twenty five bucks I'd take it."

Hollis had grown too attached to the medallion to sell it, even for a lot of money. He'd let go of his comic books for the right price, or his bike or television, but he wouldn't sell his parents or Risley or the medallion. It was a nonstarter.

"You and Jar Jar Binks," Hollis replied. "Come on, let's ride. This is gonna take forever."

They hopped on their bikes and peddled in the direction of downtown, which was still a fifteen minute ride. Staying mainly on the sidewalks, they had to wait for several crossing lights and at times the wind in their faces made their eyes water. The middle of town was a veritable parking lot, as always. They dropped their bikes along the side of the building at Relics and More and shuffled through the shop's spring-loaded door. The tin can radio, almost imperceptible in the background, played music that Kirby recognized.

"Oh, I know this dude," said Kirby. "This is Elvis. I don't care what anyone says, Elvis was the man!"

"What, the music?" asked Hollis. He'd grown accustomed to Kirby's apparent depthless pool of musical knowledge. It was impossible to stump the kid. Where Hollis was the school's undisputed king of science and math, Kirby was a music trivia master. Teachers and parents stood in awe of the fifth grader.

"Yeah, he was, like, a rock and roll god."

Hollis thumbed through a stash of classic comic books on the front shelves. "He seems okay."

"*Okay*? Check it out, jerkasaurus, he ushered in modern music. He had the hips, man!" Kirby spun a two-foot globe on its axis, stopping it with a finger. "Pacific Ocean," he said. Hollis didn't reply. Kirby spun it again, once again stopping its motion with his index finger. "Chad! Hey check it out, this country is called Chad!"

"No duh," said Hollis.

"What, you know it?"

"I've heard of it."

"Yeah, well it's a stupid name."

Hollis delved into an early copy of the Fantastic Four as Kirby moved on from the globe to a 1940s-era replica tank. "Cool," he said, picking it up. "Man, toys used to be really heavy. What is this, made out of a real tank?"

Hollis glanced over and Kirby held it up for him to view. Then Hollis surveyed the cash register area. "Where's Fern, do you think?"

Kirby shot an eye over the display cases. "I don't know. Out back?"

Hollis returned the comic book to the milk crate where he'd picked it up and edged closer to the back of the store, examining trinkets along the way.

"Get a load of this," said Kirby, "a space bus." He held up an old tin bus with robots and astronauts painted in the windows as passengers.

Hollis nodded to his friend and rested his arms on the display case in front of the cash register. "Mrs. Mori?" he hollered.

Kirby joined him.

Hollis shouted toward the office door, "Fern?"

There was no response.

"You think we should come back?" Hollis asked Kirby.

"No, she's here. Maybe there's a basement or something. She wouldn't leave the door open if she left." Kirby slipped by Hollis behind the counter. "Mrs. Mori?" he said, stepping toward the office door.

As he entered the back room, Kirby froze.

"We're not supposed to go back there without her," Hollis said, moving in behind his friend. He peeked around the corner to see what Kirby was staring at, laying a hand on his friend's arm. As he peered over Kirby's shoulder, he noticed Mrs. Mori lying on her back on the far edge of the room, an accumulation of dark liquid pooled underneath the upper half of her body. Her legs, clad in tan slacks, were bent unnaturally, her ruffled sweater soaking up the congealed puddle. There was nothing in her eyes, no spark, no life. They were wide and fixed on the wall. In the center of a mangled forehead, a bullet hole.

"Jesus!" Kirby mumbled, knocking Hollis off balance as he bolted past him into the shopfront. Hollis staggered back to the display case, bumping into Kirby, the color fading from his face.

"Aw Jesus," said Kirby. "Aw crap. She's dead Hollis. Someone shot her."

Hollis didn't reply. He was focused on the open door to the back office. They had just talked to Mrs. Mori. They were in here with her yesterday. Now there was blood all over the floor and she was shot. That was definitely a bullet hole in her forehead. She didn't look real, like someone had vandalized a pale and waxy mannequin. He began to wonder if he was smelling blood. Would the metallic odor carry this far away from the body?

The stereo's tinny speakers cut through an unnatural silence in the store, the bouncy keyboard in Elvis Presley's "Bossanova Baby," a macabre contrast to the bloody scene on the other side of the office door. The boys remained frozen. Thirty seconds? Five minutes? They couldn't tell. Time had ceased to move at its normal pace.

"We need to call the police," Hollis said, unable to avert his gaze from the door.

"Are you mental?" Kirby replied. "They're gonna say we did it! We gotta get outta here!" Kirby started for the front door, but hesitated when Hollis wouldn't budge. "Come on, man! Let's go!"

Hollis turned toward his friend, his face pale and sunken. "We can't. We need to call the cops."

"Didn't you hear me? They'll pin it on us. That's how this always goes down."

"We don't have a gun," Hollis replied. "Do your parents have a gun?"

"No."

"Well neither do mine. They're not going to say two kids without a gun shot her. Kids always find bodies. This was like a robbery or something."

Kirby eased up a bit and stepped back toward Hollis. "Okay, then you call them."

Hollis scanned the counter behind the display case. Fern's cell phone was next to the cash register. He edged along the case, staying as far from the office door as he could, he lifted the phone. "It's locked," he said. "No, wait, there's an emergency thing." He clicked the screen and struggled to slow his breath. "Um yeah... Someone shot a lady here," he said.

Kirby's attention bounced between the office door and Hollis.

"No... I think she's dead... Yeah... We're at the antique store."

Kirby took a step toward the office and peeked around the corner at Fern's body.

"She wants to know," Hollis said to Kirby, who drew his attention back to the matter at hand. "She wants to know what antique store. What's the name?"

Kirby looked stumped, raising his palms to the ceiling.

"Well go look." Hollis pointed to the front door and Kirby darted outside, returning a couple seconds later.

"Relics and More," said Kirby.

"It's Relics and More," Hollis explained. "Yeah... yeah, okay. I don't know. This isn't my phone. I think it belongs to the lady... Okay." Hollis hung up the phone. "She said there's a unit on the way."

"Oh man Hollis, what if this has something to do with us?"

"Why would it have anything to do with us? It was a robbery. I told you."

"Think about it. We were in here yesterday asking about your necklace and today she's dead."

"So what does that mean?"

"Maybe it's worth something." Kirby peeked into the office again holding steady on the periphery and tapping his fingers on the doorjamb before tiptoeing inside.

"What are you doing?" Hollis shouted. He slinked to the doorway and looked in at his friend who was making his way deeper into the room. "Get out of there! What are you doing?"

Kirby stepped through Fern's twisted legs, avoiding the pool of blood underneath her upper body, and climbed onto the chair in front of the computer.

"Kirby... Kirby! Cut it out! Get out of there!"

"I'm just looking, man. I'm just making sure." Kirby woke the computer and opened up the browser, clicking on the bookmark Fern had used the day before. Within a few seconds, the message board on which she had posted her query appeared. "This is it, Ant-eeks." He scanned the page, scrolling down every few seconds.

"Kirby, this is serious," said Hollis. "This isn't like detention, this is like police and jail."

"It's not here," Kirby said.

"What?"

"It's not here, I'm telling you."

"What do you mean?"

"I mean the post she put on here yesterday about your necklace, it's not here anymore."

"What, like it was deleted?"

"That's what I said."

Hollis inched closer, sticking close to the wall, taking a short awkward hop to avoid the puddle. He stepped over Fern's gray motionless arm, her sweater having acted like a sponge with the clotting blood. On the far side of Fern's body, Hollis leaned in toward Kirby and studied the webpage.

Kirby scrolled up. "See the dates? That was last week. They're in order. Look." He scrolled up some more. "See, here's yesterday. There's only two and neither one is ours. And see, here's today. Someone posted one this morning. Ours is missing."

XI

From inside Relics and More, Hollis could see a strip of yellow police tape blocking access to the shop. The police had cordoned off the sidewalk out front and just past the tape, two lanes of cars crept by, their drivers rubbernecking to catch a glimpse of what was going on. Twilight was upon the city. The streetlamps were casting a yellow glow outside and the lights and neon signs in the rest of the shops and restaurants were sparking to life, indicators of the shortening days.

A detective in a white shirt and tie was interviewing Kirby near a display of typewriters, writing notes on a small pad. Kirby had convinced Hollis not to mention the missing message board post, telling him they'd be blamed for inadvertently causing Fern's death. Hollis didn't agree, but his friend was the first to give a statement, so what else could he do? He'd have to omit the fact himself. An African-American with a clean shaven head and face, Detective Pacquet seemed amiable, especially considering the circumstances, and he wasn't giving the impression that the boys were suspects, contrary to what Kirby had figured. All of the adults were treating them like they were fragile.

Hollis was seated motionless on an old rocking chair, hands in his lap, waiting to give his version of the events to Detective Pacquet. A female police officer was crouched by his side, offering words of comfort. She only made him more nervous. There was another patrolman guarding the office and the background music had been turned off, so the only noise in the store was the low conversations of police officers and Detective Pacquet talking to Kirby. Pacquet turned toward the entrance when the bell on the front door jangled.

Two more men in ties entered—each carrying canvas satchels— politely greeted the officer near the entrance and made a beeline for

Pacquet. The detective laid a hand on Kirby's shoulder, said a few more words to him and rose to greet the new men, motioning to the back office.

As the three men marched toward the crime scene, the entrance bells on the front door jingled again. It was Lonnie Whittaker looking as distressed as Hollis had ever seen her. She had raw, red marks around her eyes and the blouse she wore was untucked on one side. She glanced around the store like a cornered animal before spotting Hollis. Lonnie darted to her son, crouched down and held him in a long embrace, reaching out for Kirby to join them. She wrapped her arm around Kirby as well and the three of them fell silent with only an occasional sniffle coming from Lonnie.

Her eyes had puffed up and turned moist by the time she finally released the boys. "What happened?" she asked.

Hollis took a deep breath and glanced around the room, seemingly distracted by all of the store's artifacts. "Me and Kirby met Mrs. Mori yesterday. We came back to look around the store again. She wasn't out here, so we looked out back..." He pointed to the back office door and let out a single uncontrollable sob, before pausing a moment to catch his breath. "Kirby found her. There was a whole bunch of blood underneath her and she was just lying there."

The police had told the boys to call their parents when they'd first arrived on scene and Hollis had already laid out the whole ordeal to his mother. "Shot," she said, confirming what she already knew.

Lonnie grabbed both boys again, pulling their heads in and smothering them in the crook of her shoulders.

"My mom's on her way," Kirby mumbled through Lonnie's blouse.

"Your mom works an hour and a half away," Lonnie replied as she released them. She placed a clammy hand on Kirby's cheek and stared at him. "You're coming home with us until she gets here."

"I still have to talk to that man," Hollis said, pointing to Pacquet.

"That's fine dear. We can wait," his mother replied.

~ ~ ~ ~ ~ ~ ~ ~ ~ ~

Graham Whittaker barreled down the hall into the Whittaker kitchen where Lonnie was sitting with the boys. There were three half-glasses of milk, a table full of crumbs and an empty package of Chips Ahoy cookies. He clenched his fists a few times, pausing under the doorframe, sweating and clearly short on breath. "How's everyone doing?"

"They're fine," Lonnie answered.

"They're fine, they're fine," he muttered to himself, stepping toward the table and placing the remaining seat next to Hollis. He sat down and rubbed the boy's back.

"The police said they have a trauma specialist who'd be in touch," said Lonnie.

"Trauma specialist? Good, that's good." He laid his hand over Hollis' head, practically enveloping it, then looked at Kirby. "How you doing, champ?"

Kirby had been staring into space, but was brought back by Graham's question. "Good," he said, before taking a swig of milk.

Graham turned his attention to his wife again, his free hand tapping on the kitchen table. "Did the cops say anything about it? Was it a robbery or something?"

"They said maybe. The one in charge, the detective, said this was the first murder in Delacroix since a bar owner a couple years ago. That one was a robbery, but he didn't know about this one. It's possible there was something in the antique store that was valuable."

"I remember that one. It was at the Green Velvet, where Ponchos is now."

"Oh yeah," Lonnie replied. "I always wanted to try it. That's why it closed?"

Graham nodded as the doorbell chimed. "I'll get it," he said. "Probably Kirby's mom."

Lonnie took a sip from her glass and shot a bemused look toward Graham's back. "She couldn't have gotten here *that* quick."

A hallway off the kitchen connected to the foyer at the front of the house, running by a set of stairs to the second floor. On either side of the foyer was a room, and in its center, the front door. Lonnie heard Graham talking to a woman, but it wasn't Kirby's mother. She didn't recognize the voice. It was raspy.

After hearing the front door close, Hollis could make out the floorboards creaking under the hallway carpet. Probably a police officer, he figured.

Graham returned to the kitchen followed by a man and woman in dark suits. Risley growled from underneath the table, yapping with as menacing a bark as he could muster, but not moving to intercept the visitors.

"Riz, quiet down," Lonnie said, nudging the dog with her foot. The bulldog stopped barking, but continued letting his displeasure be known through his growls. Lonnie grabbed Risley by the collar and led him out the glass double doors to the back yard, the dog barking and snarling the whole way. Even after the doors were closed Risley wouldn't keep quiet.

The solemn looking man bore a bony face and thick coffee-brown hair trimmed above his ears. Entering a few paces into the kitchen, the man grasped his hands together in front of himself. He was taking in the room, but his gaze always returned to the two boys.

The woman, whose face was framed by a dark Jennifer Aniston haircut, was a foot or so shorter than her counterpart. She wore a smile that seemed to be concealing a natural scowl.

"The boys have some visitors," Graham said.

Lonnie moved toward the counter. "Can I offer either of you a cup of coffee or a water or something?"

With full attention from the room, the woman stepped toward the table, her jowls becoming more apparent. "No thank you. My name is Agent Grey," she said, motioning to her partner behind her, "and this is Agent Breiner." The man didn't react, his eyes carefully dissecting everyone. "We're working on the Fern Mori investigation, and we wanted to talk to the boys if we could."

"By all means," Lonnie replied, returning to the table. "Is it all right if we stay? They've been through a lot." Lonnie wasn't really asking for permission. She sat in her chair and smiled at her son.

Agent Grey glanced back at her partner, a practiced smile on her face. "Of course. That will be fine." She circled the table and placed her hand on the free chair. "May I?" Lonnie and Graham nodded and She moved the chair to the head of the table, ensconcing herself on it.

Agent Breiner remained at the edge of the kitchen, near the hallway, as stiff as a piece of stone. Hollis glanced at him. The well-dressed bruiser was still sizing up the kitchen, taking it all in, his gaze returning to the boys, his hollow eyes stabbing through Hollis like a shark hunting its next meal. The boy slugged down a gulp of milk. "Can I have some more cookies, mom?"

"In a little while, Hollis," his mother replied. "Let's see if we can help these agents first, okay?"

Agent Grey leaned her elbows on the table and centered her attention on Hollis and Kirby. "We understand one of you brought an object in for Mrs. Mori to examine, is that right?"

Hollis spun his glass of milk on the table, barely catching it in time before it fell over. He hadn't told the police about it. How did they know?

"Hollis!" his mother said. "Stop fiddling around and answer her."

His heart quickened a step, but he knew he didn't have a choice. "It's mine," he replied after a long pause.

"Would you mind if we take a look at it?"

Hollis eyed Kirby, who shrugged his shoulders. His friend didn't understand. Agent Breiner was behind him, so he couldn't see the veins on his temples. These agents weren't like Detective Pacquet, and for the first time, Hollis thought he might not comply with a request from an adult. He didn't want to hand over the medallion.

"Is it in your room?" asked Agent Grey. "Should one of us go get it with you?"

"I can get it myself," Hollis said. He couldn't believe he was about to try something so dangerous, but he quickly worked out a plan. He would head down the hallway and then rather than traipsing upstairs to his room, he would bolt out the front door. If he handed it over, there was no way he'd ever get it back. He stood up, pushing the chair back.

"I'll go with you," Agent Breiner said, breaking his silence for the first time. His voice was resonant, much deeper than you'd expect from his rather lean build. His declaration unnerved the boy. Hollis wouldn't be able to shake the man. He was trapped.

Kirby butted in. "It's in your shirt, mentalyptus."

And with those words, all hope faded. Kirby had just offered up the medallion. Hollis' face began to turn a shade of pink. He wanted to reach across the table and rap Kirby upside his stupid head. "Oh yeah," he finally replied, pulling the seat back under his rump. He grabbed the back of his necklace and pulled the medallion from under his shirt, handing it across the table to Agent Grey. She studied both sides of the artifact while her partner pulled a phone from an inside jacket pocket and began swiping. "It looks right," Agent Grey said as she offered the object to her partner.

Agent Breiner stepped toward the table and snatched it out of her hands with a dead look on his face. He scanned the medallion front and back and checked his phone again. "That's it," he said, placing both the phone and medallion inside his jacket pocket and stepping to the opposite side of the table, a few feet behind Hollis.

"We're going to need to take it for evidence," Agent Grey said, her eyes narrowing. "I hope you understand."

That was exactly what Hollis feared would happen. From this point on, he would never see the item again. These people shouldn't have even known he had it. Did they see it on the message board before it got deleted? Or worse yet, were they the ones who deleted it... and killed Mrs. Mori?

"Do I get it back?" he asked.

Agent Grey either didn't hear him or chose to ignore the question. "Can you tell us where you found it?"

"When am I going to get it back?"

"We'll need to see if it had anything to do with the murder of Miss Mori. And we'll run it against a list of stolen artifacts," Agent Grey said. "If everything checks out, we'll make sure to get it back to you."

"How did you know I had it?"

Once again, Agent Grey sidestepped the question. "Did you find it around here?" she asked.

Hollis looked at his mother, who didn't seem at all put out that Agent Grey had taken his medallion. She nodded for him to answer.

"Out in the woods out back," he said.

"In the woods," she repeated.

"Yeah, out by a stream or something."

Lonnie leaned back in her chair, jaw dropped. "You don't really think this is the reason Mrs. Mori was shot, do you? Was someone looking for that medallion? Was Hollis in danger?"

Once again, Agent Grey didn't answer. She rose from the table, glancing back at Agent Breiner. He produced a handgun that had been holstered inside his jacket. With a stony focus, the man aimed the gun at the back of Hollis' head as an involuntary gasp escaped Lonnie's lips.

The crack of the gunshot amplified to deafening levels inside the compact kitchen.

XII

Bits of sheetrock sprinkled onto the kitchen table, and a cloud of gypsum descended from above, a new hole having been blasted into the ceiling by a Native American woman at the kitchen entrance, rifle in hand, focused on Breiner. The male agent still had his pistol leveled at Hollis, but he hadn't pulled the trigger.

Those in the room turned toward the slight, but regal woman, her silky tresses, black as a crow, draped over her shoulders. A set of icy, hazel brown eyes drilled into the armed agent, the unmistakeable smell of gunpowder dissolving into the air, ears ringing from the blast of her rifle.

"Lower your weapon," the woman said in a calm tone, her cowboy boots scuffling across the floor, as she entered the kitchen.

Breiner didn't budge or speak.

She waited a moment, then moved the barrel of her rifle two inches to the right and blew a hole in the wall behind the agents, the sharp crack from the shot once again splitting eardrums. The Whittakers and Kirby jolted at the noise, but neither agent flinched.

Agent Grey cocked her head to the side and met eyes with her partner and after a tense couple seconds Breiner lowered his gun.

"Lay it on the floor," the stranger said.

The man complied.

The woman looked at Agent Grey. "Open your jacket so I can see your weapon, remove it with two fingers and lay it on the ground."

Agent Grey paused, the synapses firing in her cerebrum with possible tactics, but eventually she did as she was instructed, her jaw set and the veins in her temples pulsing. With narrowing eyes, the agents stared down the stranger, neither blinking, not even attempting to mask the vengeful thoughts racing through their heads. The agents were the kind of people who always retaliated.

"Now one at a time, kick the weapons towards me," the woman said.

Agent Grey kicked her pistol over and then Breiner's. "We're U.S. Agents," Grey said. "You're committing a federal crime right now."

The Native American crouched down while keeping her rifle aimed at the agents with one arm, picking up both pistols by the trigger guards in her other hand. "Well, U.S. Agents, I don't like *anyone* murdering children." She rose again to her feet.

"You have no idea what you're getting involved in," Agent Grey replied. "We had no intention of hurting anyone."

The Native American squinted at Agent Grey and she pointed the rifle at her chest, but neither Grey nor Breiner seemed intimidated. If anything, the rage seemed to be busting out of their skin. They were used to being in charge and their civility was nearing its end. Breiner shifted his weight toward the kitchen entrance, his foot inching forward, and the Native American moved the rifle's barrel accordingly, stopping him in his tracks.

The stranger pried her eyes off the agents and glanced at Hollis. "Come here," she said. The boy froze, unsure of anything that was going on. "You," the woman said, obviously focused on the fifth grader. "Come here."

Hollis glanced at his mother, then rose to his feet. He moved toward the woman and from the other side of the table, Kirby accompanied his best friend as if he could somehow protect him. The woman put the arm holding the pistols around Hollis as both boys turned to face the room.

"Where's the Nííchʼi?" the woman asked.

Nobody answered.

"Where's the Nííchʼi, the medallion? Who has it?" She squeezed Hollis tighter to her body. "Do you have it or did you give it to them?"

Hollis raised his arm and pointed at Agent Breiner. "He has it."

"Throw it over here," she said, gazing into the cold stare of the male agent, who didn't move. "Now!" Her voice had grown louder and impatient. Breiner gritted his teeth and stuck out his lower jaw before opening his jacket and exposing the inside lining. He reached into the pocket and removed the medallion holding it up for the woman to see. Breiner tossed the item and it landed on the floor at Hollis' feet.

"Take it," the woman said to Hollis.

As the boy picked up his lucky charm, the sound of a chair scraping the floor broke the tense silence and Graham lunged at Breiner, slamming the agent with a meaty fist to his face. The agent stumbled backward against the wall, his legs buckling, and he fell on his haunches. No sooner had he hit the ground than Graham was on top of him, knee on his chest, pummeling the man's face with his hands. Breiner raised his arms in defense and began striking back.

Hollis had never seen his father act violently before and he failed to notice the armed woman holding onto him when she cried, "Let's go." Agent Breiner flipped Graham onto his back, gaining the upper hand as the woman tugged at Hollis' arm and stated more forcefully, "Let's go!"

In a desperate bid to help her husband, Lonnie leapt out of her seat and ran around the table, plowing into Agent Breiner and knocking him against the wall. Agent Grey reached down and yanked Lonnie off of her partner, but Lonnie writhed free and fell on Breiner again. As she did, Grey tackled Lonnie and turned the brawl into a jumble of struggling limbs.

The Native American pulled at Hollis, but the boy refused to budge. Breiner, who was again on top of Graham, reached toward his lower leg, retrieved a gun from an ankle holster and aimed it at Hollis. A split second before he could pull the trigger, Graham struck Breiner's arm and the bullet shot into the doorjamb next to the boy.

Lonnie, buried underneath Agent Grey, and unable to even look in his direction, yelled to her son, "Run!"

"Now!" the Native American shouted at the boy, dragging him by the arm out of the room and into the hallway. Kirby stayed on their tail as the woman hauled Hollis out the front door, across the lawn and down the driveway. As the storm door slammed shut, the sound of chaos inside the kitchen was muffled out. The woman was now pulling Hollis by the shirt, a rifle strapped across her shoulder and pistols rubbing against the boy's arm. Hollis was more interested in what was happening inside his home.

The early evening was already turning dark, a layer of invisible clouds blotting out the stars and turning the sky a dull gray. The streetlights cut through the cold autumn air and exposed the puffs of breath coming from Hollis' mouth.

They reached the side of an old powder blue Ford Aerostar minivan and the woman heaved open the back door, practically tossing Hollis onto the benchseat. As she reached for the handle to slide the door closed, Kirby snuck in under her arm, jumping onto the seat with Hollis. The woman stared at Kirby, her mouth agape, but only for a second before slamming the door shut and hopping into the driver's seat. The ignition churned the engine over several times to no avail and a loud crash coming from the house drew everyone's attention. It was Agent Breiner, his hair jetting out in all directions, his face pummeled and bloody. He was close enough that his snarl betrayed a set of bloody teeth as he bolted past the Whittaker's front door light. He had nearly broken the storm door off its hinges as he barreled down the front steps, firearm in his grasp.

The engine on the Aerostar sprang to life and the woman threw the shifter into gear, gunning the gas pedal and causing rubber to squeal—not due to the vehicle's power, but because of the poor condition of the tires. The minivan slowly accelerated, but Agent Breiner had momentum and for a moment closed the gap. As the van finally started to pull away, Breiner raised his weapon and pulled off two rounds hitting the rear quarter panel. From inside the cabin, the bullets didn't sound like much more than denting a milk jug.

"Are you both okay?" the woman asked, craning her neck to take in both of the boys. "Did he hit you?"

The fifth graders were silent as the woman shot her gaze in between the road and her passengers. "Hollis!" she shouted, catching his attention. "Are you okay? Is your friend okay?"

"Yeah," he replied without checking on Kirby.

The tires squealed as the minivan took a corner faster than it was designed to, cutting off a box truck, whose horn was blaring. After putting some distance between the minivan and the truck, the woman let off the accelerator keeping a steady pace down the curvy road.

The woman gasped in short choppy bursts. The rifle rested in between the front passenger seats, barrel pointing down, the pistols haphazardly tossed on the passenger seat. Hollis instinctually buckled his belt and Kirby, absorbing the scene, did as well.

"I'm sorry about that, I'm sorry," the woman said, the tension in her voice dissipating. "You're both okay." She was more confirming their condition than stating the fact, but neither of the boys responded.

About a mile after cutting off the box truck, the woman turned right onto a side street lined on both sides by maple trees and firs.

"What in the heck just happened?" Kirby asked, unsure if there would even be an answer.

The woman let out a huge puff of relief. "Those two in the suits back there, they're not good people."

"No shit, Sherlock," Kirby replied. "Are you?"

The woman regarded the boys through the rear view mirror and her eyes, having warmed, displayed the hint of a smile. "Let's just say I'm a better person than either of them."

"Prove it," said Kirby. "Let us out."

The smile quickly retracted. "Do you get what just happened back there? That man would have killed Hollis, no questions asked. And if he can find him, he'll try it again."

"What about my parents?" asked Hollis. "Did he shoot them?"

The woman was silent for a second. "Probably not," she said.

"*Probably* not?" Kirby replied.

"His parents weren't their targets," she said. "*He* was. And since they didn't get the Nílch'i, they'll probably want to leave as few ripples in the pond as possible."

"But you don't know," Hollis said. His eyes turned red and then came the sniffles and before long he was sobbing. The woman fell silent.

After five minutes of nothing but the sound of the wheels on the blacktop, Hollis had quieted himself. He stared out the window at the passing countryside. "I want to go home," he said.

There wasn't an immediate response, but the woman finally said, "You can't go back there. Not now anyway... I'm telling you, the farther away from those people you stay, the better chance you'll have."

"I need to know if my parents are all right."

"I know you do, sweetie. We'll find out. We just can't go back there right now."

"This is kidnapping, you know," Kirby offered. "You can't hold someone against their will."

"Look, *you* can go," she said to Kirby. "You're not in the kind of danger he's in. And if you both really decide that you don't want to be with me, then I'll drop you off somewhere safe with some money, but please, please, please trust me on this, he cannot go back home. They'll be waiting for him there. And they will kill him."

"Why do they want to kill me?" Hollis asked.

"Because you found the Niłch'i. Or it found you... whatever. I don't know. They want it and right now, it's yours."

"They can have it," said Hollis, realizing for the first time that the medallion wasn't as important to him as his parents. "What's the big deal?"

"It doesn't work like that," she said.

"So how does it work?"

The woman seemed disappointed in her answer even before she gave it. "All I know is you can't just give it to them."

"Well, what am I supposed to do?"

"The plan was to bring you to see my grandfather."

"And he'll know what to do?" asked Kirby.

"Probably better than anyone on earth. Listen, I'm not a kidnapper," the woman said, catching Kirby's eye in the mirror. "I'm going to drop you off." She glanced at Hollis. "I'm hoping you'll agree to come with me."

Hollis muttered in a low enough voice that it was barely audible over the sound of the shuddering minivan, "I don't want to."

The woman stayed silent for another mile or so, fidgeting with the heating controls on the dashboard. "Hollis," she finally said, "they are going to kill you. They will. You don't understand how important you are, not just to your parents, but to everyone."

Kirby pushed his friend on the shoulder. "I'll go with you."

"No," the woman replied. "Uh uh, you can't go. I'm dropping you off."

"Will you go if I do?" Kirby asked Hollis.

Hollis shrugged. "I guess."

"No way guys," the woman said more forcefully than before. "I'm not kidding. This isn't a joy ride. One of you is safe to go back home and that's where he should be. Hollis is the only one in trouble."

"I don't want to go without Kirby," Hollis said.

The woman let out a guttural moan from the depths of her lungs, knocking her head against the steering wheel several times. "No, no, no! This is not happening. Guys, come on. I'm trying to help here, but you have to meet me halfway."

Hollis spoke a little louder. "I'll go if Kirby does and if we can find out about my parents. Otherwise, I'm not going."

"This is just perfect," she said. "Everybody else I know just gets to go to work, come home and watch TV, but not me..." She trailed off speaking to herself in an irritated tone.

XIII

Silence spread throughout the minivan as the heater blew lukewarm air and a musty, burning odor out of the vents. Staring out the side window at the stretching shadows of passing trees and overgrown meadows, Hollis was lost in the afternoon's events. He relived the scene over and over, his father wrestling with the physically superior agent and losing, his mother jumping into the fray and being attacked by the female agent. His stomach had never felt like this before. This was nausea, brought on by the thought of his parents lying on the kitchen floor as dead as Mrs. Mori. His skin was glazed with sweat, and not from the minivan's lackluster heat.

This was all his fault.

As tears tried to force their way out, Hollis recalled the time his parents had brought him to see Santa at the North Mills Mall. He was eight years old and couldn't bring himself to tell them that he didn't believe in the jolly old elf any more. For one thing, he figured they'd stop buying him presents if he let on. Hollis had stood in line for ten minutes as the sweaty man in thick red cotton picked kids up off the floor, sat them on his knee and ho-ho-ho'd into their faces. When it was his turn, he mustered up some unconvincing enthusiasm, but he was more embarrassed than anything else. Santa was a fairytale for kids and he was old enough to know better. Santa's suit was redolent of B.O., his white beard splotchy and attached by wires to his ears, and the oversized buckle on his plastic belt seemed cheap. Hollis had considered confiding in the man that he didn't believe anymore to save them both the humiliation, but in the end he decided that the man might spill the beans on him and then the gravy train would end. And so he played along.

What really stuck with him was the expression on his parents' faces.

He couldn't understand why the charade made them so happy. But as the reality of the past day returned to his mind, the thought of losing them created such a hole in his stomach that he understood. It didn't matter if he was adopted or not. They meant more to him than anything else, period. And he knew that they felt the same about him.

"Do you have a phone?" he asked the woman.

"Yeah," she replied, in a reluctant tone that indicated she was about to disapprove of his request.

"Can I see it?"

"What do you want it for?"

"I want to call my parents. See if they're okay." His parents had made him memorize their cell numbers just in case, and he'd always considered it ridiculous because phones kept numbers so you didn't have to memorize them. It turns out they'd been right.

"Hollis..." She paused, clearly lacking a good response to his request.

He waited for a few seconds, but she wasn't forthcoming. "What?" he said, pushing for a reply.

"If we use my phone to call your parents, those people in the suits will be able to track it. Right now they don't know who I am and that's an advantage."

"We can borrow someone else's. We'll tell them it's an emergency."

"They'll still be able to figure out what direction we're traveling. Any clue we give them is dangerous for you. We have to assume at this point that your parents' phones aren't secure."

"I can email them," he said.

"It's the same, little guy. They have ways of tracking these things. We're going to have to find some other way. Maybe we can check out the news. If anything happened to your parents it'd make the news."

The boy returned to staring out the window and Kirby, who had been quietly observing the discussion, followed his friend's lead. The minivan fell silent again.

Hollis thought back to the antique store. A vague recollection of the song that had been playing over the speakers still coursing through him. The tune seemed a lot less happy than it was supposed to be, and a lot more foreboding in hindsight. He remembered Fern lying on the floor in a pool of blood, the song playing in the background. At the time, everything else was tuned out, but now the music was glued to the scene. It didn't seem real anymore, like a fading dream.

Just this morning he had been a young star on the rise, a scientific genius who knew things that even the adults didn't. He was on the cover of a magazine and on the front page of the newspaper. TV stations were supposed to be interviewing him tonight. Even the other kids at school were treating him differently, with more reverence. Heck, the older kids were picking on him because they were intimidated.

He jerked his head toward Kirby, who was staring into oblivion, then looked down at his jeans and began digging through the left pocket. His hand clasped onto a crumpled scrap of paper at the bottom, which he withdrew and straightened out. He held the paper up in the minivan's dark interior and shook it. Kirby returned a puzzled look.

"Alexus' email," Hollis said. "We can email her and have her check on my parents."

With a set of bug eyes, Kirby acknowledged the brilliance of Hollis' idea.

"Hey," Hollis said to the woman in a more assertive tone. "Mrs....?"

The woman glanced back at her young passenger. "Cha'Risa," she said.

"Mrs. Cha'Risa?"

"Just Cha'Risa. That's my first name."

Hollis wasn't used to calling adults by their first name, but this wasn't a time for convention. "Cha'Risa, I have a friend's email. Can we email her and see if she'd check on my parents?"

Cha'Risa grew silent for another few seconds. "You know what? That will probably work. We'll see if we can find a library."

"Can't we use your phone?"

She emptied her lungs through pursed lips. "Okay, yeah, that'll be fine. We should avoid public places anyway, but let me find a good place to pull over. I want to help you write it."

As the amber twilight dissolved into shadows, she pulled the minivan onto a service road straddling a large farmhouse. It was separated from the main road by a row of mature willow trees and ran along a split rail fence that stretched as far as they could see with the minivan's dim headlights.

Cha'Risa pulled the vehicle next to the trees and parked. Reaching into the side pocket of a dirty, black spring jacket, she retrieved a phone and swiped through several screens, finally handing the phone to Hollis. "Here," she said, "that's set up on my email. Don't send anything until I check it."

Hollis took the phone and stared at the blank screen. He met eyes briefly with Kirby wondering whether or not they should throw the door open and run. They had a phone now and could call the police or just run to the farmhouse in the distance. Cha'Risa had a rifle. Would it be dangerous to flee? It might cause her to panic. He tried to process what had happened in the past 45 minutes. This woman had saved him from being killed and she seemed like she was trying to help. If she was a kidnapper, she wouldn't have given him her phone. The woman wasn't paying attention any more. She was just staring out the windshield. If she were worried about them running, she would be paying attention.

Kirby's eyes were wide open, mouth slackened. They stared at each other, hearts pounding, minds running like the hammers of hell, before Hollis made a final verdict. He shrugged his acceptance at Kirby. He was going to trust Cha'Risa.

Throwing the scrap of paper on his lap and utilizing the phone's illumination to see, he typed in Alexus' email address and began laying out their request. After a few minutes, he raised his head. "Okay."

"You're all done?" she asked.

Hollis nodded.

"What do you have? Read it to me."

This was another good sign, Hollis figured. If she didn't trust him, she'd want to read the email herself.

"Hi Alexus, this is Hollis Whittaker. A bunch of stuff happened. You can't tell anyone about this. Can you check on my parents? Make up an excuse and go over and let me know what's up. Can you tell them I am ok? Me and Kirby are going to visit this lady's grandfather, but it's dangerous for anyone to know where we are. This can't wait till tomorrow so can you do it ASAP and email me back? We live at 56 Sherwood Avenue."

Cha'Risa appeared concerned. "I don't think she should let them know about you. And you shouldn't mention my grandfather. Just see if she'll pop in and report back."

"How come?" Hollis asked.

"Well, if she tells them you emailed, they'll tell the police and then there's a good chance those people will be able to track down my email and figure out who I am. And if they find out about my grandfather, they'll know where we're going. It's just not safe."

"So what should I say?"

"Tell her you might get hurt if she tells anyone and just see if she'll go over your house for a visit. She can tell your parents she's a friend from school and you were going to hang out."

"Hollis started typing again and when he was finished, he read back what he'd written. "Hi Alexus, this is Hollis Whittaker. I'm in a lot of trouble and if you tell anybody about this I might get hurt. Can you go to my house and see if my parents are ok? Just tell them we were going to hang out and email me back and tell me if they're ok. I need to know ASAP."

Cha'Risa took in a long deep breath and let it out. "Okay," she said.

"Wait," Kirby interrupted. "So that's it? We can't even tell our parents we're all right?"

"Not yet," she replied. "Let's just make sure Hollis' parents are alright first. Ok?"

Kirby gave her a look of resignation, turning his attention to the trees outside his window. Hollis hit send, then handed the phone back to Cha'Risa.

"So who are you?" Hollis asked.

"I told you, my name is Cha'Risa."

"Yeah, but how do you know what's going on?"

"I don't really know much. My grandfather told me I had to come find you. The Nílch'i—that medallion you have—is a relic. I've never been one to believe all of the old superstitions. I don't see any spirits or shit, but my grandfather's the most important person in the world to me and if he asked me to go snipe hunting, I'd do it. And the old son of a gun wanted me to find you."

Hollis wasn't used to adults cursing, at least not in conversation with a kid, but he had more important matters at hand. "How does he know me? Did he read about me in *The Astronomical Journal*?"

"*Astronomical Journal*? I doubt that. Honestly, I thought I was on a wild goose chase. I thought I was going to drive out to the east and turn around and tell him I couldn't find you, but I read about you in the paper and, Jesus... I don't know how he knew about you. I know he'd say the Niłch'i is why you got a dose of the smarts."

Hollis retrieved the medallion from his front pocket where he'd stuffed it during the incident at his house. "You mean I knew about science and stuff because of this thing?"

"That's not me saying it," Cha'Risa responded. "But that's what he thinks."

Cha'Risa's phone made a chirping sound. "That's a new one," she said, pulling it out of her jacket pocket.

Kirby leaned toward his friend holding out his hand and Hollis placed the Niłch'i into it. "So what," asked Kirby, "those government spooks want this thing to make them smarter?"

Cha'Risa, focused on her phone, didn't answer. "Shit, Shit! Oh my god, shit! Oh my god." She faced forward and fell silent.

"What?" Kirby asked, handing the Niłch'i back to Hollis.

Cha'Risa didn't utter a sound. Hollis wondered if Alexus had replied. Maybe it was already on the news that his parents were dead. His heart sunk, the years flowing by in an instant. "What is it?" he asked. "Was that Alexus?"

Cha'Risa covered her mouth with her hand and muffled through it. "That was an Amber alert. They're saying I kidnapped you."

XIV

Cha'Risa hit the gas quicker than her brain had time to respond. The tires spit out gravel, heaving a cloud of dust into the black ether behind the van—a vehicle too old to be featured in preowned ads and a decade shy of being collectable as an antique. She pushed the engine to its limit, revving the RPMs to an anemic whine, a hundred and fifty yards, two hundred. Then she slammed on the brakes, pulling into the tree line again. The cloud of dust caught up, enveloping the van in a powdery fog, illuminated by the light of a half moon shining through it.

"So what do we do now?" Kirby asked.

"First of all, we get a grip," Cha'Risa replied. "We don't panic. Gunning this thing without any direction isn't going to do any good. We need a plan."

"So what's the plan?" Hollis asked.

Cha'Risa clutched the steering wheel with both fists, the plastic creaking as her fingers tightened around it. She eased her ebony tresses back onto the headrest, her arms extended fully and locked in front of her. "They're describing this van in the Amber Alert. We need to ditch it," and she began discussions with herself. "Of course then we need to find a way to travel. They're searching for a Hispanic looking woman with two white kids. That's pretty much us. There can't be a lot of groups matching that description. Not in Virginia... Not anywhere. So what, public transit? No way. The kids' pictures will be all over the place."

"We could hitchhike," Kirby suggested.

"Oh yeah, that's a great idea," she replied in a tone that even the kids could pick up on as sarcastic. "The entire countryside's looking for us and we're out flashing our faces to everyone driving by."

"What about a bus?" Kirby asked.

"No."

"How 'bout a train?"

Her lower jaw jutted out, eyes thinning to slits. "No, that's the same thing as a bus... What's your name?"

"Kirby."

"It's the same thing, Kirby. Everyone is looking for us. The only way we get out of this thing is on our own. We need another vehicle."

"So what, you want to trade this in?"

"No. No trading in. No hitchhiking, no buses, no trains, no planes." She pulled her phone from her jacket pocket and began swiping through it.

"What are you doing now?"

"I'm looking for a car."

"Are you going to steal one?"

Cha'Risa exhaled long and hard, shaking her head. "No, I'm not going to steal one. What do you think, they have a list of cars to steal on the internet?"

"Well, I don't know. What are you doing?"

"I'm on Craigslist, alright? Now give me a minute."

Kirby's mouth puckered in and out as he made swishing sounds between his cheeks. He glanced at Hollis across the bench in the dimly lit van. The boys' eyes had adjusted to the shadows to the point where Cha'Risa's phone made them squint when they looked directly at it. "Your mom and dad are okay," Kirby said.

Hollis, lost in another world, turned his head toward his friend and nodded.

"Her grandfather will know what to do."

Hollis didn't reply. He focused out the windshield at the ghostly trees lit up by the van's headlights. The dust from Cha'Risa's fight or flight impulse settled in a film across the windows. In front of the van, the service road faded away to an inky abyss, the trees on one side and fence rail on the other providing the only point of reference in an ethereal veil.

The farmhouse was still visible behind them, a few points of yellow light, brighter than the stars materializing from nothing in the sky, but not by much. Hollis figured without the fruits of human ingenuity, the world would be in total darkness for the entire night. What did people do before electricity? You can't even read at night without a light.

Hollis had changed even in the few months he and his family had been living in their new home. Back then he didn't see the darkness for anything other than bedtime. Now he realized that the blackness represented everywhere humans hadn't conquered. It's where the rest of the world lived, the mosquitoes and deer, frogs, monkeys and mackerel, the kangaroos, moths, lobsters and eagles. They all followed the natural rhythm of the earth's rotation. And he understood that the other side of the earth was facing the sun right now, evaporating water and feeding plants, allowing the cycle to continue. He'd known it for years, but never fully appreciated it. He considered the massive amount of light being blasted off the sun that wasn't directed at this little planet, shooting past it and traveling forever down its own service road.

He contemplated the insignificance of the minivan and its inhabitants on such a vast cosmic canvas. The dirt could swallow up the van and everyone in it right now and nothing would change. Oh sure, family members and friends would weep, but the light would continue to blaze off the sun into infinity. In fact, he thought, not much would change if the whole planet disappeared. From a distance, there'd be one more speck of light visible on our sun, one less bug blocking the solar lamp. And our sun was a grain of sand on the seashore.

A pleasant woman's voice on Cha'Risa's phone directed her to head west for two miles. Cha'Risa pulled the shifter into drive and the van crawled forward, much more cautiously this time. Hollis watched the farmhouse disappear out the rear side window. "Where are we going?" he asked.

"First we're leaving this van where hopefully no one will see it for a long time and then we're going for a hike."

"A hike? When are we going to sleep?"

"I have a tent. We can camp out in the woods."

That sounded acceptable to Hollis.

For twenty minutes, Cha'Risa whispered to herself, "please don't be a cop, please don't be a cop," with every new set of headlights. She kept the vehicle at the speed limit, which brought on a fair share of tailgaters and each time another car got too close, she found a side road to turn onto.

"You know what," she said, after taking one of these detours, "this will do." She stayed on the smaller road, keeping her speed at a minimum and eyeing the tree line. Within a few minutes, she made a three-point u-turn and crept along the side of the road, pulling onto a one-lane dirt road surrounded on both sides by columns of towering hemlocks. The phone told her to take a U-turn, but she shut off the GPS app and drove a few hundred yards into the trees, throwing the van into park.

There was enough ambient light for Hollis to make out the general surroundings, a meandering overgrown road with a center line of ten-inch grass heading up a gentle slope. The hemlocks on each side of the road blocked all light from entering the forest and past the first row of trees, he couldn't see a thing.

Cha'Risa cracked the driver's door and stepped out onto the gravel, the dome light temporarily blinding Hollis and Kirby, as a pulsing door chime sounded through the cabin. The boys watched Cha'Risa trudging through thigh-high grass and disappearing into the woods as a cold wind crept in around them through the open door. The rifle rested in between the front seats inches from the agent's handguns.

Kirby focused on the woods where Cha'Risa had entered. She had stepped into the blackness. "This is definitely where the creepy music starts and she comes back with an ax."

"What do you think she's doing?" Hollis asked.

"I think she's getting an ax."

"You think she brought us to this secluded spot in the woods where she already ditched an ax?"

"Haven't you ever seen any movies?"

"I think she couldn't take your smell anymore and scrammed."

Kirby snickered and Hollis followed suit. "I think she went to take a crap," Kirby said, causing Hollis to break out in a full belly laugh. "I think the rusty shocks on this piece of shit jalopy sent a message right up through her butt. It was like morse code. Dee dee duh duh dee. Evacuate bowels. Evacuate bowels." Kirby's voice had become computer-like and Hollis released his seat belt and doubled over, trying to catch a breath. "And she's in there looking at all these trees and there's like no leaves to wipe her butt with. There's like only needles. She's gonna come back out here with her pants around her knees and ask if she can borrow your shirt." Hollis fell on the van's floor, slapping Kirby's shoe in an attempt to have him stop.

"What's so funny?" Cha'Risa's voice came from the open door. It startled the fifth graders enough to stop the flow of laughter instantaneously. It was one thing to tell crude jokes around other kids, but adults never appreciated the humor, especially if it was at their expense.

"Nothing," Kirby replied instinctually. "What were you doing?"

Hollis cast a worried glance up at her from his position on the floor.

"Watch and learn," she said. She dropped herself onto the driver's seat and shut the door, shifting the van into drive and pulling hard left into the overgrown grass. She inched the vehicle forward and into the forest, the headlights beaming against the trees directly in front of the van, an eerie vacant blackness surrounding each lighted trunk as the van passed. There wasn't a lot of room to maneuver, but she cut the wheel left and right moving the van deeper in, the sound of organics and sticks breaking under the tires. Over decades, the hemlock needles had formed a prickly bed as wide as the forest. The branches and twigs scraped along the sides of the van as it crept on. With three hemlocks directly in front and one on either side, Cha'Risa stopped the van and threw it into park, cutting the engine and turning off the lights.

It was hard to discern anything more than a few feet away. With a forest's canopy above them, there was no longer a moon to illuminate the terrain. With the air too cold for most bugs, there was no light and no sound except the ticking of the engine cooling down. Every move they made inside the van was amplified by the otherwise abundant silence.

"Come on," she said, "help me cover the tracks." She dropped the van key on the passenger seat and threw open the driver's door, heading for the road they'd just left, the dome light forcing the boys to squint. Hollis and Kirby unlatched their seat belts and plodded back to the tree line twenty yards away, hands extended to feel for trees and sticks that might smack them in the face. At the edge of the woods, with the moon and the stars once again holding dominion, Cha'Risa was fluffing up the tall grass with her foot, masking the tire tracks as best she could. As she leaned forward, her silky hair, raven black, draped over her shoulders, wisps of it catching in the breeze. The boys mimicked her motions to a lesser effect, and when she was satisfied, they all returned to the minivan. Cha'Risa lifted the minivan's rear door and yanked out a duffel bag and a backpack, tossing them onto the ground and quietly closing the door.

"Bug out packs," she explained. "Help me gather some sticks and branches. I want to cover the van so people can't see it from the road."

Camouflage was easy to come by in the thick of the woods, especially as eyes grew more accustomed to the shadows. When they were finished, there was nothing shiny to attract anyone's attention on the dirt road, even in the daylight.

Even with the exercise over the last twenty minutes, the boys were shivering in the chilly air. Their shirts could only keep them so warm. Cha'Risa unzipped the duffel bag and rummaged around, pulling out a blanket and handing it to them. "You'll have to share it. It's all I got."

Kirby accepted it and spread it across his and Hollis' shoulders and the boys huddled close. As they warmed up, Cha'Risa retrieved the guns from the minivan, placing the agents' pistols in the duffel bag and slinging the rifle around her shoulder. "Still got the Níłch'i?" she asked.

Hollis pushed his hand into his front pocket and nodded.

"Okay then," she said. "Let's hit it." She beat a slow path in the opposite direction of the road and the boys followed, moving as one underneath the cover of the blanket.

Cha'Risa led Hollis and Kirby through the woods, down into ravines and back up long inclines, keeping a close eye on a glow-in-the-dark compass she stored in her jacket pocket, the moon—visible occasionally through the thick canopy—drifting silently across the sky as the hours passed. At a few points, the terrain was too difficult for the boys to stay together, so without any planning, they began taking turns with the blanket, only sharing it on easier ground. The hiking was keeping them warmer now.

The woods weren't the same as the ones in back of Hollis' house. For one thing, he hadn't spent much time in them when it was dark. But these just seemed bigger. He always had the feeling in his sanctuary that if he walked far enough in any direction he'd come upon another neighborhood. Not so in this forest. The trees stretched on and on. He didn't know what time it was, but he figured it was hours past his bedtime.

Hollis already suffered from a lack of stamina due to his heart problem and his weight, but the exertion of hiking for hours when he was supposed to be asleep was taking its toll. The steam from his lungs melted into the crispness of the countryside, an unneeded reminder of the frigid temperature. "How much longer are we going to be walking?" he asked, struggling to keep his breath.

Cha'Risa had opened up a little distance, but she was close enough to hear him. She doubled back toward the boys. "You two must be tired, huh?"

They nodded.

"Okay, we'll stop the next good spot we hit, alright?"

The boys agreed, and Cha'Risa returned to the front of the pack. Hollis was surprised when she hadn't stopped within five minutes. He was used to his parents, who would never push him to overexert himself. Every few minutes, he would mutter an aggravated "come on" to himself as the evening ticked away, his breath harder and harder to control. Kirby kept silent.

A half hour after Hollis had complained, Cha'Risa dropped her bags and laid down the rifle in an area where the trees had thinned. Hollis and Kirby slogged up next to her, the blanket wrapped around them both.

"This should be good," she said.

"Looks good to me," Kirby replied, eschewing the blanket and taking a seat on a fallen tree full of holes and rot. Hollis and Cha'Risa sat on either side of him. The few times Hollis had been out in the woods at night near his house, the sound of frogs and crickets dominated the landscape. The woods—at least these ones—were eerily quiet in the colder months.

"There's grass," she said. "That's good for sleeping, but there's enough of a canopy that we won't be spotted from the air."

"Yippee," Hollis said with more than a hint of sarcasm.

"Unless they have thermal," she added. "But there's not much we can do about that, is there?" She moved over to her duffel bag and started removing items and tossing them on the ground, a tent, collapsable poles and a bag of parts.

"Is that a tent?" Kirby asked.

"Yes," she answered as she unpacked the tent from its sheath.

"Awesome, I thought we were barebacking it. This won't be so bad."

Cha'Risa reached into her backpack and pulled out two more pouches and tossed them at Hollis' and Kirby's feet. "Those are heating packs. Just open them up and they'll heat up in a few minutes."

The boys ripped them open, their minds already distracted with the thought of finally getting to sleep.

"They won't make you sweat or anything, but they should help," she said.

"Can we check on my parents again?" Hollis asked.

"Yeah, of course," she replied, pulling her phone from her jacket pocket and swiping a finger across it. "There's no reception, Hollis. I'm sorry. It's going to have to wait until morning." She turned the phone off and returned it to her pocket before spreading the tent out along the ground. "Can one of you help me with this?"

Kirby rousted from his perch and pocketed the handheld warmer he'd been given, sidling up next to Cha'Risa. Hollis wrapped the blanket fully around himself, leaving only his face exposed. As he watched the pair assembling the tent, he thought back on the longest day of his life and was still unsettled by how he'd arrived here.

"So who *are* you?" he asked.

XV

"Who *am* I?" Cha'Risa repeated, feeding a pole through one of the sleeves on the tent. "I'm nobody. I'm a chambermaid."

"A chambermaid?" Kirby asked. "A pistol packin' chambermaid?"

Cha'Risa pointed to the corner of the tent's base. "Slide it into that little slot." Kirby struggled to bend the pole enough to fit it in where she'd instructed. "What do you think, a lady that cleans a room, that's all she does?"

"I don't know," said Kirby. "It just seems weird. I mean one minute you're stocking the mini shampoos and the next you're busting through Hollis' door and blasting holes in the kitchen wall."

For the first time all evening, the anxiety had drained from her voice. She seemed in her element, assembling a pole and sliding it through another sleeve. "I grew up around guns. Housekeeping's a paycheck."

Hollis moved toward the tent and took a seat on the grass, the blanket still wrapped around his body. "How'd you end up at my house?"

She stopped her work on the tent and stared at the fifth grader for a few seconds, then reached over to the backpack and unzipped the front pocket, pulling out a flashlight and a sheet of folded-up paper. The thick yellowed sheet crinkled as she unfolded it and handed it to Hollis with the flashlight. In the center of the sheet was a crude drawing of a boy's face that resembled Hollis.

"Is this me?" he asked.

Kirby crossed over the flattened tent to take a peek.

"That's you," she said.

"Where'd you get it?"

"My great-grandfather drew it."

"Did he see me on the news or something?"

"I doubt that very much."

"Is he your grandfather's dad?" Kirby asked, accepting the illustration from Hollis.

"Yep."

"How old is he?"

"He's dead."

"Oh," Kirby replied, a glimmer of shame showing. "Sorry about that. When'd he die?"

"That's okay. He would have died, let me see..." Cha'Risa looked up at the sky and began mouthing numbers, "somewhere around eighty years ago."

"Wait," said Hollis. "Huh?"

"He died during World War II. My grandfather was eight years old when he got that from his father."

"That doesn't make any sense," said Hollis. "How did he draw a picture of me way back then?"

Cha'Risa was silent for a second. "When I saw your picture in the paper..." She looked over Kirby's shoulder at the illustration, turned her palms toward the treetop canopy and shook her head, mouth wide open, like she was searching for the words, but couldn't find them.

"So like," Kirby said, "your grandfather knows something about what's going on?"

"Yeah. Believe me, he was supposed to be the one making the trip out here. He used to tell everyone when I was growing up that he needed to live to see this year because he had a mission. I just figured it was like a private joke from when he was young. He said he had a boy to help and a wrong to right. One time he goes into his bedroom and comes back with a copy of *Brave New World*. He pulls that drawing from the inside jacket and shows it to me. He says, 'This boy's going to need guidance and I promised my father I would find him.' That's when I knew he was serious. You know, today always seemed like the future, like it would never get here." Cha'Risa squatted next to the tent and began assembling poles.

"So how come he didn't come?" Hollis asked, accepting the illustration from Kirby and returning it to the backpack.

"How come?" she replied. "He's 87. He has a walker half the time and an oxygen tank. He can't see for crap. He wasn't going to be driving shit. At first he asked if I'd take him and I was like, sure Análí, but pretty soon I knew he wasn't even going to be up for the trip. And at some point, he realized it too. I've never seen him so broken, like his whole life was working toward one goal and nothing else mattered and now, on the verge of completing this lifelong task, his body was telling him it wasn't going any farther. The bones weren't doing his bidding anymore." Her hands fell idle as she stared blankly at the poles, not that either boy noticed.

"Where is he?" asked Hollis.

She continued threading the rods again. "He's not too far from Albuquerque."

"Where's that?"

"New Mexico."

Kirby dropped the rod he'd been assembling in a blatant attempt to make a point. "New Mexico? Isn't that like on the other side of the country?"

"We won't be walking," she replied.

"Oh man!" It seemed like this was going to be a problem for Kirby's schedule. "What are we supposed to do? You need a plane to get that far."

"You don't need a plane to get that far," she said. "I drove."

"Yeah, but a plane would be a hell of a lot easier than whatever else the plan is."

"We're not taking a plane."

"Why not? This is ridiculous."

"Because in case you hadn't noticed, there's a lot of people looking for us. We already went over this."

"Well how are we supposed to get there? We just ditched the van."

"I don't know," she said. "I'll figure it out. I got a line on a car."

The tent was up in minutes. Cha'Risa unzipped the front flaps and they all slipped inside. As Hollis and Kirby snuggled under the blanket, Kirby asked if there was another.

"Do I have another blanket?" she asked. "No. What am I, Kreskin? Move over, we're sharing."

"Aw! No way. This thing's too small."

"It's a regular sized blanket. It can fit me and two kids."

"The ground is freezing," Hollis said.

"Aw Christ," said Cha'Risa. "Are you two really going to be like this? This is what I have. I never thought I'd be avoiding Johnny Law in the woods with a couple of ten-year old buttercups, okay? The bugout bags were for me. Technically you two didn't bring your own blankets."

This shut the boys up. Cha'Risa pulled a bottle of water from her backpack at her feet and offered swigs to Hollis and Kirby before taking some for herself. Then she positioned herself between them and they all laid back covered by the blanket, eyes wide open, staring up at the dark impermeable fabric above them, inhaling the stale musky odor of a tent that had been stored in a backpack for years.

"Hey Hollis, show her the medallion," Kirby said. "It should be dark enough."

Hollis retrieved the medallion and held it above his chest, the faint blue glow seemingly brighter than it had been before.

"Oh my god," she said. "Can I see it?"

Hollis dropped it into her hand and she held it five inches from her nose, the blue light emanating from both sides of the object and illuminating her cheeks, its reflection faint in her eyes. "This is beautiful. I guess I had no idea what it would look like." She examined the other side. "This is a sacred relic. You should feel honored."

"I don't think I want it anymore," Hollis said.

"It was stolen from my great grandfather, but you're meant to carry it now."

"So it belongs to your family?"

Cha-Risa paused for a moment. "It never belonged to us."

"But it was stolen from you."

"Who stole it?" asked Kirby.

"Análí says it was the government."

"Great, and now they want it back. You should take it back to your grandfather."

"It doesn't work like that," Cha'Risa said. "I told you, nobody owns it. It's just something that exists. It was around long before my great grandfather had it. It doesn't even belong to you. It's part of nature.

You can hold onto a rock, but eventually you're going to die and the rock isn't. In a million years, it'll be sitting somewhere else and you'll just be a blip in its history."

"How about if we just leave it here?" Hollis asked.

She handed it back to Hollis. "Let's just bring it to my grandfather. It's still a pretty important part of our culture."

~ ~ ~ ~ ~ ~ ~ ~ ~ ~

"Did you bring anything to eat in your bugout bag?" asked Hollis. "I haven't eaten since yesterday."

"*We* haven't eaten since yesterday," Kirby corrected.

The morning sky was beginning to brighten, a late start Cha'Risa said. The trio had been traipsing through the woods for a half hour after clearing their campsite and Hollis had finally uttered what everyone was thinking. Cha'Risa removed her backpack and spun around to face the boys. "Okay, you're right. I should have broken out something before. I don't think I have much."

She dug around in the pack and pulled out a small packet of teriyaki beef jerky, opening the packet and handing out individual strips. She placed a length between her incisors and ripped off a hunk of meat as she lowered the backpack to the ground.

Kirby duplicated her eating style, but Hollis was volleying his attention between the stick of glossy brown meat in his hand and the other two members of his party. He couldn't contain a look of utter revulsion. "What is this stuff?" he asked as if Kirby and Cha'Risa were chewing on a family pet.

"It's beef jerky," Kirby answered. "It's good."

"Doesn't meat get all gross and make you sick if you don't keep it in the fridge?"

"They took all the moisture out of it," Cha'Risa explained. "So it doesn't rot."

Hollis wasn't sold on the concept. "It looks gross."

"It's really good," said Kirby. "You seriously never had jerky?"

With a glare indicating a certain amount of disdain for the meat, Hollis bit into the strip and yanked the other end off with both hands. He chewed for a few seconds and the apprehension in his face dissipated. "That's pretty good."

"I told you, dummy," said Kirby, chewing mightily.

Cha'Risa removed a bottle of water from the backpack and handed it to Kirby, who took a few sips. Hollis relieved the bottle of another couple ounces and gave it back to Cha'Risa, who was already rummaging through the bag at her feet. She took a swig of water, placing the bottle on the ground and removed a chocolate covered protein bar from her bag. Tearing open the packet, she split the bar into thirds and distributed it.

"I don't even remember being hungry yesterday," said Hollis. "Maybe I just didn't think about it."

"You had plenty of other things on your plate," Cha'Risa said.

"Is your phone working?" Kirby asked.

They sat on the ground as Cha'Risa pulled her phone from her jacket pocket and waited a minute for it to power up. "Two bars," she said. After a minute of swiping and typing, she handed the phone to Hollis. "You got an email."

Hollis read Alexus' reply aloud. "OMG Hollis! Everybody says you and Kirby were kidnapped. Can you escape? I can't go to your house because it's too late, but I'll check it out tomorrow."

He talked as he typed a response. "We weren't kidnapped. We had to get away, but we're good. Can you ride your bike over and check on my parents? Don't tell anyone you are talking to us. Thanks." Then he looked at Cha'Risa for approval and hit send.

As she held out her hand for the phone, Hollis continued hitting keys. "Hold on," he said. "I just need to see if there's anything about my parents."

Cha'Risa leaned over the boy to take a peek at the screen. Hollis had opened a news app on her phone and the national headlines were abuzz with the missing boy and his friend. One headline read, "Ten-year old planetary genius abducted." The article was adjacent to a headshot of Hollis. He opened the article, which featured school pictures of both Hollis and Kirby, and read it aloud.

Police are investigating the alleged abduction of two fifth graders from a rural town in northern Virginia. Hollis Whittaker and Kirby Cooper-Quinn were reportedly taken at gunpoint on Wednesday evening from the Whittaker household.

The suspect in the abduction is described as a woman in her mid-20s, of Hispanic or Native American origin. Detective Terrence Pacquet, of the Delacriox Police Department, added that she is petite, has long, straight black hair and was wearing cowboy boots, a black jacket and jeans. She is considered armed and dangerous.

An Amber Alert was initiated at 7:15 p.m. on Wednesday for the suspect and the two boys. Detective Pacquet said he had reason to believe the children were in "extreme danger."

Hollis Whittaker, 10, was thrust into international fame earlier this week as the discoverer of the famed Planet X, a 9th planet whose proof had eluded scientists since mathematical projections predicted its existence in 2015. Experts have hailed the discovery as unprecedented especially due to the boy's lack of scientific training.

Detective Pacquet would not offer a theory for the abduction, but said that nothing was being ruled out at this early stage, including the boy's recent rocket to fame. A sketch artist is working with Hollis' parents Graham and Lonnie, and police hope to have a sketch of the suspect available this morning.

According to both Graham and Lonnie Whittaker, two other individuals, a man and a woman, who claimed to be Federal Government agents, were also present during the alleged abduction.

Police had taped off the Whittaker household, but a visibly distraught Graham Whittaker claimed that the male agent had tried to kill his son. Graham Whittaker had lacerations and bruising around his face, which he said was caused in a scuffle with the man. He added that the agents presented badges before entering the home, but attempts by this paper to confirm involvement by any federal agencies have been unsuccessful.

Detective Pacquet said he was unaware of any involvement by federal agencies, and that he was seeking information about the two alleged agents, but that his first priority was to find the Hispanic woman and return the children safely home.

Cha'Risa put an arm around Hollis. "They're okay," she said.

Hollis nodded.

Rising to her feet, Cha'Risa motioned for the group to continue. "Come on, we don't even know if anyone's found the van or not."

The heating packets the boys had been given the night before had long given out, and the fresh ground seemed colder than the small patch they'd warmed up by sleeping on overnight. The chill in the morning air cut right through their inadequate clothing. Moving didn't seem like the worst idea.

"Who?" asked Hollis. "Those government agents?"

"The government agents, the police, a volunteer posse. I have a feeling everyone is looking for us now."

"I doubt they found the van," said Kirby. "That thing was hidden pretty good."

The woods were hushed as the group returned to the hike. Only the sound of their own footsteps on the forest floor pierced the silence. But over the course of the next half hour, another sound grew in intensity, Hollis' breathing. He was lagging behind Kirby who was struggling to keep up with Cha'Risa. At one point, he lost sight of his friend and called out to him in a weak voice. "Kirby... hold on a sec."

His friend spun around and hollered to the leader of the pack. "Hey, hang on! Hollis needs to take a break."

It was a hard pill to swallow for Hollis, but there was nothing he could do about it. He couldn't maintain even moderate physical exertion for very long.

"What is it?" Cha'Risa asked. She had doubled back to meet up with the other two.

Short of breath, Hollis spoke in stunted phrases with great gulps of breath in between. "It's my heart... I can't exercise too hard... otherwise I have trouble breathing."

"Oh my god, Hollis. Are you okay?" she asked, placing a hand on his shoulder. She crouched beside him.

"I'll be fine... I just need a breather."

"What's wrong with your heart?"

"It's a condition I've had since I was a baby... It's nothing."

"Well, take your time," she said. "We shouldn't be too far from civilization."

Hollis rolled back on his haunches, flanked by the other two, Cha'Risa rubbing his back as if it would somehow cure a defective heart.

"If you ever need to stop, just let me know. I don't want you hurting yourself," she said.

"I'll be all right... if we go a little slower."

It wasn't long before the trio were on the move again, this time at a more casual pace. Hollis was given the lead and he admittedly felt safer that he wouldn't be left behind. Beforehand he was lagging by enough that he had begun picturing a scene where the other two didn't notice him missing until it was too late. He'd concocted a storyline where Cha'Risa and Kirby reached the edge of the woods only to realize he wasn't there, then they didn't report him missing because of the Amber Alert and the government agents. He wondered if his survival skills would be up to the task.

But that was all past now. He was setting the pace. Occasionally, Cha'Risa checked the compass and told him to head a little to the left or right, but other than that, he was in charge. Conversation had fallen to a minimum as the day began to warm up. It had to have been three hours since they'd left their campsite.

Kirby was the first to hear traffic, but after he pointed it out, the sound became obvious to everyone. For a scant few minutes they made their way toward the vehicle hum and after cresting the top of a small hill, the road came into view below them, still past a mix of maple and hemlock trees.

"That *should* be Route 81," Cha'Risa said. "If we follow this, we'll end up in town."

Hollis eyed the motorists rushing by, two lanes of cars, trucks and SUVs, most with single occupants. Some held phones up to their ears, others were red from yelling, but the majority just drove by, glazed over, the daily commute an extended interruption between home and work, a necessary waste of time. He wondered what kept their minds occupied. Did they switch to autopilot? It seemed like a miserable way to spend every morning. Was that the tradeoff for attaining adulthood?

As the trio gazed at Route 81, Hollis began to see patterns, clusters of traffic and limited open spaces, a sense of flow, or lack thereof. He recognized the overarching pattern as more significant than each of the individual vehicles. It wasn't possible to determine how every car might change its path, but the whole road took on a coherent order, a system that provided him a little comfort.

At Cha'Risa's suggestion, they retreated a dozen steps so they could hear the noise from the road, but no one would be able to spot them. Then they shadowed the road with slightly lifted hearts, having emerged from the unknown wilderness back into the world of humans. Even though the motorists weren't aware of the three desperados paralleling the road, civilization was near. It was evidence that the woods wouldn't claim the hikers for its own.

They tramped over a flat landscape within earshot of the road, the din of Route 81 a constant whine of rubber on blacktop to the left, and directly opposite, the silence of the forest. Within a couple miles, the terrain slanted down ever so slightly for what seemed like a preponderance of the morning. Every hour or so, Cha'Risa called for a respite and distributed trail mix and water. She was taking more care than she had the night before and Hollis had a feeling it was because of his heart problem. He had given up the lead, but the pace was less hurried no matter who was out front.

A clearing appeared up ahead through the trees, a parking lot. They stayed back about twenty yards and Cha'Risa dropped her gear on the ground. The lot belonged to a gas station and convenience store with a wooden sign at the entrance that read "Tilly's Gas and Go" in fluorescent green lettering. A rusty metal display with flip over numbers gave the day's regular gas price, $2.96. Tilly's had a healthy turnover with a steady stream of customers vying for parking spots, filling up dwindling gas tanks and trudging back to their cars with snacks and Styrofoam cups of coffee and energy drinks.

Reaching into her backpack, Cha'Risa pulled out a wad of cash and stuffed it into her front pocket. "I'm going to get us some food," she said. "Can you two stay here?"

XVI

"Hold on a minute," said Kirby. "You're going to look exactly like the lady everyone's looking for."

The shady woods and small brush at the edge of the forest camouflaged Cha'Risa from the bustling parking lot of Tilly's Gas and Go and the harsh light of day. She froze in her steps, turning her head back to her two traveling companions. "That's a good point." She switched into self-critical mode, lowering her voice. "Gotta keep your head on straight. Gotta stay focused." She reached into her jacket pockets, pulled out a couple hair pins and bound her hair into a loose bun. Then she pulled the blanket out of the backpack, flipped open a Leatherman from her jacket pocket and sliced a strip off the blanket. She converted the slip of the blanket into a bandana and dropped her jacket on the duffel bag, leaving her just a khaki button up shirt for warmth. "How's that?"

"They're looking for cowboy boots too," said Kirby. "You want to try mine?"

"Oh, please tell me I don't have the same sized foot as a ten-year old boy," she said, pulling off one of her boots.

Kirby untied his sneakers and tossed one on the ground near Cha'Risa. "I have big feet."

She pulled it on with a bit of a struggle and tied it, putting weight back on the leg. "It's pretty tight, but give me your other one." With shoes exchanged, Cha'Risa headed on her own to the parking lot.

Kirby stomped to a nearby tree and retraced his steps back, looking down at his new footwear. "Check it out," he said, "I'm a cowboy."

"Yeah," Hollis replied. "A girl cowboy."

"Shut up." Kirby ran around the tree he'd just visited. "Plus it'd be a cowgirl, not a girl cowboy."

"What do you think of her?" Hollis cast an eye toward the parking lot Cha'Risa was just entering.

"I don't know. She's okay, I guess."

"Do you think she's dangerous?" Hollis took a seat on the ground, his back up against a hemlock.

"I think she had plenty of chances to kill us if she wanted."

"Yeah, but... I don't know. Do you think she's really a maid?"

"Sure, why not? Who's gonna make up a job like that?"

"Maybe she works for the government."

Kirby shrugged. "Maybe. But give me a break. She had a drawing of you that her great grandfather drew."

"That's what she says. How do we know she's not lying?"

Kirby folded his arms, his lips puckered. "I guess we don't. What are you saying, she's a Fed and she's competing with those other two?"

"I don't know. Maybe they weren't with the government and she is."

"Well then why would she be trying to avoid the police?"

"Maybe it's top secret."

"So what, do you want to split?"

For a moment, Hollis seemed to be contemplating the possibility. He picked up a stick at his feet and tapped it on the ground. "No. She knows more about this than we do, if she's a government agent or not. What's the worst that happens? We go out to New Mexico and figure out she's a freak and come back."

"Or she drops a turd on your head while you're sleeping. That would be worse, wouldn't it?"

"Or her grandfather lays a crap in your mouth."

"Aww, gross man! You're sick."

The pair broke into a fit of laughter that faded over the course of a minute, Kirby shoving Hollis so he toppled over onto his side like a portly tree being felled. Then Kirby lay down next to his friend and they stared at the forest canopy above.

"I hope she gets Reese's," Hollis said.

"For breakfast?"

"Yeah. Why not?"

"'Cause it's candy."

"It's got peanut butter in it."

"You don't really eat those for breakfast, do you?"

"Like I said, it's got peanut butter."

"That crap isn't peanut butter. It's peanut flavored substitute or something."

"Same diff."

"I'm thinking taquitos," said Kirby.

"What's that?"

"It's kind of like a taco."

"So peanut butter for breakfast is wrong and a taco is normal?"

"Yeah, that's what the Mexicans eat."

"They eat tacos for breakfast?"

"The whole world doesn't stuff down Fruit Loops, you know."

"What, so now I can't have cereal?"

"Try something that's not made out of sugar sometime. You ever eat Grape Nuts?"

"You eat that stuff?"

"Well no, that's like eating cardboard, but there's shit that's good that's not made out of sugar."

"Like tacos."

"Taquitos."

"Whatever. I hope they have Pop Tarts. A gas station should have them. Does that qualify as breakfast for you?"

"It's still sugar. What about this don't you get?"

"Maybe I *like* sugar."

"That's how come you're fat and your heart doesn't work."

"I'm not fat. I'm overweight and I have heart disease. It's a disease."

"Whatever, you lump of moron sauce. All I'm saying is try the taquitos. You won't be disappointed."

"Okay... but I'm not fat."

Cha'Risa returned toting several plastic shopping bags. She dropped them by the boys and squatted down next to them. Sitting upright, Hollis and Kirby surveyed the provisions as Cha'Risa pulled a jacket and sweatshirt out of one of the plastic bags. She tossed them on the ground and each of the boys grabbed for one, holding them up to examine them. They were Redskins team clothing.

"I didn't want to get two of the same thing just in case someone noticed a woman that looks like me buying two kids' jackets," she said.

"Makes sense," said Kirby as he pulled the sweatshirt on. Hollis stuck his arms through the jacket and immediately returned to searching through the bags, pulling out a packet of Pop Tarts.

"See? Pop Tarts," he said. "Pop Tarts equal breakfast."

Kirby was unwrapping a breakfast sandwich. "Don't get me wrong," said Kirby, "they taste good, but... Ooh, what is this, sausage? Nice." He chomped off a huge bite.

Cha'Risa removed a liter of orange juice and laid it on the ground, grabbing a breakfast sandwich from the same bag Kirby had rooted through. The meal was eaten in silence. Placing the remainder of the food in the duffel bag, the group continued following the highway, skirting well around Tilly's, Cha-Risa and Kirby swapping shoes again before leaving.

"Stoneville's about a mile away," Cha'Risa said.

"So what's the plan?" Kirby asked.

"There's a cheap-ass car for sale," Cha'Risa replied. "With any luck I'll offer cash and there won't be any questions."

"How much you got?"

"Never you mind... Enough to buy a cheap-ass car."

The hike to the edge of town was uphill. Hollis asked the group to stop twice so that he could catch his breath and by the time civilization seemed imminent, it was warming to the point that the boys had removed their new apparel and slung them over their shoulders.

The first sign that they were entering Stoneville was a fenced-in little league park and though it was empty, the diversion around it added up to another ten minutes. Just past the baseball field signs of life began to emerge. Miller Lite cans and empty bags of chips were scattered around rocks, aged paper plates and plastic shopping bags melted into the ground along with scores of cigarette butts. And just past the scene of a former underage party, a couple trailer homes came into view, forty-footers. They were part of a trailer park that had been carved into the woods, but decades on was in danger of being swallowed up by it, unkempt backyards covered in pine needles, discarded toys and broken Big Wheels. Cracked plastic flower pots and rusted watering cans remained as signs of an attempt at beautification a decade or two ago.

On the far side of the two trailers, rows of similar homes continued on either side of a pothole-marked blacktop road for what would have been a city block. Baby blue, beige and brown homes with American flags by the front doors, souped-up cars and beat up trucks in the driveways.

Cha-Risa halted the group and laid down her bags and rifle. "I'm going to take the lead, okay," she said. "Give me a couple minutes and then follow me, but stay far enough back so it doesn't look like we're together. I might just have to bury the rifle."

Hollis and Kirby knew if they had any chance of escaping detection, they'd need to be separated from their leader. Authorities were looking for an Indian or Hispanic woman with two white kids. They wouldn't get far if they stuck together in public.

"Put your jackets back on," she said. "And Kirby, keep your hood up, okay? The less you resemble who they're looking for the better." The boys did as they were told.

"What if something happens, like somebody recognizes us?" Hollis asked.

Cha-Risa shook her head. "I don't know. Make a run for it and meet up at the trailer park entrance when it seems safe?"

"What if the cops show up and arrest you?"

"I don't know Hollis. I don't have a plan." She raised her hands in surrender. "I guess I'd better not get arrested."

"We're kind of screwed if you do," said Kirby.

"No shit," she replied, frustrated. "What do you want me to do? Do you think I want to be the target of an Amber Alert? Do you think I woke up yesterday and said, 'Shit, you know what I would like better than anything else? To get arrested for kidnapping two kids.' I don't know what else to tell you. We need to get a car and I can't do that and stay hidden at the same time."

"How about if me and Hollis just make our way through the woods to the trailer park entrance and wait for you there?" Kirby asked. "That way nobody will see us together."

Pursing her lips, Cha'Risa nodded. "Okay, that's a better idea than mine." She dug out a package of beef jerky from the groceries she'd bought earlier and took a swig of orange juice. "I have no idea how long I'll be. It'll at least be a couple, few hours. I'll leave everything here if you guys think you can carry it all."

"No problem," said Kirby.

"The safety's on on the rifle. Do *not* take it off. Do not *play* with it. Do not *shoot* it. Got it?"

The boys nodded.

"Do you want my sneakers?" asked Kirby.

"There's no way I could walk a couple miles in those things. I'd be crippled. Thanks though." She straightened herself and fixed her hair—which had once again fallen down past her shoulders—into a bun, then she tied on the blanket bandana and stepped out of the woods into the side yard of the left trailer. The boys, obscured by trees, watched as she made it to the road unhindered, the sound of the gravel crushing under her feet fading as she moved farther away.

~ ~ ~ ~ ~ ~ ~ ~ ~ ~

The trailer park had opened onto one of the main roads into town and Cha-Risa slogged along in the breakdown lane past the first few permanent homes, single dwelling Cape Cods with chipped paint, missing shingles and rusty propane tanks hidden by scraggly shrubs. Just past them a concrete sidewalk welcomed her off the road.

Within a half mile, the homes became more consistently spaced and better cared for. The front yards sported stone walls and Christmas decorations. Family names were emblazoned on the mailboxes at the end of picket fences. The road into town had a steady stream of traffic heading in both directions.

She passed a Citgo station, followed a block later by a Shell. A few blocks past that she had clearly arrived in town. Hiking around without the two boys eased her mind a little, but Cha'Risa was still on edge. Despite the fact that residents might be on the lookout for a woman traveling with two children, her general description was still plastered all over the news and Native Americans weren't prevalent enough in this part of the country that she could easily melt into the community. So she did her best not to be noticed when she started passing other people—avoiding eye contact. A key tactic was to bury her face in her phone, with the dual benefit of conforming to modern pedestrian norms while simultaneously following the directions on her map app.

The fire station on the left was close to the middle of Stoneville, according to her phone, so she kept a lookout for Queen Street, which lead to Lee Drive, Lemley Street and finally to Melody Circle.

Cha-Risa followed the numbers on the houses, stopping in front of number 12, an alabaster and sage one-story ranch, with a large porch dominating its center. The car she had found for sale on Craigslist was parked on the front lawn next to the driveway, a silver 2005 Honda Accord. There was a cardboard sign in its window marked $1,000.

Taking up center stage on the driveway was a yellow metallic Mustang, shiny as a piece of hard candy. It was a sign that the owner was home. She marched up the driveway buoyed to be one step closer to fulfilling her mission. The doorbell brought a bony man in his forties with a crew cut, three days worth of stubble and a Slipknot concert tee-shirt. He had aging tattoos along both arms and up his neck. He examined her from head to toe. Cha-Risa let loose a moan of dread under her breath.

"Hi," she said. "I was wondering if I could take a look at the Honda."

"Yeah," the man replied in a tone that indicated the Slipknot concert and subsequent celebrations might have been last night, or even this morning. "Let me grab the keys." Leaving the door ajar, he traced his steps back into the house and returned a few seconds later, following Cha-Risa onto the driveway. She didn't like his silence. She could sense his gaze moving up and down her back, evaluating her—rating her. There was likely a sneer on his face. Why were so many men like this?

She reached the car and spun, catching his eyes moving up from her butt. Typical. He opened the locks with the remote key fob, showing no sense of shame. She opened the door and peered inside.

"It's got a hundred and thirty thousand miles, but it runs good," he said. "It's a Honda, you know."

Once again, as she inspected the front and back seats, she could feel he was focused on her backside. She just needed to buy this thing and get away as fast as she could. She sat in the driver's seat. "Can I start it?"

"Sure," he said, handing her the key.

It took a few seconds to turn over, but it started and sputtered like a car that was much older. At one point she thought it would stall.

"It idles low, but it's been good to me," he said.

She gunned the gas a few times. "Does the heat work?"

"Yeah."

"I'll take it," she said.

His demeanor improved. "Okay, are you like using a check or anything?"

"Cash," she replied, shutting the engine off and stepping out of the car. He loomed over her, not granting much space and peered down at her chest, then at her face.

"Awesome. Let me go get the title." He dawdled up the driveway, glancing back at her when he reached the porch.

Cha-Risa leaned against the Accord and crossed her arms. "God, what a scumbag," she mumbled to herself.

Within a couple minutes he had the title on top of the car's hood, filling out the few required lines. "You live around here?" he asked.

"No."

"What's a pretty lady like you doing in Stoneville?"

"Ugh," she muttered to herself before answering. "My boyfriend and I are visiting his parents."

"Oh yeah?" the man said.

She didn't reply.

"You got a license?" he asked.

"Not on me. Why?"

"I need to fill this shit out. I'm supposed to put in your name and everything."

Her heart sped up. This wasn't going to be as simple as she was hoping. "I don't have one on me. Is that going to be a problem?"

He gave her a fed-up look.

"I have cash."

"Yeah, but I'm trying to do this above board."

Cha-Risa reached into her pocket and pulled out a wad of cash. She counted it out. "I have $1,170 if you let me drive this thing out of here as is." She pulled a twenty dollar bill from the wad. "Can we make it $1,150? I'll need gas."

"Shit. What are you in trouble?"

"No, I just want to get it done and get on with my day." She held up the money toward him. "It's all I have."

"Did your boyfriend hit you or something?"

It wasn't 50 degrees, but Cha'Risa could feel the sweat beading up on her brow. The man sized her up again. Should she just walk away and try again somewhere else? What if he called the cops? "It's a hundred and fifty more than you're asking."

XVII

"Knock 'em dead sweetie."

"Thanks, Pop." Eleanor leaned across the truck's bench seat to kiss her father on the cheek, static electricity pulling wisps of white hair out from his head. His hands remained on the steering wheel, the engine clattering and shaking the truck all over as a morning breeze blew the exhaust in through the open windows.

Eleanor flung the door open using her shoulder for strength and jumped out of the cab, reaching back in to grab her handbag off the floor.

"I'll be back at five o'clock," he said, "unless I come up with something better to do." He placed his thumbs underneath his suspenders and pulled them out for a stretch before tilting his head toward her with a raised eyebrow.

"Daddy that wasn't funny when you said it yesterday and it wasn't funny the day before either." But there was something comforting about his predictability.

"You laughed the first time I said it," he replied, grabbing the steering wheel again and nodding as if he'd decided something. "Humor is cyclical. One of these days, it'll be funny again."

She waved at him and slammed the creaky door shut. Her father had bought the Chevy Coupe pickup new in 1941 and the way he figured, it was just beginning to break itself in now. Garnet red, a chrome grill and bumper and a spare tire on the driver's side, the old man did all the maintenance on it himself. He didn't like paying other people to do things he was capable of handling.

The tires crushed the gravel as it lurched forward, leaving Eleanor standing alone in front of the Potomac Research Facility. She faced the gate, a dozen feet high, capped with barbed wire and fronted by cement pylons every few feet. Just on the other side was a large half-full parking lot and past that was the actual building where she worked. There were five women in front of her at the security station, and two sets of armed MPs. A speed bump and manually operated boom barrier forced all vehicular traffic to stop before entering the facility, but staff and visitors on foot could proceed around the short end of the barrier after having their identification checked.

The last woman in line caught her eye. It was Stella Romano, an Italian in her early forties with a propensity for men in uniform and a talent for finding mischief. Her skirt matched the tone of her bag and violet mushroom hat. It took a second for Stella to recognize Eleanor, with her new movie star look, but when she did, her mouth dropped. "Eleanor Cole. What have you done to yourself?"

Eleanor twirled around. "What do you think?"

"I think you should have brought a stick to fend off the men."

This was exactly the reaction Eleanor had hoped for. It was the first sign that her fashion gamble would pay off—not that she was looking for a hookup with anyone at PRF. Quite the contrary, actually. But it was nice to know that she could turn heads.

Some of the other women in line glanced back at Eleanor, their eyes drilling through her from head to toe. She wished it were different, that women could be pleased for one another, but often enough everything boiled down to a competition. Still, she wasn't going to let it bring her down. Stella was as accepting a woman as Eleanor had ever come across and that's all that mattered to her.

"Where did the inspiration for this come from?" Stella asked.

"I needed something different," Eleanor said. "Don't you ever feel like a hamster on a wheel, running and running and nothing ever changing?"

"What, are you kidding me? At least you still have youth."

"Ma'am?" The taller of the two sentry guards was speaking to Stella who had reached the front of the line.

Stella spun around. "Oh! Sorry about that." She started digging through her handbag, pulling out her ID and handing it to the man. He scanned the card and stepped to the side for her to pass, then he moved in front of Eleanor, expectant.

Eleanor had her identification ready and presented it, and within seconds was strolling across the parking lot with Stella to the main building.

There were fifteen to twenty men for every woman at PRF, a majority military, a few dozen civilian, and most of the men were professional and respectful, but there were some hands-on slimeballs and arguably the worst was Colonel Emory Clay, the man in charge of the facility and also Eleanor's direct boss. His arrogant and condescending personality was equally renowned and detested among the secretarial staff, and even with a lot of the men. As Eleanor approached the guard by the building's front door, her stomach began to churn with the thought of spending another day with the swine.

After another ID check, the women entered the building, the stench of industrial cleaner heavy in the air and the silence of a government building broken only by muted conversations and footfalls on tiled flooring. Stella took an immediate left and Eleanor climbed the two flights of stairs to the third floor and her office.

A dozen or so women streamed into the Potomac Research Facility during the few minutes before nine a.m., all secretaries for higher ranking army personnel. The base housed a company of two hundred soldiers, and the majority of the work that went on within it was highly classified. Eleanor wasn't privy to the most secretive details inside, but as the assistant to Colonel Clay, she had high clearance, high enough to attend most, but not all meetings with which he was involved.

Her new look was intended to raise a reaction, but she didn't want it from the one man guaranteed to turn it against her. That was the tradeoff, she'd need to work under the chauvinistic gaze of her boss for eight hours. He would start with an off-colored comment, then hover too closely behind her throughout the day, his mouth next to her ear and hand on her shoulder so that he was almost embracing her, all the while feigning interest in her work. It was a daily battle to prevent her fist from introducing itself to his jaw. His breath, redolent of cigars and poor dental hygiene often brought her to the point of breaking.

And it was about to begin. Their office door was ajar, he'd already arrived. At least he wasn't in the reception area. That was her domain and the one saving grace of their setup. He had a private office to the side and occasionally he kept the door closed. Eleanor entered the office and shot a quick eye at his door. It was open.

Her desk was at the center of the reception area, shelves of official literature and military knickknacks all along the rear wall. The door to Clay's office was to her left, by an official portrait of Harry S. Truman, the new president. Overall, it was a dull room, painted a muted sea green with cream-colored filing cabinets and a clock by the door that seemed to move more slowly the longer the day progressed.

She laid her bag on the desk and made her way as quietly as she could to her chair, the smell of musky aftershave and the stench of cigars already heavy in the air. As she sat, Col. Clay was barking on the phone, out of sight, gruff as ever with his thick Louisiana accent. There was a stack of papers she'd filed away the night before that needed to be run through the ditto machine, but she took a moment to eavesdrop on his conversation.

"Fourteen hundred," he said abruptly. "If you'd like me to come down there and shove a fist straight down your pie hole, I'll be more than happy to do it."

My god, Eleanor thought. *He never eases up. From the first minute of the day to the last, he's always demeaning someone.*

"Do you think Uncle Sam pays you to be idle?" Clay roared, pausing for a reply. "I *am* Uncle Sam! And I'll be standing in front of your crappy little desk at thirteen fifty-nine and fifty nine seconds, and I am not waiting two seconds, by god, or you will have my wrath!" He slammed the phone down and muttered a few obscenities to himself.

Eleanor placed her bag on the floor and lifted her chair to stand as quietly as she could. The best few minutes of the work day were before he knew she was in. She tread lightly to the filing cabinet and rolled the upper chamber open slowly, removing a sheaf of papers and closing the drawer with a soft click. Two steps over at the ditto machine, her back was to the room, but it didn't take any figuring to know when Col. Clay had entered. He let out a long descending whistle, the calling card for degenerates the world over.

She glanced back at his door. He was leaning against the jamb with his arms folded in front of his chest and a repulsive smirk on his face, a folder in his clutches with papers spilling out the side. Col. Clay was in full ogling mode and his eyes moved from her bare calfs to her new coiffure, stopping for more than a second on her buttocks.

The Potomac Research Facility's Commanding Officer had oversized ears and a receding hairline that was evident despite a crewcut. He spent hours every day exercising, and was in good shape.

"You know my birthday isn't until October," he said. "But if you wanted my attention, you got it."

Eleanor flashed him an uneasy smile and returned to the work at hand. When would it ever be acceptable to tell a man off when he was being inappropriate? Her chest tightened, anxious about what was coming next. Would he keep commenting, move in on her, or let the matter drop?

"Woo! Spin around and let me get a good look."

Of course he wasn't going to let it drop. She tried her first line of defense—ignoring his remarks. "You said you needed three copies of the 1348s?"

The folder he'd been holding slapped down on her desk and she heard his footsteps closing in on her. "I'll do triplicates of the 1348s and 1480s." Eleanor wondered if she should try to make it past him to her desk to minimize the chances that he'd touch her, but knew it would be pointless. She was stuck in an office with him and it was best to let him do what he was going to do.

Col. Clay placed his hand on her shoulder and spun her toward him. She relented, facing him full on. He gave her the up and down, his warm calloused hand still on her shoulder catching on her blouse like it was barbed, the stink of cigars and bad breath invading her space. He had a formidable frame, towering over her at a good six foot two. She stared at his belt buckle, trying to avoid eye contact.

With his free hand, Col. Clay lifted her chin. "Eyes up here, doll. Get your mind out of the gutter."

Her artificial smile had disappeared, replaced with a blank stare.

"That's better," he said as he laid his free hand on her other shoulder. "You look good enough to eat. I oughta sop you up with a helping of biscuits and gravy." His sinister grin hinted at the thoughts in his head.

The life had gone out of her. She needed this job, or at the very least a reference from this man. Who would believe her if she reported his constant harassment? He was a colonel in the U.S. Army in charge of top secret information. And it would be her word against his. Clay had even molded his wife into a malleable shell, unwilling or afraid to oppose him. She'd back up her husband if called on. No, Eleanor would be labeled a jezebel and lose her job if she blabbed to anyone. There was nothing she could do but take the abuse and minimize it where possible.

Shaking off his meathooks, she turned her shoulders and edged past him back to her desk. She needed to keep standing. If she sat, he'd have his hands all over her. "Did you need a copy of this?" she asked, snatching up the file that Clay had delivered. Some of its contents had ejected when he'd dropped the file and she stuffed them back into the container, pausing on a picture of an Indian family: a mother, a father, and a young boy. They were clad in their Sunday best for a family with a meager existence. Their hair all long, their faces all solemn. But it was the boy's eyes that cut right through her. She saw the boy's soul through them. He was inquisitive—a mischief-maker. It didn't show in his stern expression, but she could see it. For a moment, she was lost, the face of a young Indian boy burning into her heart. But it didn't last.

Clay approached and she tucked the photo back into the folder.

"You really don't want me getting any work done, do you?" he said. "I tell you what." He took the folder out of her hand. "Why don't you run along and fetch me a cup of coffee? Be a good girl." He gently pushed her shoulder toward the door and when she began walking, he patted her on the butt. "That-a-girl."

XVIII

Present Day

The ground inside the woods was covered in dried pine needles, a brittle, scratchy brown carpet created layer by layer over the decades. The trailer park, 50 years old if it was a day, was crowded with saplings and overgrowth inching further onto properties and partially engulfing some of the homes on the park's outskirts.

Hollis was seated on the cold forest floor, far enough into the trees so as not to be noticed by residents coming and going in the trailer park. Earth and air married in a crisp breeze, fresh and healthy. A stone's throw away, Kirby was tiptoeing through the woods, the rifle's strap weighing heavily on his shoulder, its stock nearly hitting the ground as the boy moved. It was a little unnerving to see his friend sporting a firearm that measured most of his height, but Kirby seemed content in his role as security guard. He'd roam deeper into the trees and listen for a few seconds before determining they were safe and moving to a different area to repeat the exercise. After pulling sentry for awhile, he'd return to Hollis and tell him that the coast was clear.

The afternoon wasn't overly cold, but sitting motionless in the same spot for too long took its toll on Hollis. He'd stand up and walk around the same 20-foot area whenever his butt reached the same temperature as the soil, always regrouping with Kirby at the end of their rounds.

It had taken them a good half hour through the woods to reach the trailer park entrance, and it was hours on top of that since Cha'Risa had trudged off in hopes of securing another car. The entrance to the park, Hemlock Estates, was a couple dozen feet behind Hollis, marked by a rotting wooden sign chipped with green and white paint, its centerpiece a barely discernible trio of evergreen trees.

Hollis shifted a foot, revealing the dirt below the needles and realized that everything around him was intriguing, from the soil to the trees, the blue sky through the clearing, even the air he was breathing. He grabbed a fistful of pine needles from the soil and crushed his thumb into them, before rolling them in his fingers, their oils releasing a strong pine bouquet. He'd never appreciated how fascinating the world was, even its minutiae.

The sound of a truck's diesel engine entering the trailer park shook Hollis from his thoughts and brought Kirby sprinting in from his post. They leapt to a large tree trunk and peeked around it into the road. "Oil truck," said Kirby. "Yeah," Hollis replied. Every so often, vehicles pulled in or out of the park, stirring the boys into action. And each time they were disappointed.

"What are we gonna do if she doesn't come back?" Kirby asked.

"Why wouldn't she come back?"

"Would you?"

Hollis shrugged, but his attention was drawn away by the sound of children. He couldn't tell if the voices were coming from the park or from the woods behind them. He eyed Kirby silently, each one concerned that the other kids might be playing in the woods. Kirby remained still as a rock, mouth ajar and hands raised upward and for a long tense moment there was no more noise. Hollis weighed the possibility of a group of neighborhood kids ratting on him and leading to his arrest, into the hands of rogue FBI agents bent on killing him, the male agent, Breiner, with his malevolent grimace and icy stare.

"Wait up!" one of the local kids shouted. The voice wasn't coming from behind Kirby and Hollis, which was good. That meant the strangers weren't in the woods. As quietly as they could, the boys crept toward the Hemlock Estates entrance where three kids on bikes were riding past the entrance sign, out of the grounds. The first two boys—about the same age as Hollis and Kirby—stopped just on the other side of the sign and turned to wait for their friend. The one in the lead was African American, with closely cropped hair. He was all bones, with big front teeth, a flannel shirt and an orange down vest.

The second kid could have passed for one of the von Trapps, with a clean-cut part in his blonde hair, and the third could easily have been his little brother. After the young one reached the first two, they all rode out of the trailer park up the side of a busier main road.

From the relative safety of the woods, Hollis and Kirby watched the kids peddle like they were in a race and when they were at their closest point, about 15 feet directly in front of them, the younger von Trapp shot a glance into the woods and met eyes with Hollis. Hollis' breath stopped short. How did the boy know to look into the woods? Would he tell an adult he'd seen kids in the woods? Was Hollis recognizable?

The bikers raced on and the young rider didn't even seem fazed.

"Crud," said Kirby. "Did you see that? Did that kid see us?"

"Yeah," Hollis replied. "He looked right at me."

"Shit! What do we do? What if he tells someone?"

"Do you think he will?"

"I don't know. I wouldn't. I mean, would you go out riding somewhere and then come home and say, 'hey mom, I saw a couple kids in the woods?'"

"Probably not. But what if he recognized me?"

"What do you think, the kid watches the news or something? He was like seven years old."

"I guess," said Hollis. "So what do we do, just keep waiting here?"

"We could run over to the other side of this entrance. At least that way we're not in the same place if anyone comes looking."

Hollis glanced at the trees on the far side of the Hemlock Estates entrance, probably only forty feet away. They could watch for traffic and make a run for it when the coast was clear. "Yeah, let's do that."

They picked up the bags and crept to the edge of the trees, crouching down in wait and listening for cars. A pack of vehicles shot by the entrance along the main road and were gone.

"Let's go," said Kirby. The boys leapt onto the blacktop, arms fully loaded, and Hollis heard another car approaching. "Go back! Go back!" he whispered. The boys pivoted and bolted back into hiding as the car approached along the main road. They took cover behind a tree, faced the woods and hunkered down on the ground.

The vehicle sounded like it was slowing down and then it came to a halt, crunching twigs and rocks under its tires.

"Shit!" Kirby muttered. "Did they see us?"

Hollis didn't respond. The car idled for a few seconds and then a couple short bursts of a horn startled the boys. Kirby peered around the tree and saw Cha'Risa standing outside the driver's door scanning the woods.

"It's her," Kirby said. They grabbed their belongings and jumped down onto the road, landing only a few feet from their new transportation. Cha'Risa opened the trunk of the car and the boys threw the bags and rifle in. Kirby hopped in the passenger seat, which left Hollis to take the back. The car's tires spat up dirt as the trio left the trailer park behind.

"How'd it go?" Kirby asked Cha'Risa.

"Some men are scumbuckets," she replied. "Do me a favor and don't turn into one."

"You got it."

"But on the flip side, I don't have any more cash."

"You got a credit card?"

"A debit card, but it belongs to my Análí."

"How come you don't have one?"

Cha'Risa let the words hang there, and after a moment, Kirby turned his attention to a trio of bike riders up ahead. He slinked down into his seat. "Hey Hollis, man, get down."

"What is it? Hollis asked, lying down across the back seat.

"It's those kids."

Cha'Risa glanced at Kirby scrunched up below the window line. "What kids?"

"Just some kids that rode by. One of them saw Hollis."

"Aw Christ, she said. "What do you mean one of them saw Hollis?"

"It was nothing. The young kid saw him, but whatever. He's not going to recognize him or anything."

The boys on the bikes didn't even seem to notice Cha'Risa as she drove by. They were too interested in peddling as fast as they could, and used to cars zipping by them on the main road. "We passed them," she said. Hollis and Kirby uncurled themselves and looked back at the bikes fading into dots in the rear window.

"Can I check my email?" Hollis asked.

Pulling the phone from her jacket pocket, Cha'Risa swiped through a few screens and handed it to him. "My battery's getting low, so make it quick."

A moment later Hollis was reading off the reply he'd received from Alexus.

ur parents r ok there are all these newz vans in front of ur house and five-o and yellow tape and everything i had to tell this 1 cop we wer frenz and I hd cookiez for ur rents and he hd 2 go chek and ur dad wavd me in every1 wz in living room and your moms crying alot i told her i thought u were aite hope that ok she hugged me the whole town iz 5150 they cansld skool ur on front page and every1 thinkz ur kidnaped i can't even i want to tell them ur ok but i no i not sposed 2 wen r u comin bck

"So, good," Cha'Risa said. "Confirmation that your parents are alright."

"Yeah dude, they're okay," Kirby added.

Hollis stared at the phone. "I'm gonna write back," he said as he started typing.

Cha'Risa held her response for a second. "Just do me a favor and read it to me before you hit send."

"I know, I know."

~ ~ ~ ~ ~ ~ ~ ~ ~ ~

"Honey, I think we need to talk about Hollis and Kirby."

Alexus was sprawled out on the sofa watching a video on her tablet, a compilation of sneezing little pug puppies. She didn't look up when her mother addressed her. "It's okay, I'm okay."

"Could you put the tablet down? This is important."

"I know, Mom. I'm okay."

"Alexus."

The girl paused the video and lowered the screen to her lap, rolling her eyes toward her mother.

"Honey, I'm not sure you get what's going on. This is very serious stuff here and I think we should talk about it."

"I know. Hollis and Kirby are missing and everybody's worried. I get it."

"We *are* worried. And how do *you* feel about it?"

"I'm worried too."

Her mother let out a slow breath through her nose. Alexus knew immediately that her mother didn't believe her, that her tone wasn't convincing enough. "I'm worried," she repeated, sounding more annoyed with her mother than anything.

"It's not just that they're missing, you know. They've been taken. Adults can be scary sometimes."

"I know."

Alexus' mother sat on the arm of the sofa looking down at the girl. "I thought that was a very sweet thing you did earlier, bringing cookies over to the Whittakers."

"I guess."

"How are they doing?"

"Mrs. Whittaker is kind of broken up."

"I bet she is."

Alexus stared into her mother's eyes. She could tell her mother was upset and she wanted desperately to offer up what she knew, that Hollis and Kirby were safe, but she had made a promise and Hollis had convinced her that they'd be better off if no one knew. She wondered how much trouble she'd be in if her mother ever found out. When she was eight, she'd made $3 selling her lunch at school and her mother still brought it up. Needless to say, this was on a whole other level. "How are *you* doing?" she asked in an attempt to flip the conversation.

Her mother broke into a proud smile that said *look what I've brought into this world*, and brushed her daughter's hair with her hand. "I'm upset about Hollis and Kirby. I'm sad for the Cooper-Quinns and the Whittakers." Her face turned more serious. "And honestly I'm worried about this world and what people are capable of... You know I'll always do whatever I can to make sure you and Marcus are safe."

"I know."

"And you know you can always tell me anything, right? No secrets," her mother said, holding out her pinky finger. They entwined pinkies and snapped the fingers apart in a well-rehearsed move. "No secrets," Alexus replied.

With a reassuring hand on her daughter's shoulder, Mrs. Facchini rose from the sofa arm and headed back toward the kitchen.

Alexus swiped at the tablet in her lap and raised it up. She sat up and craned her neck over the back of the couch to make sure her mother was gone. Then she tapped on the mail app. There was a reply from Hollis. She clicked on it.

> hi alexus idk wen were coming back we need 2 take care of something 1st thats awsum that theres no skool i kinda wish we were back so we dint have to go ether but i guess we arent going anyway we camped out lst nite it was cold but kirby is funny i wish u 2 got along kuz he's a good guy and i bet u wud like him if u gave him a chanz

Alexus hit reply and began typing out a response:

> ive nown kirby since lk k and he nvr liked me so thats y i dont like him idek y he dsnt lk me i think hes funny and everything but he always calls me a btch wich i hate i evn invited him to my bday in 1st grade and he sed the prty sucked cuz it wz myn

"Honey?"

Alexus jolted, her head whipping around in surprise. Her mother was leaning over the back of the sofa squinting her eyes at the tablet.

"Honey, what are you writing? Is that about Kirby?"

Alexus flipped the tablet on its side instinctively trying to hide it. "No," she said, a panic in her voice.

"Let me see it."

The girl froze.

"Alexus Facchini, you hand that tablet over this instant!" The tone was undeniable. Her mother was serious. Her hand was extended.

"I'm not supposed to," the girl said, an obvious guilt in her voice.

Mrs. Facchini reached over her daughter for the machine, grabbing it out of her hands. She pored over the girl's email to Hollis, a look of devastation on her face. She swiped upward through the thread of emails Hollis and Alexus had been sending back and forth and brought a hand up to her chin as she read. For a moment the girl thought her mother might break into tears and she didn't know whether it was because everyone was looking for Hollis and Kirby or because she had kept a secret from her.

XIX

Alexus' bedroom was covered in movie memorabilia: posters and printouts from *The Hunger Games*, *Harry Potter*, and *Goosebumps*. She'd read all the books as well. On one manic Saturday afternoon last year she'd ripped down all of the posters from her childhood, mostly cartoons for little kids and had been replacing them as her new favorite collectables made themselves available. The bookshelves and top of her bureau were neatly arranged homages to Harry Potter: official replicas of Harry Potter's and Hermione Granger's wands; a framed autographed black and white photo of Robbie Coltrane, who played Hagrid; a Hogwarts Sorting Hat; and the full set of novels.

Her room, like the bureau and bookshelves, was organized. It bugged her to have clutter in the way. Whenever she visited friends' houses, there was clothing and junk strewn everywhere. She even tried to secretly straighten up her friends' rooms when she visited them, pretending to thumb through a book she found on the floor and returning it to the bookcase or trying on clothing from the foot of the bed and hanging it up afterward. When she was younger, a psychiatrist suggested that Prozac might help her, but her mother wasn't interested in medicating her only daughter. Anyway, what was the big deal? It's not like she *needed* to have things clean, she just preferred it that way.

The girl lay on her back on the bed casting a glance around the room for anything she could straighten up. But it was all in its place. Her eyes were wide, her fingers drumming the bedspread.

Of course she should have told her mother about Hollis' emails. What was she thinking? She was going to be grounded until college. And worse than that, she'd lost her mother's trust. It's not like she hid things all the time, but Hollis told her he'd be in danger if she told anyone. She was trying to keep her friend safe. It's not like her mother could fault her for that.

But she could.

The whole incident was unfair. She was trying to do the right thing. What if Hollis was right? What if her inability to keep his secret was really going to put him in danger? The woman who took Hollis and Kirby fired a rifle inside the Whittaker's home. What was more dangerous than that? But even Hollis' parents said the mystery woman had saved Hollis.

Alexus shifted onto her side, her socked feet pulling up so she was in a fetal position. She wanted to bolt out of the house, but there was nowhere to go and she was in enough trouble as it was without running away. Maybe Jayden could come keep her company. She was going crazy lying here all alone. No, the chance of a friend coming over after she'd aided and abetted in a kidnapping: zero.

The silence was almost worse than being yelled at. Without any indication of what was coming, nerve shattering scenarios played out in her mind over and over. She wondered if she'd messed up the only opportunity to save Hollis and Kirby, that the adults had been right all along and she'd actually been a pawn in the kidnapper's game. She thought of Hollis and Kirby being held captive in some basement afraid for their lives... or worse.

She heard the erratic clomping of footsteps on the wooden floor in the hallway. It was a group of people approaching her bedroom, not a good sign. Her door flew open without the customary knock.

"Alexus, this is Detective Pacquet and Officer Anagnos. They need to talk to you." Her mother's voice was stern. Behind her stood a bald black man in a suit and a female officer, each wearing a minimal smile. Her mother led the two visitors into Alexus' room. The officer had a gun holstered on her right side and the sight of the weapon in her bedroom caused Alexus' breath to stop short. She pushed herself up so that she was seated on the edge of her bed.

The adults looked down at the girl, a foreign smell invading the girl's space. Musky. Cologne.

"Alexus," the man said, "no one's mad at you. You're not in any trouble. We're just trying to find your friends Hollis and Kirby. Do you think you could help us help them?"

Alexus nodded.

"Good," Pacquet replied. "Look, don't be nervous. Do you mind if I sit down?" He motioned to her bed.

"Okay," Alexus answered.

Pacquet sat next to the girl and folded his hands in his lap. "You know, I have a daughter just a little bit older than you."

The girl nodded again.

"I'm just like your mom, here. She goes off to work every day, right?"

"Yeah."

"Well, I do too, and so does Officer Anagnos. It's just that our job is helping people that are in trouble and right now your two friends are in trouble. I know you thought you were keeping them safe, but trust me when I say, we can protect them from whatever's out there. It's just that first we need to find them. Now, the emails didn't really give us any insight into where they are yet, but they're probably going to be pretty useful to us. Have you talked to them at all?"

"No. I only got those emails."

"You're sure about that? Remember, you're not going to get into any trouble."

She nodded.

Pacquet stared at her for a few seconds silently, as if he didn't believe her. "Okay then. Now, we're going to be commandeering your email. Do you know what that means?"

"It means you're taking it, right?"

"That's right. You're not going to be able to get back into it and I'm sorry we have to do that, but I need you to promise me that if they contact you in any other way, you know, via phone or text or Facebook or whatever, that you'll tell your mother. Do you think you can do that?"

"I guess."

~ ~ ~ ~ ~ ~ ~ ~ ~ ~ ~

"Can I check my email again?"

"In a little while, all right Hollis. I don't want to turn my phone back on until I have somewhere to charge it." Cha'Risa turned on the car radio, which crackled out a blend of modern country and static. "See if you can find something, will you Kirby?"

Kirby fumbled through the buttons in the car's darkened cabin, changing radio stations every few seconds.

"I just don't know why Alexus didn't get back to me," said Hollis.

"Ugh, not that. It sounds like it's made out of plastic," Cha'Risa said to Kirby, bubblegum pop bouncing off the windshield. She turned her attention back to Hollis. "We'll find a motel soon. We'll check the news, emails, everything, okay?"

"I was hoping you'd say that. How about this?" asked Kirby. He had settled on a song from the 1960s.

"I can live with that."

"The Animals," said Kirby.

"That's the song?"

"That's the band," Kirby replied. "We Gotta Get out of this Place, 1965. But they didn't write it... Hey, it's the right song for us!"

Cha'Risa chuckled. "Are you a big '60s fan?"

Hollis answered before Kirby had a chance. "He knows, like, everything about every song."

"You don't say?" Cha'Risa replied.

"Go ahead, ask him something."

"Okay," she said, pausing for a few seconds. "Something before your era. 'Turn! Turn! Turn!'"

"You're probably thinking of the Byrds version," Kirby answered. "But they stole it from Pete Seeger, who really just took it from the Bible."

"Holy shit!" Cha'Risa said. "How the hell did you know that?"

"I don't know," Kirby replied, as if it wasn't a big deal.

"Give him another one," Hollis said.

"Okay, hang on. Let me get a good one."

Kirby turned the radio's volume down.

"Okay, here's one," she said. "Electric Avenue."

"Eddy Grant."

"Cut it out!" Cha'Risa pushed Kirby's shoulder. "You are way too young to know that. All right, one more. Let's see. 1970s. Okay, Shadow Dancing."

"Pfft," said Kirby. "Andy Gibb. Give me a hard one."

"That is unbelievable."

"Hey," said Kirby, "Hollis found a planet."

"Well, yeah, I know, but this is *Andy Gibb* we're talking."

"You didn't grow up in the '70s, did you?" Hollis asked.

"Oh, no, that was before my time," said Cha'Risa. "But a girl can dream, can't she?"

The trio had been searching for appropriate accommodations since they'd made it west of Nashville. It had been dark for a long while as the warm air continued coming out of the car's vents. Three exits in a row off Route 40 had produced nothing Cha'Risa had felt comfortable with and the eye strain from the lights of oncoming traffic was beginning to get to her. She was just about willing to try anywhere not too pricey. There was a general description of her on the news, but she was betting no one this far away from northern Virginia would put two and two together. She'd once again tie her hair up in a bun and check in without the two boys. It should be pretty safe.

Cha'Risa pointed to a highway exit sign. "I'm going to try this one. One of these towns has to have somewhere cheap."

The exit ramp looped around in a familiar cloverleaf pattern and onto an intersection with a road that had brightly lit gas station signs in both directions.

"You know if you brought a car charger, we could have just found a hotel on your phone," said Kirby.

"Shut up," Cha'Risa replied as she turned the radio volume to low.

"What?" Kirby said in response. "You can't find a hotel while the radio's on?"

"Shut up!" she repeated louder. "You know what? I changed my mind. You're not a musical genius, you're a pain in the ass."

"He can be both," said Hollis.

"It's just a habit, okay? People turn down the radio when they're looking for something. I don't know why, but I guarantee you'll both be doing it when you get your licenses." She stopped the car and glanced in both directions. "Which way do you want to go?"

"I'd try right," Kirby said. "Looks like more."

"It does? Where?" she asked.

"I can see some stuff down there." Kirby struck the passenger side window with his finger a few times. Then he looked down the road past Cha'Risa. "That side's all dark past the gas station."

Cha'Risa squinted to where Kirby had pointed. "To the right it is." She pulled out onto the deserted road, the Accord's headlights revealing unremarkable countryside littered with bright bits of styrofoam and papery trash that sped by like ghostly apparitions, here and then gone in the night. Within a few hundred yards, the lights Kirby had spotted became clearer. They were lighting up signage of some sort.

"I think it's a hotel," said Kirby to no response. As the car drew nearer, it was obvious he'd been right. The Braithwaite Inn.

"I will never doubt you again," Cha'Risa said as she pulled the car into the parking lot. It was poorly lit, which was exactly what she'd been hoping for. That meant there probably weren't any security cameras. "I'm gonna go check in. You guys give me a minute and head around back. I'll see if there's a door back there and let you in."

"Want us to bring the stuff in the trunk?" Hollis asked.

"I'll bring in my bags. We'll leave the rifle in the trunk. Even in Tennessee, someone walking into a motel with a rifle will raise suspicions." She stepped out of the car and slammed the door shut, grabbing her bags from the trunk and heading for what seemed to be the front office with yellowish fluorescent lights flickering above the entrance. Hollis and Kirby watched her disappear inside.

Something about the parking lot came across as seedy to Hollis. It was as if the Braithwaite Inn had neglected the grounds for decades, like it was the natural extension of the trash on the side of the road they'd just passed. The car was off, its headlights still beaming through the overgrowth, illuminating the weeds but not the inky blackness beyond them. Crumbling tar coated the half-empty lot, large chunks missing in spots, replaced by the gravel rising up from below. What little lighting there was, highlighted the inn's cold concrete structure. It was painted a flat teal.

The headlights shut themselves off after a minute and Kirby cracked open the passenger door, the car's dome light causing Hollis to squint. He was tired.

"Think we should go?" Kirby asked.

Hollis didn't reply. He picked up a plastic bag of food from the car's floor, slid across the cloth back seat and opened the door behind Kirby. They waited until there was no traffic on the road and made their way to the rear of the inn, which was deserted, just a glass door, a lighting fixture beside it and more overgrowth and trees past the empty parking spaces. The single incandescent light bulb only lit up so much. Beyond its reach the night seemed to stretch on forever. The boys leaned on the wall by the door, their breath misting in the cold night.

Neither spoke. It was obvious that Kirby was as drained as Hollis. They both just wanted to hop into bed and fall asleep. It had only been a day since they'd escaped from the government agents, but it felt more like a week. Hollis' head was pulsing from fatigue. He thought about his own bed, about his parents. He wanted everything to go back to normal.

The glass door shot open and Cha'Risa leaned her head out. "Come on," she said.

Hollis and Kirby followed her a few feet into the hallway and up a set of stairs. The wallpaper, a mix of beige and brown rounded squares, was peeling from its edges, a remnant of a bygone era. The apricot carpet was worn down in the middle of the steps to just its mesh backing material. Hollis didn't care. At the top of the stairs, Cha'Risa led the boys down a hallway covered in the same wallpaper as the first floor to room 236. She inserted a bulky key into the lock, its green plastic fob clattering as she opened the door. She placed a Do Not Disturb sign on the outside handle and closed the door as the boys scoped out their temporary home. Two beds with shiny, floral bed coverings, a thick brown rug, sturdy drapes, an old-style television and a crappy wooden bureau. A faux leather chair near the heating unit was losing stuffing due to a tear, and a strong mildew scent permeated everything.

The boys kicked off their shoes and crawled under the blankets of the first bed, Kirby picking up the TV remote from the nightstand between the beds. He hit the power and the TV slowly emerged from its slumber, casting a flickering glow across the room. The volume had been cranked, so he nudged it down to a more reasonable level. Jimmy Fallon was in the middle of an interview with a woman Kirby didn't recognize, so he began shuffling through the stations.

"I got some toothpaste at the front desk," Cha'Risa said, "and one toothbrush. I didn't want to draw suspicion. One of you can use it. The other's stuck with his finger. Sorry." The boys didn't hear her; they were more intent on watching television, so Cha'Risa took the first turn in the bathroom.

Meanwhile, Kirby settled on an early episode of The Walking Dead. That was fine by Hollis. It was one he'd seen before, where Hershel still believed the walkers in his barn could be cured. In the middle of Hershel's monologue, Kirby muted the TV. He held a finger up to his lips to indicate that Hollis should be quiet and pointed toward the bathroom door. It was a little muffled, but Cha'Risa was obviously talking to someone in a hushed tone. Her voice was calm at times, quietly agitated at others.

"He's sweet, yeah," she said. "The thing is, I kind of have one of his friends too... I didn't have a choice... I can't... No, I can't, I'm telling you... 'Cause we're in friggin' Tennessee. Look, I didn't call for a lecture... I don't know... I had to ditch my van... Do you not get the news out there? There's a nationwide manhunt on for me, Amber Alert and everything... I had to. You were right, the government had people already there... Two... Yeah... No, they were going to kill him, no doubt... They had the gun at the back of his head... No, in his house... Yeah... I had to buy a car... Cash. And I just put a motel room on the card. That's why I'm calling. I need you to put some more money in the checking account... No, I used everything... Look, I wasn't planning on buying a car, all right?... The more the better... I don't know, a few hundred at least... Okay, thanks... I don't know, a couple days... Yeah... Do you have a plan?... Well, you're going to have to do better than that... I'm looking at serious jail time here and that's not even thinking about Hollis... I know... He's just like the picture... Yeah, I showed it to him... I don't know, he seems just like a regular kid... Okay, listen I gotta go, can you do that in the morning, first thing?... Try for a grand... Yeah... Yeah, I love you, too, Análí... Okay, yeah... Análí, I have to go... I'll talk to you later... Yeah... Okay, thanks, bye-bye."

XX

Hollis' parents eyed Agents Breiner and Grey.

"Would you mind if we take a look at it?" Agent Grey asked. She looked shorter than Hollis remembered. Everything looked different from this angle. He was watching from above the adults' heads—not from his chair—though he could see himself too, sitting at the kitchen table, right where he was supposed to be. He realized he'd already experienced this moment, but not like this. This was more like an instant replay. Everything else seemed right, an empty container of Chips Ahoy, three glasses of milk and a table full of crumbs. Kirby was there.

Hollis was only an observer in the room, floating and fluid, imperceptible to the actors. He was behind Agent Grey as she examined the Níłch'i, holding it in front of her face and squinting at each side. "It looks right," she said, offering the object to her partner.

Agent Breiner studied both sides of the medallion as Hollis watched from above his shoulder. The agent checked out his phone and looked back at the object. On the phone's display was a black and white image of the Níłch'i with a ruler laid next to it for perspective, and when the agent swiped the photo, a black and white image of the other side of the object appeared, once again accompanied by a ruler. Breiner compared the image to the medallion in his hand. "That's it," he said, placing both the phone and Níłch'i into his jacket pocket and moving around the table.

As Hollis scanned the room, he understood it, not the situation unfolding, but the basics in the room: the elements of the people, the furniture, the walls, the entire light spectrum from extremely low frequency to gamma rays, the energy. It was all following the rules. He could sense the binding forces between the atoms in everything he saw, the neutrinos so minuscule that they shot through the spaces inside the atomic particles without even coming close to them, the push of everything to the center of the earth, even infinitesimally small particles that popped in and out of existence instantaneously. He began to discern the octillions of particles making up everything in the room.

"We're going to need to take it for evidence," Agent Grey said. "I hope you understand."

The ethereal Hollis floated over the table and focused on the material version of himself with the murderous Agent Breiner looming behind. He could see the chemicals and synapses firing inside his own head, the adrenaline entering the bloodstream.

"Do I get it back?" his solid form asked. The air left his lungs and vibrated his vocal chords, sending the sound in varying frequencies through the room, where it bounced and dissipated. From above the table, the phantom Hollis recognized the amplitude of the soundwaves. It all seemed perfect.

Gradually, the conversation became background noise. He could hear the words, but they were no longer in focus. The particles and energy filling the room became clearer than the kitchen and everyone inside it. Everywhere Hollis looked, there was energy. Time itself was woven into the molecular fabric and it was all interconnected. Without time, there were no particles or waves; without particles and waves there was no energy; without energy, there was no time. Everything was reliant on everything else, a perfect balance. Change one and you change them all. The room and everything in it began to separate into basic components dispersing evenly throughout Hollis' field of vision. The walls faded, the people and furniture, each breaking down and dissolving like vapor. Beyond their house, the trees and roads did the same, the earth itself losing its form.

As the world's makeup lost its focus, so did time. And when the hazy soup of light began to coalesce once again, the boy felt that time had changed as well. The earth took shape, the firs and the pines coming together around him, solid forms out of dust. The ground firmed, the breeze blew. He drifted directly through the pines and firs as if they were just figments, shadows of their solid cousins, and he saw inside the trunks whenever he passed through them. The treeline ended abruptly in a clearing and Hollis could hear a commotion. Though it was nighttime, the area was well lit. There was a road and three old-fashioned cars.

As he exited the woods, four men in suits and hats converged on him, one of them holding a pistol. The fear that should have been the natural reaction in Hollis never took hold. After all, he was only floating through this world. He wasn't part of it. But what did these men want? And how were they seeing him given his ghost-like state? It became apparent that their eyes weren't on Hollis. They were focused on the ground. Hollis turned his attention below him where a woman in a blouse and wool skirt lay on her stomach. Blood was pumping out of a hole in her back and Hollis thought of Mrs. Mori.

One of the men stooped beside the woman and frisked her and Hollis felt a growing sickly, sweaty heat seeping through his core—nausea. The woman was incapacitated and this man was rifling through her clothing as if she were insignificant. The man muscled the woman onto her back, her body limp like a lifeless doll and her eyes staring up at the sky. There was a mixture of emotions inside Hollis as the woman gurgled with each breath, first sorrow for her and then anger. The man searched the woman thoroughly with no recognition of her pain or dignity and Hollis wanted to jump on top of him and knock him off the woman. But the boy knew he wasn't really at this spot at this time. He was just an observer. And though he couldn't say why, and he knew this was long ago, there were similarities between these men and the agents who had tried to kill him in his kitchen—a lack of humanity.

The man gave up his search. "It's not here," he said.

Not far beyond the cadre of men, an older woman stood by the driver's side door of one of the old cars. Sporting a skirt suit and a hat straight out of a black and white movie, the woman was anxious, but her concern wasn't for the woman on the ground. This other woman was in no danger from these men. "What do you mean, 'it's not here?'" the woman barked. It was her cold tone that frightened Hollis as much as the men. He'd only ever witnessed such callousness in the agents at his house. There'd been cruelty in movies, but there was something in him that didn't believe people could act this way in real life. It was outright malice and even a ten-year-old boy could see it.

The man that was crouched at Hollis' feet kept his eyes on the injured woman. "I mean it's not here," he shouted back in response.

Hollis floated toward the woman in the hat as she rushed around the car. The woman lifted a white garment off the pavement. "Here," she said as she searched through the fabric. Her fingers, wrinkling and pale, began to merge with the cloth, particles passing between her hands and the garment, and the world slowly began to lose focus again, sounds and smells becoming less distinct for Hollis. He floated toward the tree line on the far side of the road as the makeup of the road fell away.

"Goddamit!" he heard from behind as he entered the woods and the rigid reality of the scene faded to mist. In a moment the woods coalesced around him again. He sensed he was home, but instead of his house, there were only trees. In fact the whole neighborhood was gone. This was before it was even built. He floated through the maples and the hills, passing straight through it all. He knew the route. He was floating toward his secret spot, the wind rustling the leaves, the sound of a stream flowing in the distance. The holiday scents of firs and pines brought some comfort from the scene he'd just left, memories of Christmas, thoughts of times he'd spent alone in the woods as ruler of his own kingdom. A satisfying warmth spread through him, happiness more intense than he'd even experienced during the best of times. This was the feeling of full contentment.

As he approached the stream, the sound of footsteps emerged from the distance. Someone was getting closer. He floated toward the sound and the woman he'd just seen victimized came into view. She looked tired, her breath labored, her eyes raw as if they'd run out of tears. The woman walked in measured steps, her stride limited by her tight tartan skirt. She kept her eyes on the ground, trying to be careful of what she stepped on as her shoes obviously weren't meant for outdoor hiking. As she reached a slight incline, she broke into a jog and Hollis floated beside her as she ascended the hill, the scent of perspiration and perfume emanating from her clothes and blending with the leafy smell of the forest. She was struggling to find the energy to continue.

Something kept pressing her forward. Her footsteps became heavy as she slowed again at the top of the hill, clearly running out of breath. Though the temperature didn't bother Hollis, the air was hot and humid, hardly conducive to someone running.

She muttered to herself and Hollis could barely decipher her words. "... couldn't just be halfway decent... They're going to have the whole damned army out... end up in jail for the rest of my life." She stifled a scream and mumbled, "What the hell was I thinking?"

As the woman started descending the other side of the hill, she paused and eyed the river—Hollis' river. She pinched the shoulder of her blouse and raised it to her forehead in an attempt to wipe the sweat from her brow, but the shirt was soaked already and the move was fruitless. She trod down the hill toward the water, reached underneath her dingy, untucked blouse into the waistline of her skirt and removed the Nílch'i, clutching it tightly in her hand. Standing on the banks of the swollen stream, she studied the medallion, then tossed it into the river. "Good luck finding that, chucklehead."

The woman trudged away from the water and the scene broke apart like it had done before, leaving Hollis in the midst of a dense fog made from all of its particles and energy. He felt a strong connection to the woman he'd just observed. She had been the last one to touch the medallion before he picked it up, and judging by the cars and her outfit, it was a long time ago. He remembered the woman lying on the ground bleeding from her back. She'd been killed for the Nílch'i and Hollis knew he'd only been lucky in avoiding his own bullet.

When the fog settled into forms again, Hollis was staring at a fenced-in facility patrolled by the military. He could make out pockets of men in uniforms and suits, a parking lot and several buildings. And though he didn't recognize this military base, he knew where it was in relation to his home, only seven or eight miles away. The guards at the main gate didn't look at Hollis. They couldn't see him. He gazed up toward the barbed wire on top of the fence and floated through the barrier as if it weren't there. Gliding toward the biggest building's main door, he heard his name. "Hollis!"

He unzipped his eyes and stared at Cha'Risa through the slits. "Wake up," she said. He turned his head to try to fall back asleep, but she shook his shoulder. "Come on, Hollis." He could feel her reaching over him to shake Kirby, who was stirring, but just barely. "Kirby, get up." She grabbed Hollis' shoulder again before stepping away from the bed. "Let's go, sleepy heads. Rise and shine. It's six a.m. We gotta get going."

XXI

Dawn had yet to usher in any warmth from the evening before and the Honda Accord was colder inside than out. The boys piled in. The sky awoke with a crisp golden-orange light spreading out of the east, the entire countryside coming alive. With a shiver in his lips, Kirby joked to Hollis, in the front seat, that he should open the window to let in some heat. Cha'Risa turned the key in the ignition and the starter struggled for the energy to shake the motor from its icy slumber. It was an uneasy moment as the trio waited for the reassuring sound of a running engine, but the car spurred to life and the two boys and Cha'Risa offered up quiet sighs of relief.

As the car pulled away from the Braithwaite Inn, Kirby spread out on the back seat, closing his eyes and pulling his arms inside his Redskins sweatshirt.

"Can I check my email?" Hollis asked.

Cha'Risa pulled her phone from her jacket pocket and handed it to him. Within a few swipes he was reading aloud what Alexus had replied.

> I've known Kirby since like kindergarten, and he never liked me so that's why I don't like him. I don't even know why he doesn't like me. I think he's funny and everything, but he always calls me a bitch, which I hate. I even invited him to my birthday in first grade and he said the party sucked cause it was mine, so you need to talk to him instead of me. Oh my god, how far away are you guys? Are you still in Virginia? That would be so cool to go somewhere awesome. What's it like?

"That party did suck," Kirby mumbled from the back seat. "But I never said it was because of her. It was because it was all girl stuff, you know, like unicorns and clothes."

"Yeah, but you do call her a bitch a lot," said Hollis.

"She's just so full of herself."

Cha'Risa broke into the conversation. "She's probably just being defensive. Do you know what it's like to have someone calling you a bitch all the time? I mean, what are you supposed to do, pal it up with the person after?"

"Hey," Kirby said. "Either of you known her since kindergarten? That's *six* years! I think I have a pretty good handle on her by now."

"How do you explain that she's trying to help us now then?" Hollis asked.

"I don't know. Must be something in it for her. She's probably ratting us out."

Hollis and Cha'Risa fell silent for a moment before Hollis started up again. "I'm going to get back to her, okay?"

"Yeah," Cha'Risa replied. "But you know the drill."

"Don't tell her where we are and read it to you before I hit send."

"Exactly."

Hollis clicked on the phone for a few minutes, his eyes still adjusting to the morning light. After receiving an approval, he sent the email and offered the phone back to Cha'Risa, but pulled back as she reached out for it. "Should I check the news?" he asked.

"Yeah, sure," she said. "That'd be pretty smart. Better to know everything we can."

The boy tapped the phone a number of times and fell silent as he scrolled through the morning's news. "Um," he said. "Cha'Risa?"

"What? What is it?" The apprehension in her voice was palpable.

"There's a picture of you," Hollis responded. "They know who you are."

The Accord pulled to an abrupt stop on the edge of the road, the gravel slipping under its tires. Cha'Risa grabbed the phone out of Hollis' hands and read the article aloud.

DELACROIX, Va.——Police identified the woman believed to have kidnapped two fifth grade boys at gunpoint from one of their homes on Wednesday. Cha'Risa Gutierrez, 24, of Agóyó Pueblo, N.M., has been named as the primary suspect in the Amber Alert abduction of 10-year-olds Hollis Whittaker and Kirby Cooper-Quinn, both of Delacroix. Gutierrez, who was last seen driving a blue Ford Aerostar minivan with New Mexico plates "506 KUP," is considered armed and dangerous.

Police would not comment on a motive, but the case has drawn national attention due to the meteoric rise to fame of one of the abductees in the past week. Whittaker was labeled a "child prodigy" by world-renowned astronomers recently for his discovery of a long-elusive ninth planet. Scientists were stunned that the discovery came from a child with only a fifth grade education.

Detective Terrence Pacquet, of the Delacroix Police Department, told a crowded room of reporters and well-wishers that Gutierrez had a "substantial criminal record" with multiple arrests including criminal threatening, unlawful discharge of a weapon and disorderly conduct.

"At this time, we are not ruling anything out, including serious bodily harm to either of the two children," Pacquet said. "Ms. Gutierrez discharged a rifle inside the Whittaker home during the abduction and anytime a firearm is used in an abduction, there is obvious reason to be concerned."

Pacquet described Gutierrez as petite, a Native American with long black hair. At the time of the abduction, she was reportedly wearing a black jacket, jeans and cowboy boots, though he added that she may have changed her clothing or hairstyle.

Adding to the mystery, Pacquet revealed that both Whittaker and Cooper-Quinn were the first on scene at a homicide earlier in the day. The two boys, Pacquet explained, "happened upon" Fern Mori, 66, owner of Relics and More, an antique store in Delacroix. Mori had been shot while at her place of business and her case is still under investigation. Pacquet would not call Gutierrez a suspect in that homicide, but also would not rule her out.

"I think the fact that we have a homicide involving the two boys raises a lot more questions than it answers," Pacquet said. "There are aspects to both of these cases that I am not prepared to discuss. Ms. Gutierrez is the number one person of interest, but at this time I am not prepared to name her as a suspect in Ms. Mori's case. I can only say that we would like to talk to her."

Pacquet declined to comment on a man and a woman allegedly present at the abduction claiming to be government agents. Hollis Whittaker's parents told reporters that the male "agent" had tried to kill their son when Gutierrez interrupted and abducted the boys. Graham Whittaker, Hollis' father, was visibly shaken and appeared to have been involved in an altercation when he described the supposed federal agents as "murderers."

Pacquet denied any knowledge of involvement by federal agencies. He said that his department had neither contacted the federal authorities nor been notified of their interest in either of the cases. There was a second firearm discharged during the abduction, he noted.

"I can say that we have recovered a slug consistent with the Whittakers' description of events. It was a different caliber than the first weapon, which leads us to believe that there are, in fact, two other people out there who know something about this. They aren't suspects in the boys' abductions, but they certainly seem to be involved in some way and we believe that they are also armed and dangerous."

The man was described as being in his early to mid 30s with brown hair and average to above average height. The woman is shorter and believed to be in her mid 30s as well, with dark hair. A police artist is close to releasing sketches of the two individuals.

"Substantial record? What am I, Charles Manson? Multiple arrests?" Cha'Risa shouted as she re-read parts of the article. "Including criminal threatening, unlawful discharge of a weapon and disorderly conduct? There's no 'substantial record.' That's it. They make it sound like I'm a career criminal. Those were the only ones!"

Hollis and Kirby eyed each other. Cha'Risa was glued to the phone, grumbling to herself.

She shoved the phone back into her jacket pocket and let out a long, heavy breath through her nose, staring out the front windshield. "That's just bullshit," she said. "Only one of those was real, and I was fifteen. Kids do stupid things. And that should be sealed, shouldn't it? I was a juvenile!" She looked at Hollis for some commiseration, but the boy only shrugged.

She jammed the car back into gear and barreled back onto the road, pushing the car well above the speed limit.

"Shouldn't you be keeping it slower?" Hollis asked.

With her lips still pursed and her knuckles turning white on the steering wheel, Cha'Risa wasn't ready to let go of her anger, but she slowly eased up on the gas. Her lower jaw jutted out. "It's just bullshit, you know what I mean?"

"Yeah," the boys replied in unison.

Over the next few miles, Cha'Risa's grip loosened and her breathing calmed. "Sorry," she said. "I'm sorry about that. I'm not a criminal."

There was no response.

A criminal record didn't tell any of her story. It was just a mark upon her for the rest of the foreseeable future. She'd been told that eventually she'd be able to get all of her convictions expunged, but just not yet. And what did that matter anyway when she was now staring at kidnapping charges?

Twenty minutes after Cha'Risa's outbursts Kirby stirred in the back seat. The heat had warmed up the cabin and he had settled in. "Hey Hollis, turn on some tunes," he said. Hollis didn't reply, so Kirby hit him on the shoulder. "Hey man, turn on some music."

Cha'Risa glanced over toward Hollis. His face had gone blank, his eyes turned upward in his head, only the whites showing.

"Hollis!" Cha'Risa shook the boy's shoulder. He offered no resistance, slumping toward the passenger door. "Oh my god, Hollis!" She grabbed his shoulder and yanked him back toward her, jerking the vehicle toward the side of the road at the same time and screeching to a stop. Kirby pulled himself up to the arm rest between the front seats.

Cha'Risa threw the car in park and grabbed Hollis by both shoulders, turning him to face her and shaking him. "Hollis, wake up!" The boy remained unresponsive. "What is this, a seizure? Has he ever done this?"

"I don't know," Kirby replied. "I don't think so."

"Did he ever mention having seizures?"

"No."

"What about medication? Is he on something for this? Holy shit!"

"I don't know." The increased pitch in Kirby's voice was matching Cha'Risa's.

She removed Hollis seat belt and unzipped his jacket as two cars whizzed by on the road. "Shit! Oh my god, we have to get off the road." Checking in the rear view mirror, she gunned it out of the side of the road and frantically searched for a place to turn in. "See if you can wake him," she said.

Wedging his torso between the two front seats, Kirby began shaking his friend, but Hollis was out. "He's not doing anything," said Kirby.

"Keep trying." Cha'Risa kept her speed at a reasonable rate to avoid any unwanted police attention, but the wild in her eyes betrayed her. This was getting out of hand. If anything happened to Hollis, she might just collapse into a puddle of weepy bones. She might not even forgive her grandfather, and he was the most important person in her life. Her hands were moving from one part of her face to another, and back down to the steering wheel, nervous energy trying to find a way out of her. Her gaze drew back to Hollis every few seconds, Kirby poking his friend in the shoulder, cheek and stomach in an attempt to rouse him.

"What's this?" She slowed the car as they approached a thin dirt path heading into a wooded area. It was big enough for the car to fit as long as it didn't get stuck on the rough terrain. She didn't have a choice. She turned in and gunned the accelerator to get up a small embankment and pulled in far enough to block the view of the road.

She motioned Kirby back and shook Hollis by both arms. Inching closer to him, she opened the boy's mouth and peered inside. "Did he choke on something? Did you see him eat something?"

"No."

She put her cheek up against his face for a few seconds. "He's breathing. That's good."

Pulling her phone from her pocket, she swiped it a few times and held it up to her ear. "Análí? Análí, it's me. Something's wrong with Hollis. He's passed out or something... I don't know, his eyes are turned up into his head. He's not responding to anything... What? Wait, I'm going to put you on speakerphone."

She tapped the phone and laid it in the drink holder between the seats. "Say that again, Análí."

An ancient voice came from the phone. "Is he breathing?"

"Yes," Cha'Risa replied. "I checked."

"This wasn't supposed to happen for some time," her grandfather said.

"What wasn't? What's happening?"

"It happens to all Nîłch'i caretakers. It takes its toll on the body. I don't know that it's ever been passed onto someone so young. Does he have any health issues?"

Cha'Risa looked at Kirby. "He's got a heart thing, right?"

"Yeah," said Kirby. "He can't run too far. He's on drugs for it."

"Has he taken the drugs?" Análí asked.

"He hasn't," Cha'Risa responded. "We didn't exactly have a chance to get his doctor's approval. I don't think he had any on him." She looked at Kirby again. "Did he?"

"I don't think so," said Kirby.

"Okay," the grandfather said. "Hold on, let me look at something."

Kirby and Cha'Risa stared at Hollis, waiting for a miracle answer from the old man. A minute passed.

"Análí?" Cha'Risa said. "Are you there?" There was no response. "Oh, come on," she said with more than a hint of anxiety to her voice. Another thirty seconds passed before her grandfather picked up the receiver again.

"Okay," he said. "There's a doctor. Grew up in Agóyó. She's a good woman. She has an office in Arkansas. You're what, past Nashville?"

"Yeah, a little bit," said Cha'Risa.

"She's in between Nashville and here. Probably a couple, few hours."

"Is he going to get better? Will it be okay to wait that long?"

"All I can tell you is that the first time usually lasts a few hours. It can be quite draining."

"A few *hours*? The *first* time? Are you serious? What am I supposed to do with a passed-out kid?"

"I don't know," the man replied. "Pretend he's asleep? You must remember I have had very little contact with the Níłch'i, just fading memories and legend. I was very young when it was taken."

"What if he doesn't wake up?"

"I do not believe he is in imminent danger. He will wake up, but you must bring him to the doctor. Mary Ruth Deschene is her name. She is in River Bend, Arkansas. I will call her."

Kirby leaned in toward the phone. "What if he does wake up?"

"I would still bring him to see Dr. Deschene. She will provide heart pills, I am certain. I do not know the severity of his heart problem, but the Níłch'i can be a burden even for healthy adults in the beginning."

"Can she be trusted, the doctor?" asked Cha'Risa.

"I believe so. She is from a good family. I will tell her that all discretion must be practiced."

"Okay, thank you Análí. I guess we'll see you when we see you."

"Very good Cha'Risa. Good-bye."

Cha'Risa stopped before tapping end on the phone. "Análí. Análí! Are you still there?"

"I am here," the man said as if coming back to the receiver.

"How often does this thing happen?" Cha'Risa asked.

"I don't know. As I say, I have little one-on-one experience with the Níłch'i. My father was the expert and he was killed before he told me much about it."

XXII

Dan West felt his kitchen was too far detached from his living room. Whenever the JWE math teacher and his partner entertained, at least one of them ended up being removed from the action for awhile. Sometimes both of them. There were always hors d'oeuvres to check or drinks to refresh. Why did they ever build houses this way? He and his partner, Ethan, had been in Delacroix too long, saving money, but this was the year they'd be upgrading to a real home, one with an open concept design. And a great location. It would be a longer commute for both of them, but Oakbridge definitely suited their personalities better; its culture consisted of more than football and Miller Lite. There was a folk club and music hall and a theater that was far better than anything you'd expect to find in a small Virginia suburb.

What was he thinking? How had trivialities even entered his mind? Two of his students had been abducted.

"Milk or sugar?" he shouted.

"Both," the woman said from the living room. "Thank you."

Reaching inside the fridge, Dan pulled out a half gallon of one percent and placed it on a tray next to a polished stainless steel sugar container and two coffees. He picked up the tray and made for the kitchen exit, but spun around at the last second, taking a few steps back and grabbing a package of shortbread biscuits from the cupboard. He shook them in his hand, mumbling to himself.

"Here we are," he said, laying the tray on the coffee table in the living room. "As I said, I don't know if there's anything I can tell you that I didn't tell the other detective."

The woman on the sofa was in dire need of a shovel's worth of Xanax, as if her idea of letting her hair down was *only* working 60 hours a week. The tension showed in her brow and her shoulders. It also looked like she'd just devoured a basket of lemons.

Her matching gray slacks and suit jacket reminded Dan of a JC Penney mannequin, with the top button on her white blouse unbuttoned just as it should be. This woman didn't give any thought to what she was wearing. She saw what was expected of her and stuck to that. What did it matter, he asked himself, as long as she was good at her job?

She'd introduced herself as a detective from the Delacroix police department. "Thank you," she said, taking a coffee from the tray. "I'm not expecting to learn anything we don't already know, but we like to be thorough."

Dan took a seat on the couch and reached for his coffee. "I understand. Detective Atterberry, was it?"

The woman nodded her head and took a sip of coffee.

"Have you heard anything about the two people posing as federal agents?" he asked.

"We haven't," she replied. "Have you?"

"Just what's around the rumor mill. Nobody seems to think they were really federal agents."

"It would seem unlikely," she said.

"People are up in the air about who killed Fern Mori. Was it the woman who kidnapped the boys, or was it these two people? I mean none of it makes any sense, does it?"

"Not yet, but it's my job to put the pieces together," she replied. "Why don't we start with the medallion. The Whittakers said there was a big deal made about it. You're the one who directed the kids to the antique store, is that right?"

"It is. It looked old, so I figured maybe it was a collectible. I didn't know if it'd be worth anything, but I think it's great when kids learn from real world experiences, you know? I thought maybe they'd find out a bit of local history."

"Did you handle it?"

"Briefly. I took a look at it, but I didn't recognize it as anything."

The woman wrote short notes throughout the 15-minute interview, and when she was ready to leave, Dan walked her to the side door. The floodlight at the head of his driveway lit up his Jeep Compass and the newer model Toyota Camry behind it. It was a cold night, but not bitter. He waved as she backed her car out of the driveway. With little more than a silhouette to go by, it didn't seem she returned the gesture. Maybe she hadn't seen him. The car accelerated toward Spring Street and Dan admired the Christmas decorations around the neighborhood. Some were beautiful, others clearly garish. He stepped back inside.

~ ~ ~ ~ ~ ~ ~ ~ ~ ~

Lewis Bowman returned the can of Mountain Dew to the collapsible tray table, which was wobbling next to the recliner. He buried his head in the plush headrest of the chair and stretched his wiry recumbent body as if he'd just woken. His left sock had a few threads still holding it together as it dangled over the end of the leg rest. The other foot was planted squarely on the carpet.

A bowl of salsa had been finished off a couple days prior and was gathering crust on the coffee table in front of him among a dozen or so magazines, a pizza box, a few beer cans, and greasy paper plates. The focus of his attention was the 50-inch flat screen a few feet in front of him, broadcasting across the room in a harsh blue light. NCIS had just wrapped up and there was a college game starting on channel 36. He pointed the remote at the TV, but stopped.

"Have you seen this woman?" The news anchor was teasing one of the big stories for the upcoming half hour. "Authorities say she kidnapped two children at gunpoint and is on the run. The latest on the national manhunt for a boy genius and his captor... And the latest cell phone scams, how can you avoid falling victim? Victoria Jacobs will let you know, coming up at six."

Lewis sharpened his gaze. He squinted at the picture and lowered the remote back down to the arm of the chair as a cheap commercial for Hunkins Furniture took over the screen. A man in a Hawaiian shirt, oversized sunglasses and an umbrella hat yelled into the camera, "We're not crazy! I'm telling you, we're not crazy! But our prices are. Hi everyone, I'm Tom Hunkins and here at Hunkins Furniture, we have the craziest prices in the state, maybe even the country. Our prices are so low, you'll think we've gone crazy. But we're just crazy about giving you the best deal on furniture, like this bedroom set, pillow-top king-size bed with real hardwood headboard, two, count 'em two hardwood nightstands and a big, did I say big? I meant *really* big chest and mirror, all for nine-ninety-nine. You heard right, *nine-ninety-nine!*"

Lewis lowered the leg rest on his recliner and leaned in toward the television as Tom Hunkins kept howling. The commercial gave way to another and Lewis sighed in frustration. "Come on! Goddamned commercials." When the news anchor returned to the screen, Lewis turned the volume up with the remote.

"Good evening. Our top story: Authorities in Virginia are asking the public to be on the lookout for this woman." A mugshot of Cha'Risa as a younger woman was inset into the right side of the screen. "According to police, Cha'Risa Gutierrez is wanted in connection with the abduction of two young boys from one of their homes in Delacroix, Virginia. She was last seen in a blue Ford Aerostar minivan in the small northern Virginia..."

"No she wasn't," Lewis said to himself with a wheezy chuckle. "You little minx." He shuffled through the mess of garbage on the coffee table and retrieved a smart phone, swiping it on. The cracks in the screen became less prevalent. Then he punched in the phone number displayed on the bottom of the TV screen. "Oh sweet cheeks, let's hope they got a reward for you. I knew you was hiding something."

He muted the television, then spoke into the phone. "Yeah, I seen that woman you're looking for." He placed a hand in the pocket of his grimy jeans, and pushed himself back into the recliner, a smug grin spreading across his face.

~ ~ ~ ~ ~ ~ ~ ~ ~ ~

Agent Grey backed out of the driveway and headed toward Spring Street. The rental vehicle still had that new car smell, which she liked. She yielded to traffic on Route 202, then slowly accelerated onto the road. She wasn't in any hurry. The meeting with Dan West—where she'd played a Delacroix detective—hadn't been much help and unless her partner had had better luck, their operation was stuck in limbo. Eventually the myriad of eyes and ears would alert them to something important, but for the time being all they could do was wait.

She did her best thinking while driving alone. The first step was always to clear her mind. She turned the heater on for its steady sound more than anything else. It helped to cut down on outside noises. She checked her mirror, no tailgaters. Good. Then she let her thoughts go, leaving the driving to instinct. This was her version of meditating. In through the nose, out through the mouth. Focus on the breath. It was during moments like this that she had breakthroughs, connections that should be obvious, yet hadn't occurred to her. Sometimes she could visualize solutions to complex problems; it was all a matter of time and the right state of mind.

When she checked the car's clock, it was because her next stop, Lucy's Kitchen, had triggered her to pay attention again. Eight minutes had passed with no new insights. She slowed the vehicle and veered into the parking lot, the fairly nondescript restaurant lit well for a non-chain. The lot was mostly empty. She exited the Camry and locked the doors with the fob. Everything was kept locked; never make it easy for your foe.

Concrete stairs led up to a vestibule, into which a line of hungry patrons would overflow during the busy hours. But dinner had passed and there were no crowds in this podunk little town. Everyone was safely tucked behind the glow of a television being fed a stream of mind killing entertainment and advertising. Agent Grey had already begun dreaming of the home baked goods inside that would serve as her dinner. Pies were admittedly a weak spot.

She glanced at the gumball machines in the vestibule and the cork board filled with flyers for guitar lessons and cancer benefits. Just like every other town, she thought.

She pulled at the glass door, which had more heft than would be expected, and crossed the threshold. For some reason the red tile floor was the first thing that caught her eye. It was well-worn, especially around the entrance, the welcome mat notwithstanding. A glass case displayed a plethora of wonderful baked goods, cakes and muffins, cookies and pies. It was the most inviting sight she'd seen in weeks.

Pondering for a moment, she settled on the flaky goodness of a bear claw. She'd order at the table.

The display case/cashier station was located in the center of two dining areas. She looked right and spotted Agent Breiner by the far wall, a dirty plate pushed to the side of his table and a cup of coffee in front of him. He was one sorry son-of-a-bitch, from his clichéd love of coffee to his macho sense of humor. He did his job well, but he was hell to partner with.

Breiner had his nose in his phone. He didn't acknowledge Grey until she placed her jacket on the empty chair next to him.

"How'd it go," he asked.

"He handled it," Grey replied.

That caught his attention. "He *handled* it?"

Grey took the free seat with a nod and Breiner shoved a menu toward her. She opened the menu and flipped through the pages. "Good selection," she said.

"Make it quick."

She raised her eyes over the menu, intrigued. "You got something?"

Breiner leaned back in his chair and pushed his shoulders back. "We got the bitch."

"Something new?"

Breiner nodded. "She switched cars." He gulped down the remainder of his coffee and placed the mug back on the table. "It looks like she's going home."

XXIII

12:07 p.m., Wednesday, August 22, 1945

The Potomac Research Facility was small compared to most military bases, but it was a secure compound and it had the basic amenities anyone working there would need—specifically a mess hall—which served the two hundred soldiers stationed on the grounds and the dozens of civilians who flowed in and out during regular working hours.

Like all of the buildings at the PRF, the single-floor mess hall was a permanent structure, a pragmatic rectangle of mustard yellow brick. The smell of organics as you walked by the kitchen windows—animal, vegetable, or other—gave away the structure for what it was, but once inside, the overwhelming and ubiquitous stench of industrial cleaner won out. It was hardly conducive to keeping an appetite, but there was a general consensus that the food had the same effect. Any agreeable flavor in the fare routinely absconded by the time it reached the tepid serving dishes, despite the claims of Corporal Oscar Paczkowski, the head cook, who maintained that he had poured great effort into the offerings on any particular day.

Without fail, he'd make time to chew the fat with Eleanor as he slopped the day's gruel onto her tray. "I made the pork chops with an extra dose of love today," he'd say, before pinching his hand to the side of his mouth and kissing the air. "And a shovel full of garlic," he'd whisper. He was one of the service men she truly enjoyed chatting with on the base.

Unless it was a stew day, you were guaranteed a root vegetable soup, a lump of meat of indiscernible animal origin, vegetables sides, and two slices of bread and butter. It might not win any culinary awards but it was free, and due to the base's seclusion, it was the only real option for lunch.

Eleanor laid her stainless steel tray onto the rack and inched along the cafeteria line, waiting for the soldiers in front of her to fill up on double rations as they made perfunctory wisecracks about the suitability of said morsels for human consumption. A trio of cooks accepted trays, filled them up and returned them with absentminded grins, more important thoughts flooding their cerebrums. They'd heard all the comments before and what could they do? They weren't in charge of cooking the food.

Corporal Paczkowski stood at the end of the cooks in the same frame of mind as the other two. Move the boys through and make way for the next bunch. Eleanor knew he'd come to life when he saw her and occasionally that made up for the food. She glanced around the crowded room and caught Stella sitting alone, picking at her lunch, a sneer tattooed on her face. They were each other's guaranteed date at noon, though sometimes other secretaries would join them, Joanne Miller or Marjorie Reynolds.

The chow line moved up and Eleanor handed her tray to the first man, who lopped down a spoon of mashed potatoes without losing eye contact. He passed the tray to the next man with an elbow to the arm and the next man looked up, let out a soft whistle and flung on slices of bread and butter. The extra attention wasn't overly unusual given that women were the exception rather than the rule at the PRF, but undoubtedly Eleanor's new look stepped it up a notch. The disruption to the normal routine attracted Corporal Paczkowski's attention, who caught sight of Eleanor and laid out a broad smile, straightening up from his fixed position hunched over the stew. There were times he figured slowing down the assembly line was warranted. This was one of them.

Some faces never age, even with wrinkles, and even in his early 50s, Corporal Paczkowski looked like the kid who always managed to get caught whenever there was a group prank, with a chubby face that screamed guilt and jowls nearly as old as he was. His stature made it clear he was no longer a child and a buzz cut helped to mask his graying hair, but you could still see him being placed on the teacher's watch list, even after 30 years in the military.

"Oh my dear," he said in his heavy Jersey accent, lowering his ladle back into the dish of stew. "Let me get a look at you." He held both hands up as if he were going to embrace her despite the fact that the cafeteria station separated the two.

She smiled, happy at last with one man's recognition, and turned her head for a profile view. There was something about Corporal Paczkowski that made his compliments a joy to receive, like he was gifting them to her. The comments and whistles from the other men seemed to be more for their own gratification than hers.

"Absolutely stunning," he said. "I didn't know you could be improved upon and once again, you've proven me wrong. Do me a favor and don't tell my wife." He accepted her tray from his still gawking assistant and dispensed a serving of stew. "It's because of this very moment that I'm glad I took extra care this morning preparing today's meal. I knew you would be visiting my little establishment. Do you know what I added to this for an extra dose of succulence?"

"I haven't a clue," Eleanor answered.

He leaned in and lowered his voice, as if confiding in her a family secret. "Fresh thyme." He closed his eyes and sniffed the steam coming off the stew.

"I can't wait," she said accepting the tray. It would no doubt be as bland as every other meal he'd prepared through the years, but complaining would only cause a good man to feel deflated. "Thank you Oscar."

"My dear Eleanor, if you were the only patron I served I could die a happy chef. Now go and tempt me no longer. Make the world a happier place."

She waved a thank you to the corporal, grabbed a glass of water and made a beeline for Stella, who was talking to herself at one of the green granite Formica tables built for two. "I just adore him," Eleanor said, as she perched herself in the chair opposite Stella.

"Oscar?"

"Yeah."

"I just wish he was a better cook." Stella sifted through the stew with her fork, separating the peas to one side of the tray. "Why do they have to put peas in everything?"

Eleanor shrugged. "Color?"

"They're the same *color* as the rest of it! I bet if you asked, he'd take the peas out. He likes you."

"I'm not going to ask him to take the peas out."

"Why not? They could serve them on the side."

"Do you really want me to ask if he'll take the peas out?"

Stella filled up half a fork's worth of stew and slipped it into her mouth. "I guess not."

Eleanor took a bite and grimaced, forcing a smile out of her companion.

"Maybe you could persuade him to take a home economics course, just some basics for cooking, that's all I ask," Stella said.

"Oh my." Eleanor washed the stew down with a large gulp of water. She glanced at Oscar, who was once again hunched over the grub and in his own world. "He's such a nice man. I wish he would find another calling."

"Speaking of nice men, how's the Colonel?"

Eleanor dropped her fork and put up her hands in defense, her lower jaw sticking out, bearing her teeth. "I need to get away from that man. He is repugnant."

"He must have had a field day with your new look."

"My god, Stella, I was this close," she said pinching two fingers together, "this close to pummeling him over the head with the typewriter."

"You should do it next time."

"I don't think you understand. I'm getting worried I won't be able to stop myself next time. He's just so horrible. I don't even think a slap would suffice. That man needs a lesson in humility."

"Let me know before you snap. I want to see it. Do you know, he once said I'd be a doll except for my nose, then he asked me why Italians had big noses."

"What did you say?"

"What am I supposed to say? He's the C.O. I said 'I don't know.'"

Eleanor tightened her jaw again and clenched her fists. "Ugh! That's the worst thing about it. I considered a formal complaint one time."

Stella chuckled and picked at her food. "Good luck with that one."

"I know. That's what I figured. He's in charge of a top secret installation. What am I? A secretary."

"Your word against his."

"It's not even that. They'd sweep it under the rug. I'd be worried they'd come after me for making an accusation against their golden boy."

"I heard General Groves loves him."

"*He's* the one who put him in charge here. I bet Clay doesn't grab the general's ass."

Stella let a snort out of her nose. "No, but he probably kisses it enough."

Her lunches with Stella helped Eleanor to release some of the pent-up tension from the morning. Just discussing the situation with another woman, a peer, brought her blood pressure back down to a simmer. But lunch was only a temporary respite. Eventually she and Stella would bus their trays and head back to their respective offices.

"So what are you going to do?" Stella asked.

"What am I going to do? I'm going to do what I always do. I'm going to walk back into the office and keep quiet as long as I can so he doesn't realize I've returned, then I'll try to stay out of arm's reach and look busy so maybe he won't talk to me. And tomorrow I'll do it all again."

"I'm sorry Eleanor."

"I spent all morning on a new hairstyle. I don't know what I was thinking. Who am I trying to impress? I should have known he wouldn't be able to keep his hands to himself. Why don't I *think* of these things?"

"There's nothing wrong with a new hairstyle. You should be able to do something nice for yourself and not have to worry about a male chauvinist ruining it for you. You're too good to work for that man, Eleanor."

Eleanor picked up her fork with a barren stare and stabbed the mashed potatoes, twirling them around and trying a bite.

"Did you hear me Eleanor? I said you're too good to work for that man."

Eleanor swallowed the potatoes and offered a halfhearted response, "I don't want to be doing this in fifteen years." It was a reply that took some of the wind out of Stella's sails. For a minute they fell silent, each nibbling at their lunches.

"I don't want to grow old," Eleanor continued. "The two of us grumbling over lunch every day about how horrible everything is. I don't want to settle down with some fellah I meet here, and do the laundry and the dishes, spend the day cooking. I don't know. I always thought when I was a kid that life would be what you make of it. I didn't know all I had to look forward to was a choice between a boss who'll fire me when my ass starts to droop or a husband who'll want his dinner on the table at 6 and a clean starched shirt in the morning." She took a sip of water. "What do you want?"

Stella took a bite of bread. "I wouldn't argue with something involving a daiquiri and a swimming pool."

"I want to be remembered," Eleanor said, "like Amelia Earhart, Susan B. Anthony, Marie Curie."

"You do realize you work on a military base?" Stella asked. "You couldn't have picked a field less likely to move you up the ladder. Do you think Clay is going to open a door for you?"

"I wouldn't even want him opening a door for me. He'd expect to be paid, if you know what I mean. Let me say, there are things I want, but there are also things I'll *never* do."

"Oh no," Stella said under her breath, in a tone that had Eleanor concerned.

"What is it?"

"Clay just walked in."

Eleanor craned her head toward the entrance and caught eyes with the colonel. She groaned without moving her lips just low enough that Stella could hear it. Colonel Clay slid his cap under his arm and marched for their table, service men stepping aside for him. He towered over the table, looking down at the women.

"I thought I'd find you here," he said. "Who's your friend?"

"This is Stella Romano, sir."

"Stella, is that right?" he replied.

"Yes sir," Stella said. "We've met."

"You would think that would stick in my mind," he said, winking at her.

Stella smiled uncomfortably, but he didn't notice.

"Well you two little gossiping beauties will have to finish up some other time." He nodded at Eleanor. "I need you to return to your desk."

"Yes sir," Eleanor replied.

Clay lifted his nose into the air and inhaled deeply. "Mmm! Don't you two smell lovely." Then he spun around and beat a slow retreat.

XXIV

Present Day

After steering the Accord back onto the county road, Cha'Risa handed her phone to Kirby in the back seat. "This car is running on fumes," she said. "See if you can find a gas station."

The boy took the phone. "What about Hollis?"

"We need gas to get him anywhere."

Kirby was on the phone for a few minutes when Cha'Risa started to get flustered. "What's taking so long?"

"The reception sucks," Kirby replied. "Okay, never mind. There's one about three miles away." He directed Cha'Risa to an Exxon station near a highway and she pulled into the lot.

"Scoot down back there," she said, and Kirby released his seat belt and scrunched below the window line.

The gas station was fairly modern, with a convenience store and eight pumps. "What the hell side is this thing on?" Cha'Risa mumbled to herself.

From the floor of the back seat, Kirby answered. "Your side."

"Are you sure?"

"Yeah, I saw when we got in."

She parked next to one of the pumps and stepped out of the car. "Let's hope there's something in this account." She fumbled through one of her pockets and retrieved a debit card, inserting it into the machine and punching in the PIN number. Removing the pump, she placed it into the car's gas intake and watched as the machine gave her the go-ahead. She filled up the tank and sat back down in the driver's seat, then turned the engine over and set off again out of the

Exxon station. "Straight forward, that's what I'm talking about," she said. "Now let's go find this doctor."

~ ~ ~ ~ ~ ~ ~ ~ ~ ~

It seemed like just another southern strip mall, stucco walls rising to red clay rooftops, a Supercuts and a Dollar Tree. The parking lot was half full, palm trees towering over a large landscaped island, and along the edges of the mall. The sun, directly overhead, was at full strength without a cloud in the sky, the thermometer under the Stony Creek Shopping Center sign displaying 71 degrees.

Cha'Risa pulled the Accord to a stop on the outskirts. "You've got to be kidding me," she said.

"What?" Hollis asked, having regained consciousness on the ride to Riverbend, Arkansas.

"What do you mean, what? This so-called doctor is located across from a Golden Corral."

"So?"

"So, just keep your heads down, will you? I'm going to check it out."

"I think I'm okay."

"I don't care what you think. You were completely out of it, a limp noodle. That's not normal."

"Yeah, but we could get spotted."

Cha'Risa relaxed into the seat. "Yeah." She paused for a moment. "I don't know what to tell you. I gotta make sure you're alright."

"I said I was fine."

"I'll be back in a couple." She patted him on the head, and looked back at Kirby before throwing the door open and making a beeline for the doctor's office on the far right side of the mall. The Stony Creek Medical Center looked like a former Chinese restaurant, white curtains in the windows separating the inside from passing shoppers. Cha'Risa stepped in through a pair of glass doors to a spartan waiting room, the odor of antiseptic strong in the air. An old couple read periodicals in green plastic chairs toward the back and a blonde woman in her fifties sat behind a chest-high reception desk, her head just visible on the far side and her curly locks stiff from too much hairspray. She reminded Cha'Risa of the Nixon era, a pair of pearl rimmed glasses dangling at the end of her nose. She was typing on a computer as Cha'Risa approached.

For a full 30 seconds the woman ignored Cha'Risa, but when she finally looked up, she seemed more pleasant.

"Sorry about that," she said in a Texas drawl. "How can I help y'all?"

"I'm here to see Doctor Deschene."

"Okay, what's your name?" The woman asked.

"I don't have an appointment, but she should be expecting me."

"Oh," the woman replied. "And what was your name?"

"Cha'Risa."

"Okay, well if you wouldn't mind having a seat, I'll see if she's available."

Cha'Risa returned the smile and took the nearest chair next to an end table covered in dated magazines. She picked one up and held it in front of her face, her eyes on the doctor's office. No one was paying any attention to her, but that didn't mean they wouldn't. And it certainly didn't mean she was safe from being recognized. Maybe the receptionist had already identified her and was calling the police. She looked at the old couple, each one huddled in their own magazine, oblivious to all distractions. How could people be like that? Cha'Risa always checked people out whenever someone new entered a room. Wasn't that just normal?

The receptionist mumbled a few words into the phone that Cha'Risa couldn't make out and hung up.

Landscape panoramas lined the white walls, a snow-covered mountaintop, the New York City skyline. There was a striking wide photo of the Shiprock Navajo Indian Reservation in New Mexico, the famous 1,800-foot rock jutting out of the flat brown of the Four Corners. In the foreground, a lone dirt road winded past the rock under the blanket of a beautiful indigo sky. It set Cha'Risa's heart at ease to know that although Shiprock wasn't their reservation, the doctor still apparently had an affinity for the Navajo.

Minutes later, a woman, not too many years Cha'Risa's senior, strode down a hallway from the back, a middle-aged man by her side. There was a healthy glow to the woman's cheeks, a strong jaw. She looked vaguely familiar, maybe from when Cha'Risa was a teenager. The doctor bade goodbye to the man she had accompanied and turned to the waiting room. Her eyes locked on the only other Native American in the room.

"Hi Cha'Risa," the doctor said as she approached. They shook hands and Dr. Deschene motioned to the examining room with her head. "Do you want to...?"

Cha'Risa followed her down a corridor decorated with a mix of Navajo artwork and cityscapes. "You look familiar," the doctor said. "I think I remember you from Agóyó."

"I was thinking the same thing," Cha'Risa responded.

Inside the back room, Dr. Deschene closed the door. "Go ahead and sit down," she said.

The room was small and nondescript, an examining table, a sink and cabinets, a table and two chairs. Dr. Deschene hopped up onto the examining table, the fresh sanitary paper crushing as she sat. Cha'Risa took a chair.

"So what's the problem?"

"Did Análí explain anything?"

"Not much. He said you were with a sick boy."

"He's out in the car," Cha'Risa replied.

"Well, do you want to..."

Cha'Risa interrupted her. "The thing is, there has to be total discretion. I have to know you won't tell anyone."

"As far as I'm concerned, your grandfather is all I need. I'd do anything for that man."

Cha'Risa exposed a halfway relieved grin. "Okay, let me go get him. I have to trust someone."

She made her way through the waiting room, the receptionist not even paying her any heed, and out to the parking lot. Above her, the palm tree leaves fluttered with a pleasant gust of wind. A pair of women talked outside a black jeep, one with her arms weighted down by bags, but neither woman looked over.

Cha'Risa popped her head in the Honda's side door, the boys laying low. "You two ready?"

"Yep," Kirby replied.

Hollis was a little more reluctant. "I guess."

"Try not to draw any attention," said Cha'Risa.

"How are we supposed to do that?" Kirby said, the sarcasm in his voice evident.

"I don't know. Just shut up."

The trio made their way into the office and out back where Dr. Deschene was still sitting on the examining table. The doctor had an instant recognition when the two boys entered. "Oh my god," she said. "Oh my god, Cha'Risa, what are you doing?"

"Don't believe the news," Cha'Risa replied.

Dr. Deschene sat in silence for a few seconds and Cha'Risa wondered whether she should grab the boys and make a run for it. Respecting her grandfather might not be enough of an incentive for the doctor to aid and abet a kidnapping.

"Are you boys okay?" Dr. Deschene asked.

Kirby and Hollis both nodded.

She threw up her hands. "Okay then. Talk to me. Who needs help?"

"It's this one," Cha'Risa said, pulling Hollis closer to her side. "Hollis here was totally lifeless a few hours ago. I mean, out of it."

"How do you feel now, Hollis?"

"Good," the boy replied.

"Okay. Does he have any conditions? Is he on medication?"

"I have heart disease," said Hollis.

"Any idea what kind?"

Hollis shrugged.

"Well you're probably too young to have plaque buildup. Would you recognize the name? Is it congenital, heart valve problems, cardiomyopathy?"

"That's it," said Hollis.

"Cardiomyopathy? Ok, we're getting somewhere. Do you know what kind? Hypertrophic, dilated?"

"Yeah, dilated."

"Dilated, okay. So you must be on some medication, right?"

"I take a blue pill and a white one every day."

"And you haven't had those today, right?"

"No."

"Do you know if they were ACE inhibitors, beta blockers?"

"No."

"No, that's not right?"

"No, I don't know."

"Oh boy. Do you think you'd recognize the name?"

"My mother usually just gives them to me."

"Great," said Dr. Deschene, squishing her cheeks as she thought. "Did she ever tell you your injection fraction?"

"What's that?"

"A percentage. It means how efficiently your heart is pumping, forty-percent, thirty-percent."

"It's supposed to be thirty-five to forty percent."

"Alright then. Why don't you hop up here?" She jumped off the examining table and patted it with her hand, and Hollis climbed up onto the crinkly paper. The doctor reached inside a drawer beneath the sink and retrieved a stethoscope, placing it on her ears and holding the business end on Hollis' chest. "Take deep breaths," she said, moving it to several locations across by his ribs, neck and back. Then she took his blood pressure with a cuff she pulled from the wall.

The doctor's voice rose so that she was clearly addressing Cha'Risa. "When you say he was out of it, what do you mean, exactly? What happened?"

"We were driving and he just wasn't responding to anything. His eyes were rolled back. He was like a rag doll."

"So, totally unresponsive? Does he have a history of seizures?"

"No," said Hollis.

"What was he doing before? Did he eat anything, do anything strenuous?"

"It's definitely been an intense couple of days," Cha'Risa replied. "But we were just driving for awhile, not doing anything really."

"And how long did it last?"

"He started coming to about an hour ago, so he was out of it for a good three to four hours."

"Four hours?" Dr. Deschene was beginning to sound angry. "You should have brought him to a hospital."

"It's just that Análi said it would be okay."

"With no offense to your grandfather, I can't expect he has much experience dealing with heart disease and kids."

"No, but he does have... He's the only one who knows about..."

The doctor let Cha'Risa's words hang for a few seconds. "He's the only one who knows about what?"

Cha'Risa didn't want to answer, but the doctor looked like she was about to lose her patience. "He has the Nííchʼi."

Dr. Deschene's mouth dropped open. "Hollis has the Nííchʼi, *the* Nííchʼi?"

"Unless you've heard of another one."

"That's unbelievable. Does he have it now?"

Hollis pulled the medallion from underneath his shirt and let it drop back down in the open. It was glowing stronger than it had been before, even evident in the office light.

"Oh my god, I was pushing that thing around. So that's it, that's the Nííchʼi?"

"That's it," Hollis replied as if it weren't a big deal. "You wanna hold it?"

She didn't respond, so Hollis removed the necklace and held it out, offering it to her. She reached her hand out a bit reluctantly, took the object and held it close to her face, examining both sides. "This is unbelievable. How do you know this is it?"

"Trust me," said Hollis. "That's it."

Dr. Deschene's eyes widened, fixed on the Nííchʼi, the whirring of the ventilation system the only sound in the room. A few blinks shook her out of the moment. "Okay, I'm going to admit your grandfather knows more about what's going on here than I do. I thought those were all just folk tales, you know?"

"I know," Cha'Risa replied.

The doctor handed the medallion back to Hollis. "Well, this is obviously yours then. You know what I'd like to do? Okay, a couple things. First, I'm going to give him the pills I'd prescribe if he were my patient to tide him over, with the stipulation that you find out exactly what he's been taking, dosage and everything."

"We'll figure out a way to do it," said Cha'Risa.

"I'd also like to check Hollis out with an fMRI. We'd have to get him to Duke Community."

"A hospital?" Cha'Risa exclaimed. "No. Uh-uh. There is *no way* we can do that."

"I think it would be safer knowing if there's something going on with his brain. He shouldn't have passed out because of his heart. I think we owe it to him to figure out what the Nítch'i is doing to him."

"Yeah, well, let's just say that ain't gonna happen. Anything we learn would be outweighed by possible lead poisoning."

"Lead poisoning?" Kirby asked.

"It's a euphemism," Cha'Risa explained.

"What's a euphemism?" Kirby asked.

"You have to bring these boys to the police," said Dr. Deschene. "If someone's really trying to kill him, you can't protect him."

"You've heard the stories. You know who took it. It's true. I stopped one of them from putting a bullet in him. They can get inside police stations. They can get him. We have to stay away from them long enough for Análí to figure something out."

"Figure something out? What are you going to do, keep him hidden for the rest of his life? What about his parents?"

"I don't know!" Cha'Risa hollered, her face flushed pink, her eyes wide. "What do you want from me? Last week I was making beds." The room grew silent, her eyes redder. "Do you have any idea how much I'd rather be making beds?"

XXV

It was a reality of the modern era that parents had to take turns watching each other's children. Who could afford babysitters? And there was no way in hell Alexus' mother was going to leave her daughter alone after the email fiasco. Prior to today, she'd begun experimenting with giving the girl freedom for an hour or two at a time, but after this morning, she would be grounded until she was twenty. Emailing Hollis created a rift that might never heal. While her mother was working, there was no choice but to leave Alexus at a friend's place, in this case, Jayden's apartment.

"So like, they're okay?"

"Yeah, I think so, but Hollis said they'd be in trouble if anyone found them," Alexus replied. She glared directly into Jayden's eyes, as if the weight of Hollis' and Kirby's safety had fallen directly on her.

"But that lady kidnapped them and, like, the cops are trying to find her," said Jayden.

"That's just what they want you to believe. You know those other people the police are looking for? Hollis said they're the ones really trying to hurt them. The lady saved them."

Alexus and Jayden had been best friends ever since Jayden moved into the school in the third grade. Jayden, with her corkscrew cinnamon hair and pronounced freckles, was the only one Alexus really felt comfortable confiding in.

The dining/living room was cluttered and in need of a vacuum, which made for an uncomfortable visit every time for Alexus. It also smelled like their overcrowded and disgusting fridge, but that was something that could be ignored for once. The two girls sat inches apart on the sofa, facing each other, the kitchen table piled high just a few feet away, a coffee table piled higher in front of them and a flat screen TV on the opposite wall.

They spoke quietly so as to keep the conversation private. "That's stupid. This lady can't protect them better than the cops can." Jayden wasn't going to make this easy. And honestly, Alexus was having a hard time figuring out her own feelings on the subject. "Why wouldn't they just go to the cops and they can put them in witness protection or something?"

"What if the cops get them and then the government comes in and gets a warrant and kills them?"

"A warrant to kill him? That's not how it works. And why would the government kill him?"

"I don't know."

"You're totally insane-o." Jayden's voice was getting louder. "And plus, you said you felt bad lying to your mother."

"*Shh.*" Alexus hushed her friend and lowered her own voice. Jayden's living room wasn't the most private spot for a discussion of this magnitude. "I did. I do, but, I don't know. Sometimes adults don't know everything. Just look at Harry Potter."

"Oh my god, Harry Potter isn't real. You *do* know that, right?"

"No, but there are a lot of good lessons in it."

"Like adults aren't always right."

"They're not. Adults make mistakes, too."

"You know you're freaking me out, right? What do you want to do, call them and, like, tell them everything, that this cop guy is pretending to be you and they, like, know everything?"

Alexus spread herself out on the sofa, her head against the armrest and her socked feet pushing into Jayden's hips. "Kind of."

"Oh my god, Alexus, are you in love with Hollis or something? This is stupid."

"No."

"Trust me, that is not the way to get him back here."

"I totally am not," Alexus said, speaking over Jayden. "He just seemed like he was fine."

"You were only talking through emails. For all you know, it was this lady."

"How would she even know who I am, and why would she email

me?"

"I don't know. You gave Hollis your email, remember? She might have taken it out of his pocket and now she's using you for information."

Alexus was quiet for a few seconds. "I don't think so."

"You need to just leave this one. We're only kids. You know that, right?"

From down the hallway, Jayden's mother shouted to her daughter. "Jayden, I told you to make your bed this morning."

The girl tried to ignore the order, but her mother wouldn't be easing off. Parents never left well enough alone.

"Jayden! Do you hear me?"

"Ugh," the fifth grader moaned before shouting a response, "I will."

"Jayden!" Her mother cried.

"You want to help me make my bed?" Jayden asked.

"I totally do," Alexus replied without budging.

Jayden rolled her eyes. "All, right Mom! Give me a break. Alexus is here."

"She can help if she wants, but you're making this bed right now, young lady."

With all the energy she could muster for the task at hand, Jayden pulled herself off the couch and plodded down the hall toward her mother's voice.

Alexus turned her attention to the television, which was fixed on the Disney Channel. Her eyes glazed over, eventually focusing on Jayden's iPad atop the summit of crap on the coffee table. This was ridiculous. She couldn't possibly get involved and let her mother down again. But it was now or never. Her own email had been confiscated and her mother wasn't going to let her have another account maybe ever. She could warn Hollis. The adults didn't understand. She threw her head over the back of the sofa, peering down the hallway. Jayden and her mother were talking. It would take a few minutes to make the bed.

She sat up and grabbed the iPad. The woman's email address was easy to remember. She tapped out a quick email and hit send before she had a chance to chicken out. Then she put the tablet back to sleep and reclined onto the sofa again.

~ ~ ~ ~ ~ ~ ~ ~ ~ ~

Cha'Risa returned to the car from the ATM machine. The trio were still in the parking lot for the doctor's office.

"You know I only said we shouldn't do that test because it's too risky, right?" Cha'Risa was talking to Hollis, who was in the Accord's passenger seat. Kirby was in the back, checking out the other stores in the strip mall that they wouldn't be able to visit.

"I know. I don't care," Hollis replied. "Do you think I want to go get all sorts of tests and stuff at the hospital?"

"I just worry about you. What if it's not the Níłch'i? What if it's something to do with your heart? All I know is seizures are never good."

"I *feel* good."

"Sometimes it doesn't matter if you feel good. Your body can have all sorts of things wrong with it, even if you feel great."

The boy tried to turn on the radio, but the car wasn't started, so Cha'Risa turned the key, chugging the automobile to life. He reached for it again and a mix of static and music streamed out of the car speakers. He fiddled around with the buttons.

"I feel like someone's watching us," Hollis said, causing Cha'Risa and Kirby to straighten up, alert.

"What do you mean?" Cha'Risa scanned the parking lot, worried that his increased intelligence clued him into things she couldn't sense.

"Not us, I guess, me," he said. "I feel like there's someone watching me."

"Like the agents or something?"

"No, nobody bad. I don't know. It's just a feeling."

"You think there's somebody *good* watching you?" Cha'Risa sounded a little incredulous.

"And I think I'm getting smarter."

Cha'Risa drew out her response. "Okaaay."

"I was only getting flashes before. I could see patterns, but now I'm seeing them all the time. Everything is set up in shapes. I can feel the bonds holding everything together, that lamp post over there and the tar and all the stores, and us."

"What do you mean you feel them?"

"Just... like I know them."

"Like in the *Matrix*?"

"What's that?"

"It's a movie. Never mind."

"I'm hungry," said Kirby.

"Alright, we'll grab something. The cash machine worked. Análí must have found some money to put into the account," Cha'Risa replied, glancing at Hollis, who had yet to find anything suitable on the radio. "Maybe we *should* bring you to Vegas and give you a shot at blackjack."

"Wouldn't that be dangerous?" Hollis asked.

"Don't worry. We aren't heading to Vegas. That was another movie reference." Cha'Risa figured she had enough money to last until New Mexico. But she began to wonder if Hollis could be like a younger Rainman, if he could count cards or even predict the outcome of a roulette wheel.

"How many cars in this parking lot?" she asked.

"Seventy-six," Hollis answered.

Cha'Risa had no idea if he was right, but she decided to test him further. "What number am I thinking?"

"I don't know," he responded. "Ninety-seven."

"Okay, no. That's wrong."

"What number am *I* thinking?" Kirby chimed in.

"That one didn't work, Kirby," Cha'Risa said. "We need something concrete." She reached across Hollis and opened the glove compartment, retrieving the owner's manual for the car. She held out the book toward Hollis and fanned through it, stopping on the last page. "How many pages in this book?"

Hollis didn't miss a beat. "Three hundred and two."

She checked out the booklet. "Hold on. This doesn't have the..." She thumbed back a few pages, then flipped to the front of the book and went page by page for a few sheets. "Yes," she said with a smile. "Three hundred and two."

"Awesome," Kirby said, inserting his face between the front seats.

"Give him another one. We should totally go to Las Vegas. We could get rich."

"Rich and dead," said Hollis.

"You can count cards," said Kirby. "My cousin told me you can do it with a computer, but we've got you."

Cha'Risa butted in, "They don't exactly let children gamble, even in Vegas."

That settled Kirby down a bit. "Aww," he said, sinking into the back seat.

"Plus, getting rich isn't exactly a priority right now." Cha'Risa pulled her phone out of her jacket and swiped through it. "Let's just check this shit before we go." Hollis settled on a pop music station and leaned back in his seat.

"Hey Hollis," said Kirby. "How about giving us a break? Do you think me or Cha'Risa wants to listen to this crap?"

"So much for super intelligence," Cha'Risa mumbled, squinting her eyes at the phone. "What's this? This is from Alexus."

Hollis sat up at attention and held out his hand for the phone, but Cha'Risa was reading.

"This is someone else's email," she said, her eyes combing over the screen. "This isn't good. Shit! This isn't good."

Kirby sat up in his seat again and both boys stared at Cha'Risa. "What?" asked Hollis.

She finished reading and held the phone down by her chest. "Alexus says the cops are using her email and pretending to be her. That's gotta be how they know who I am. They found out through my email address."

"Do you think they know where we're going?" asked Kirby.

"They have to. I live with my grandfather. Shit!" Cha'Risa had started swiping through the phone again. "Let's see what else there is."

"So what are we going to do now?" Hollis asked.

She didn't reply.

"Oh man," said Kirby, lying back on the seat. "So we can't even go meet with her grandfather then, can we?"

"You think they'll be staking out his house?" Hollis asked.

"That's what I'd do," Kirby replied. "So if we go meet up with him, they're totally going to be there and nab us."

"Shit!" Cha'Risa shouted. "That fucker!"

The boys drew in again as she continued. "This is all over the news. That little bastard I bought the car from must have squealed."

"What?" Hollis asked.

"They know what we're driving again. That little prick! I knew I should have kicked him in the groin when I had the chance. So now, not only do they know where we're going, but they know what we're driving. We've got every cop in the country looking for this car now."

"What the hell," said Kirby. "So *now* what do we do, walk?"

"We're not walking to New Mexico from here," she said.

"You think we should hotwire something?"

Cha'Risa glanced out the window toward the doctor's office.

XXVI

A blue Volvo pulled off a moonlit road, easing to a stop along the gas pumps at a trucker service station. The station's industrial lights cast the busy lot in a harsh yellow glow. Men wore Peterbilt caps and cowboy hats, greasy jeans, flannel and leather vests, and they wouldn't pay attention to anyone else at the facility as long as that person didn't stand out in some way. There was ample room for tractor trailers, a set of showers and a diner serving down home cooking: fresh flapjacks any time of the day, slow cooked brisket and Texas chili.

"You two keep down, alright?" Cha'Risa said as she stepped out of the Volvo. After paying cash inside the facility, she pumped $30 into the tank and returned to the driver's seat, churning the engine over.

"You don't see those much these days," Kirby said.

Cha'Risa hit the gas and made for the station's exit. "Don't see much of what?"

"Pay phones," the boy replied. One of the classic coin-operated machines was taking up wall space along the convenience store's painted cinder block exterior.

"True that," she said as the Volvo's tires hit the road. She was heading west, but flung the car back into the truck stop at another entrance.

"What are you doing?" Hollis asked.

"Dollars to donuts they're tracking my cell phone, so I don't even want to turn the thing on. But they aren't tracking a pay phone." She pulled the car into a spot near the phone and rummaged around in her pockets for change. "Give me a minute," she said, as she climbed out of the driver's side and made her way to the phone. She picked up the receiver and dropped in a couple quarters, punching in a New Mexico number. "Uncle Abraham? It's Cha'Risa.... I'm well aware of that.... They're fine. They're in the car.... Listen, I need you to do me a favor."

~ ~ ~ ~ ~ ~ ~ ~ ~ ~

The night had only grown darker as the Volvo eased along a rusty chain link fence, its wire diamonds illuminated by the peripheral headlights and veiling the black nothingness beyond it. The eight-foot high fence was weaved through with a mixture of vines, weeds and overgrown greenery. The dirt road along its perimeter was long deserted, just two gravel paths for tires cutting through long blades of grass. The sound of the grass brushing along the underbody of the glossy sedan made the abandoned area seem even more desolate. There was no civilization out here, just two headlights, and beyond them, shadow as far as the eyes could see. The air blew warm out of the vents and eyelids were heavy.

A structure came into view, a hundred yards on the other side of the fence seeming even blacker than the night sky. Cha'Risa aimed the headlights at it. The facility, whatever it was, looked as if it hadn't seen a human in fifty years. She straightened the car back out and inched it along the fence line around a corner, eventually stopping by a chain link gate.

She stepped out of the driver's seat and inspected the gate, which wasn't locked. Pushing it open, she climbed back into the Volvo and drove the car inside the fenced off area, closing the gate again. The area was blacktopped, or at least it had been. Now there were more weeds than tar. The building, looming large across the lot, was a former factory, its corrugated steel siding rusted and coiling away at the edges.

There was no way they would have made it this far without Dr. Deschene's help. The doctor had offered her car to the trio, along with its contents: a blanket, first aid kit, tarp, poncho and duct tape. The doctor had also given them some money, but had laid down the caveat that she'd need to report the car stolen within 24 hours. That was the only credible way to avoid being an accomplice to the kidnapping.

Cha'Risa had until 3 p.m. tomorrow to reach Análí, and after that, things would be worked out. She told Dr. Deschene that she'd abandon the car somewhere it could be discovered, making sure to wipe it down for fingerprints first. It seemed like a win for everyone.

But that was tomorrow; this was tonight.

The Volvo stopped in front of one of the delivery bays along the factory's side and the engine chugged to a halt, ticking in the cold air. There was a set of stairs leading up to a door, which Cha'Risa checked. It was locked. Hollis and Kirby exited the car as she descended the stairs and hoisted herself up onto the edge of the delivery bay. Grabbing a rusty handle at the bottom of the bay door, she heaved enough to raise it a couple feet, but she couldn't budge it any more.

"That's enough for me," said Kirby, struggling to pull himself up onto the loading dock. Cha'Risa jumped off and retrieved her bags from the car before helping Hollis onto the platform and jumping up again herself. Once they'd all crept under the bay door, the darkness seemed complete. Cha'Risa unzipped the backpack and rifled around until she found a flashlight. Its bright LED bulbs were no match for the vastness of the factory's interior. From where they stood, the floor—once a bed of smooth concrete—was more akin to the salt flats, littered with broken iron machine bits and chipped paint, which had dropped from the metal-beamed ceiling decades prior. The far walls were indiscernible as the flashlight faded into nothingness past the first 20 feet, but a row of windows two stories up revealed the night sky, just this shade of bluish gray against the factory's inky blackness.

It was much colder than it had been outside, like they'd walked into a freezer.

"You seriously want to sleep in here?" Kirby asked.

"Yeah, why not?" Cha'Risa replied. "Off the beaten path. There's a roof over our heads. Easier than setting up the tent."

"Whatever happened to hotels?"

"What do you mean 'whatever happened to hotels?' We're fugitives. What don't you get about that? They know who I am. I am in serious shit here. You want Hollis to get caught? I go to jail for the rest of my life and Hollis gets reintroduced to his agent friends. Hotels are *not* safe."

"Alright," said Kirby. "Don't get all pissy."

"Did you just say 'don't get all pissy?' Kirby, I am two seconds away from kicking your scrawny ass."

Hollis chuckled.

"Okay, okay," said Kirby. "Whatever. We're all under a lot of stress here."

Hollis broke out in laughter.

"Hey Dick Clark," said Cha'Risa, "just stick to your music trivia. Sleep in the car, if you want."

"Who's Dick Clark?" asked Hollis.

"The world's oldest teenager," Kirby replied. "Host of American Bandstand. He knew a lot about music."

"You're a freak," said Cha'Risa, unpacking a blanket from the duffel bag, the illumination from the flashlight flittering around randomly as her hands moved.

Hollis went mute for a moment, biting the underside of his lip. "How can anyone be the oldest teenager?" he asked.

"You're kidding me, right?" Kirby answered. "You're the genius and I'm somehow a freak."

Cha'Risa snorted a laugh out of her nose.

"What?" asked Hollis in a slightly riled tone. "What did he die like a millisecond before his twentieth birthday or something?"

Cha'Risa crouched down to her knees hugging the blanket and the duffel bag. Her belly laugh had become involuntarily silent and the flashlight's beam bounced on the floor as her diaphragm convulsed.

"What?" an increasingly irritated Hollis repeated.

~ ~ ~ ~ ~ ~ ~ ~ ~ ~

Kirby felt a hand shaking his shoulder and cracked his eyes open. Cha'Risa was kneeling next to him, gentle and quiet. "Wake up. We need to get going."

The factory was still draped in shadows, the dark gray sky providing the only light through the second floor windows.

"What time is it?" Kirby asked, raising his head a few inches off the backpack.

"It's time to get up."

"It's still nighttime."

"Come on," she said softly, as she reached for Hollis, sleeping under the same blanket as Kirby.

"Hollis," she said, shaking the boy. "Hey buddy, time to get up."

He didn't budge.

"Oh my god," she said, a crack in her voice. "Come on Hollis!" She shook Hollis harder, but his eyes were upturned into the back of his head. "You've got to be kidding me." She kneeled next to Hollis and sat him up, cradling the boy in her arms and running a hand through his hair.

With the commotion, Kirby was quick to spring to life. He tossed the blanket aside and scrunched down next to Cha'Risa, eyeing his best friend. "Is he out again?"

Cha'Risa's nod was barely visible in the dimly lit concrete room. She threw her head back and let out a heavy breath and for another minute nobody said a word. Dr. Deschene hoped that the heart medication she'd given Hollis might alleviate the problem, but obviously it wasn't having any impact. The only solution, at this point, was to get Hollis to Análí as soon as possible.

"The car keys are in my jacket," Cha'Risa said, motioning with her head to the group's belongings. "Do you know how to start a car?"

Kirby was on his feet before she finished her question. "I can start it without the keys, if you want."

"Put the heat on," she said.

Kirby rummaged through her jacket and marched to the bay door, which they'd sealed shut before falling asleep. With his best heave and a guttural grunt released from his tiny frame, the door moved up a couple feet. He slid underneath and disappeared from sight.

Cha'Risa gazed down at the helpless boy in her arms, his eyes wide, but motionless, her voice soothing. "Don't worry Hollis. We'll take care of you. Kirby's a good kid and Análí will know what to do. We'll get you better, I promise."

Through the opening in the bay door, she heard the Volvo's engine churning over and idling, effectively killing the calm she'd felt for a handful of seconds. "All right, buddy, here we go." She raised herself onto one knee and hoisted Hollis up into her arms, carrying him to the open door. She had to crawl underneath the opening and drag him through before bringing him down to the car's back seat. She opened the door with a pinky while holding on to Hollis.

"Don't forget the stuff," Kirby said from the front passenger seat.

She shot him a fed up look. "You're killing me, Kirby. Something wrong with your legs?"

"I'm monitoring the heat." He placed a palm in front of one of the vents and adjusted the thermostat.

She lay Hollis down on the leather seat and rolled her eyes, slamming the rear door shut. Mumbling to herself, she climbed back onto the bay door platform, crawled back into the factory and exited the building a minute later. She packed up the trunk still muttering.

When she finally sat down in the driver's seat, the radio was tuned to classic rock and the vents were blowing warm air. She prided herself on being self-sufficient and not whining, but it was admittedly nice to have a little warmth after a night in a giant concrete structure. "Nice job on the heat," she said.

"Some people call it a talent," Kirby responded.

"Some other people call it laziness."

Kirby remained focused out the front windshield. "Ouch!"

She threw the car in reverse and craned her neck to see out the back window, which was useless because there was no light. She burned a few inches of rubber as she gunned it.

"I got some good tunes rolling," Kirby added.

Cha'Risa threw the car into drive and beat a path for the fence gate as the radio belted out Marvin Gaye's "Ain't No Mountain High Enough." "Alright pip squeak, I'll give you that one."

"Do you want to check the news on your phone?"

"Uh-uh. The phone is off for the foreseeable future."

"Oh yeah," said Kirby. "Just in case they're tracking, right?"

"Correctamundo."

"How much farther to your grandfather's place?"

"That depends on what kind of obstacles there are between here and there."

"What's your ballpark?"

"Average obstacles? I'd say twenty years to life."

XXVII

Agents Breiner and Grey stared down at Agóyó Pueblo from atop an escarpment, their ingot silver Ford Expedition running to keep the interior warm. The altitude of the New Mexico mountains brought an unexpected chill.

The closest home, a half-mile away, was a single-wide trailer on the outskirts of the pueblo. It was a 1970s unit, white with umber highlights. A brown corrugated metal awning provided shade for three folding chairs outside the trailer, an old grill sat rusting by the front door and a satellite dish capped off the home. A single cable connected the trailer to a utility pole where an old rusty Chevy truck was parked.

Vegetation was scarce in this part of New Mexico, a smattering of sagebrush shrubs, a mix of yellow grass and dirt, some motionless tumbleweeds.

"Why on God's earth would anyone live like this?" Grey asked.

Breiner didn't reply.

"Do people really live in those things?" She was referring to the traditional adobe homes making up the pueblo, just beyond the trailer from their viewpoint. They were the same rectangular buildings the natives had been living in for centuries, topping out at three stories. Most of the dwellings had cyan doors and tiny windows. Wooden beams ran through the adobe walls, supporting the roofs.

"Yeah," Breiner replied. "They're traditional homes."

"They're horrible."

"I don't know. I don't think it would be so bad."

Grey remained silent.

The armrest supported a pair of high power binoculars. Breiner picked them up and raised them to his eyes. "That's definitely them," he said. "Two of them." There were two Native Americans who stood out. They weren't interacting with anyone else in the pueblo and they looked too alert for pueblo residents. For hours they'd wandered aimlessly around the grounds never straying too far from the main path through the pueblo, nor too far from the trailer the agents were watching.

"Feds?" Grey asked.

"Mmm hmm." He lowered the binoculars and placed them back on the armrest. "We're going to have to take them out if they get to them first."

Grey didn't reply.

"We're sure she's still living with her grandfather?" Breiner asked without breaking his focus on the pueblo.

"As sure as we can be. I just don't know if they'll actually show. I mean, would you come home if everyone was looking for you?"

"Fucking retards. Why would they tell the media they knew who she was?"

"I assume they thought the kids were in danger and someone would spot them."

"Fuck that. They screwed this whole thing up."

"You can complain all you want, but this is the hand we were dealt. Is there somewhere else you want to try?"

"No. This is the best place we have... I'm sick of cleaning up after amateurs." Breiner grabbed the binoculars again and peered through them. "Hang on. Something has our friends' attention.... Who's this?"

A Toyota Camry slowly emerged from the pueblo, dust kicking up in its wake. The car was heading for the trailer.

"Is it them?" Grey asked.

"I can't tell. I don't think so. It's not an Accord."

"Maybe they switched cars."

The Camry pulled up next to the trailer and a Native American man stepped out. He was medium-build, a modern-day cowboy, with a jean jacket and Stetson hat. He approached the trailer's door, knocked and entered.

"It's not them," Breiner said.

"Who the hell is it?"

"It's a fucking Indian, how should I know? I can get the plate. Write this down."

Grey pulled a phone from her bag. "Go."

"New Mexico, one, three, eight, whisky, lima, bravo."

"I'll call it in," she said.

Breiner studied the scene for another minute while Grey called in the license plate number. Maybe this man was bringing the grandfather to meet the girl, or maybe he was delivering a message. They could be arranging to meet somewhere. Of course, maybe it was no one. There was no reason to believe that Cha'Risa Gutierrez was planning on involving her grandfather, but the reports indicated she was closer to the old man than to anyone else. Whatever was happening, Breiner didn't like it.

"It's an uncle," Grey said, while putting away the phone. "Abraham Gutierrez, the grandfather's son."

"Just visiting, you think?"

"I doubt that," Grey replied. "Your niece is on every television station in the country. You think he's just stopping off for a coffee?"

"I *don't* think. I say we wait until the uncle leaves, take care of the old man and wait for the target to walk into our laps."

"Sounds good to me."

But the agents didn't budge. They both knew the best chance at success was to be patient.

They waited silently for 45 minutes. And then there was movement. Breiner watched through the binoculars as both men exited the trailer, the uncle and the grandfather. The uncle came out first and stopped to help the old man down the stairs. The grandfather had a plaid jacket, a baseball hat and was pulling an oxygen tank. Uncle Abraham helped the grandfather into the truck and then returned to his Camry, both men waved goodbye to each other and drove back through the pueblo. The Native American federal agents who'd been casing the scene walked briskly toward the parking area, but Breiner and Grey had already shot back onto the main road and made a beeline for all the action. The road they were on intersected the one leading from the pueblo. They would pick a covert area and wait for the old man to drive by.

~ ~ ~ ~ ~ ~ ~ ~ ~ ~

Dobie's General Store had a mixture of just about everything for sale: groceries, clothing, cookware, liquor, knives, livestock feed, postcards, mugs, home decorations, tools, books, fishing supplies (worms and flies, too) and there was always something unexpected. There were four gas pumps and one diesel, plus a kitchen serving a variety of freshly made foods for eat-in diners. The adobe structure was the main gathering point for residents in the sprawling village of Navan, New Mexico, population 231. With the first Spanish settlers arriving in the Navan area in the 1730s, the village was the much younger sibling of Agóyó Pueblo, just 15 miles away.

Dobie's parking lot was half full of cars and trucks, mainly locals. A family just passing through the area had stopped their RAV4 for gas and to let their dog have a bathroom break. In the front of the store, a man was dumping 50-pound bags of poultry feed into the bed of his F-150.

There was also a blue Volvo.

Behind Dobie's there was nothing—desert ground dotted with blue grama grass, sagebrush shrubs and untold numbers of hibernating rattlesnakes. Cha'Risa, Hollis and Kirby skirted along the side of the store and around back where an unused, faded neon store sign leaned against the wall, partially covered by a blue plastic tarp. Past that there was a screen door that lead to an employee only area. Cha'Risa creaked open the spring-loaded door and peered inside. There was a woman in her 50s with her back to the door working on a computer, a small radio beside her playing U2. The woman, a Navajo, turned when the door hinges squeaked and she beamed at Cha'Risa.

"Rissa!" she said, leaping from her chair. She rushed to the door to greet her guests, her arms outstretched. Cha'Risa stepped inside and hugged her, as Hollis and Kirby wandered in behind her.

"My dear, I have been so worried," the woman said.

"I'm good," Cha'Risa replied. She turned to the two fifth graders. "Guys, this is Mary Nez. Mary, meet Hollis and Kirby."

"They're so cute," Mary said. Hollis and Kirby rolled their eyes. "Are you boys okay? Do you want a milk or something? A hot dog?"

"Sure," said Kirby.

Cha'Risa interrupted. "Later, okay?" She turned to Mary. "Have you talked to Análi or Abraham?"

"I have. Which one has the Nílch'i?"

Hollis reached up to his neck and pulled the medallion out of his shirt, letting it dangle across his chest. The metallic blue glow from the Nílch'i was becoming evident, even in the daylight.

"Oh my," said Mary. "That's it?"

"That's it," Cha'Risa answered.

"It's so beautiful." She studied it, speechless for a moment.

The back room was cluttered, a large area stuffed with backup stock that had yet to make it to the front of Dobie's. Boxes teetered on chairs, and more boxes were piled on top of that. Crates of Pepsi and Coke products were stacked six feet high. Even the desk that Mary had been working on looked like it had found itself in the path of a small cyclone.

Cha'Risa was trying to get a read out of Mary on the situation. Mary was older and had heard more stories through the years of the Nílch'i and she certainly would have given the old superstitions more clout than Cha'Risa. "Do you know anything about it?" Cha'Risa asked.

Mary crouched down in front of Hollis, placed her hands on his shoulders and stared into his eyes. "I know that this young boy has been given both a gift and a burden. I can only imagine what he has seen in the short time he has possessed it, but it must be overwhelming for someone so young. I know there will be many people jealous of him, and those who will want to take it from him."

"And many who will want to take *him* from it," a voice proclaimed from the other side of the screen door. It belonged to an old man, a Native American clad in a jean jacket and a Stetson hat.

"Análi!" Cha'Risa shouted, her relief evident. She charged toward the door as her grandfather stepped inside.

"Hello my little flower," he said. "How was the journey?"

They held each other in an extended embrace, the room falling silent except for the tinny sounds of Bono over a cheap radio. And then Análí's eyes fell on Hollis. He moved toward him with his hand extended. "Hello my friend. I have waited a long time for this moment." He shook hands with the boy, glanced down at the Nilch'i and smiled, his wrinkled and weathered face contented.

"Análí," said Cha'Risa. "Where's your oxygen? What are you doing?"

"That reminds me," said the old man, struggling for a deep breath. "I'd better sit down." His shoulders hunched, he took a couple steps toward a rolling chair and carefully set himself down on it, revealing the failings of an aging body.

"Where's your oxygen tank?"

"Your Uncle Abraham has it. There is no such thing as sneaking out with an oxygen tank."

"Well, where is *he*? You need that."

"He is in my truck riding east. I told him to put at least two hours between us and only to stop where there are people. I pray that he is safe."

"How did you get here?" Cha'Risa asked.

"I took *his* car. We exchanged clothes. He took my oxygen and truck. We were hoping it was enough to mislead those who would follow us." He took a labored breath. "I took detours and turned around several times and I noticed no one trailing."

Mary interrupted, "Just because you didn't notice them doesn't mean they weren't there."

"This much is true," Análí responded. "But we must start somewhere."

Cha'Risa turned toward Mary. "I don't suppose you have any oxygen in the store, do you?"

"The store is well stocked," Mary said. "But not that well."

"We need to find him some."

"I'll make enquiries," said Mary. She marched to the far door which led out to the storefront, making sure to open the door as little as possible before slipping out.

The temperature outside was hovering in the low 40s, but Dobie's back office was sweltering, brought on by a decades-old heating system with too few zones. The front of the store was cavernous and needed a constant supply of heat to keep it from escaping out the busy outside doors and overall drafty walls and windows. There weren't many realistic options. Mary could pay someone to insulate the building better; she could purchase a new heating system; or she could keep the office's back door open. Option three had been working for so long, she never even really thought about it anymore.

Análí pulled a handkerchief from his trouser pocket and wiped his brow, resting his hands on his knees afterward. "And who is this young man?" he asked, looking to Hollis' left.

"I'm Kirby Cooper-Quinn," the fifth grader replied. He offered his hand, which the old man accepted with a grin.

"You are special, too, Kirby Cooper-Quinn. An old man has ways of knowing these things."

"Cool."

Análí reached inside his jean jacket and retrieved sheets of folded paper from an inside pocket. They were yellowed from age and crinkled as he flattened them out on his knee. He laid them out on the top of cardboard boxes next to him. There were several sheets covered in Navajo text and illustrations, but the top one contained drawings of both sides of the Nílch'i, with more text and symbols in the borders surrounding it. The papers looked as if they were from the same batch as the one Cha'Risa had shown the boys on their first night in the woods—the drawing of Hollis' face.

"The Nílch'i Bee Hane'e was with our people for a long time—millennia," Análí began. "It had always been handed down from one bearer to the next whenever death was imminent. And that is one of the key dictates. Once it has imprinted on someone, it is that person's for life. It can only be utilized by the true bearer. Many have tried to abscond with it through the centuries, but the Nílch'i Bee Hane'e will do nothing for the thief. Hollis, you are the true bearer. The Nílch'i will be little more than a beautiful object to anyone else."

"Unless he dies," Cha'Risa said, a hint of understanding in her voice.

"Unless he dies," Análí repeated. "Then the Nílch'i will begin its quest for another bearer. It does not seek a moral person, nor a wise person, a man or a woman. It settles on anyone who possesses it long enough. That is why the government killed my father. They needed the medallion to imprint on one of their own men in order to use it. And use it, they did. For centuries we used the Nítch'i Bee Hane'e for the amelioration of our people, but once it was discovered, there were those who wanted it for destructive purposes. In the few years the military held the object, it was responsible for dreadful advances in technology. It allowed for the creation of the first atomic weapon. I cannot think of the future if it falls into the same hands as it did those many years ago."

Kirby leaned against a side wall. "So it just makes your brain bigger or something?"

"Not bigger, no. Nítch'i Bee Hane'e is the Navajo word for radio. A close enough translation would be 'news over the air.' But it is much older than radios," Análí replied. "Nítch'i means wind or spirit. It makes a connection to the gods. It allows the bearer and the gods to share one mind."

"Geez!" Kirby cried, gazing at his friend. Hollis' face had gone pale, his jaw slacked. All eyes were upon him.

Hollis had felt another being in the doctor's parking lot, when he thought they were being watched. But it was more than that. He realized it now. Análí's explanation fit better. It was as if he was sharing minds with someone else. Hollis hadn't ever given much thought to the notion of gods. He only knew of the one they'd made Christmas about, and everyone had told him there was only one god anyway. Was this the same god he'd been sharing his mind with or was he going to have to learn about a whole different set of them?

"What's up with the seizures?" asked Cha'Risa. "He's had a bunch of them. Just another one this morning."

"Another one so soon?" Análí asked. "I've never heard of anyone experiencing them so close together. These are usually spread out over years, even decades. It is imprinting on him, a process that can take a long time even before the seizures start. I can only assume it is because he is so young and his mind is more malleable than anyone who has borne the Nítch'i before. The succeeding bearer was always chosen by the current bearer years before he or she had passed from this life, and so it has never gone to anyone so many years from adulthood. Perhaps his body is absorbing it faster."

The radio's volume seemed to increase as everyone gathered in the room fell silent. Then the sound of rustling broke the stillness. Heads darted toward the screen door, where a beautiful woman stood, wrapped only in a blue plastic tarp, her bare shoulders and legs exposed. She was shivering.

"Who are you?" Cha'Risa growled.

The woman spoke from the other side of the screen. "My name is Eleanor. I'm sorry to interrupt. I was at work and... I can't explain it. Suddenly I was lying next to the bushes out back."

XXVIII

Análí shrugged his shoulders and Cha'Risa took the hint. If *she* didn't know the naked woman at the door and her grandfather didn't know her, the misfit wasn't welcome here. And the woman's timing couldn't be worse.

"Get lost," Cha'Risa barked. "We don't have any smack and we don't have any money." She showed her back to the screen door, Kirby and Hollis ogling the stranger, open mouthed.

Eleanor jerked the plastic tarp tighter around her torso and turned to take her leave.

"Wait," said Hollis, a finger raised into the air and all eyes focused on the fifth grader. The woman at the door stopped, but didn't face him. She waited to hear what he wanted.

"I've seen her before," he said.

"What do you mean you've seen her?" Cha'Risa asked.

"In a dream."

Análí spoke up. "You say you have seen this woman in a dream?"

"Yeah," Hollis answered. In his dreams, Eleanor had been shot and was dying on the side of the road.

"When was this? What happened in this dream?" asked Análí.

"She was..." Hollis trailed off. "There were other people there, an old lady and a bunch of men."

Eleanor turned her head and looked in through the screen door at the boy.

"Are you sure?" Cha'Risa asked.

Hollis nodded.

Cha'Risa met eyes with Eleanor for the first time. There was a moment of silence as she strongly considered disregarding Hollis. What could this bimbo do for them other than cause disruption?

What if she was some sort of government agent and Hollis was being used? But it made no sense that anyone coming to sabotage their plans would present themselves wrapped only in a tarp. Cha'Risa didn't have the faintest clue what the Niłch'i was capable of, and if Hollis said he knew the woman, than perhaps she should just let the whole incident play out. Cha'Risa motioned with her hand. "Come on in."

Eleanor pulled the door open and stepped inside, yanking the long trail of the tarp through so the door could close. It bunched up behind her legs and she studied the faces, sheepish but thankful for a bit of warmth and the possibility of help.

She wasn't used to being the center of attention and each of the strangers was gawking at her. She glanced over the others in the room settling on Análí. There was something about the stern old Indian man that captured her attention. She tried not to stare at him, but couldn't help it. It dawned on her that he wasn't stern at all, he was calm. He looked curious. Inquisitive. And then Eleanor's breath stopped short. His eyes. They were the same eyes from the young boy in the folder that Col. Clay had dropped on her desk. Except this was an old man. It wasn't the man from the picture who she presumed was the boy's father. Was this the boy's grandfather?

Análí met her gaze, interested. "When you say you were working? When was that?"

It took a moment for her to reacquaint herself with the present. "Just now," Eleanor replied. "A couple minutes ago. I was pulling a stack of paper out of my desk and suddenly I'm looking up at the sky out back here."

"I see. And where do you work?"

"At the Potomac Research Facility."

With a raised eyebrow, Análí indicated to Cha'Risa that he had never heard of it. Cha'Risa shrugged her reply. She hadn't either.

"I know it," said Hollis. "It was in my dream, too. It's not too far from Delacroix."

Eleanor nodded in agreement.

Cha'Risa shook her head. "Hold on..." She looked at Análí who was nodding as if he knew something. "What? What is it?"

"This is something that is beyond my understanding," he said.

"Where are we?" Eleanor asked.

Análí responded, "Dobie's General Store." His reply drew no response from Eleanor. "Navan." After more silence Análí cocked an eyebrow. "New Mexico?" He kept a focus on the woman as she scanned the room, her gaze darting to the computer screen for a moment before becoming fixated on the drawings he had strewn over the boxes. There was a look of panic on her face and he knew that she recognized the illustration of the Nílch'i. "Do you know this object?" he asked.

She didn't reply, but Hollis—in a motion to which he'd grown accustomed—held up the medallion for the mysterious woman.

"I've seen something very similar, but it wasn't lit up like that."

Análí let out a long continuous breath through his nose and refilled his lungs with a slight wheeze. "By chance, would you know the year?"

"Are you serious?"

"I am," he replied.

She seemed hesitant to answer, but did so in a quizzical tone. "1945." The room grew still.

"You have not seen something similar to this amulet. You have seen this one. It was stolen from my father in 1941 and the gods have brought you here for a reason."

The blood drained from Eleanor's skin, her blood vessels dilating with nerves, her eyes shooting back to the computer and at the plastic cases of Pepsi.

Análí could feel her anxiety; he could see it in her brow. She was about to shatter into splinters. It was the same sense of overpowering fear he'd seen in fellow soldiers during the Korean War, and in those returning from Vietnam. He'd witnessed men and women coming back from Iraq and Afghanistan with the same look on their faces. The woman before him hadn't been through a battle, but her mind was coming unraveled, nonetheless.

"Sit," he said. He motioned with his arm for Kirby to drag over a chair, which the boy did. She sat, absent-mindedly, the blue tarp crinkling underneath and her eyes darting from object to object around the room.

"Get her some clothes," Análí said to Cha'Risa, who marched out the office door.

Análí leaned in toward Eleanor, speaking softly, "What did you do at the facility?"

She barely acknowledged him, her gaze shooting from the radio to the box of foil wrapped PowerBars resting on the office desk.

"Eleanor?" Análí said.

She looked at the old man, a new focus in her gaze.

"What do you do for work at this facility?"

"I can't say."

"You need to know," said Análí, "that it's not 1945."

"It's 2020," Kirby interjected.

"I don't understand," said Eleanor, her face turning a sickly moistened pale.

Análí just nodded.

Her brow started to tremor as if something might snap inside her. She pulled the tarp tight around her.

The office door shot open and Cha'Risa entered with a set of flip flops and socks in one hand and a pair of gray sweat pants and a New Mexico Lobos sweatshirt under her arm. She tossed the clothes to Eleanor, who caught them with a surprised breath and a rustling in the tarp.

Análí looked at Hollis and Kirby. "We need to give this woman some space to get dressed." He struggled to his feet, Kirby helping him, and the males made their way out the screen door.

The outside air was crisp and biting, a cool, dry, desert air. Análí motioned to Kirby, who helped lower the old man to the ground. He wrapped his arms around his knees and stared into the side of the store wall. Hollis had taken up a resting position by the old neon sign, which was covered by a plastic tarp not that long ago. He stared past Análí across the desert, the patchwork shrubs and grasses dotting the landscape.

"This is so cool," said Kirby, striding between his friend and the old man. "Is that lady really from 1945?"

Nobody replied.

"Cool," the boy repeated.

"I know of nothing like this in the history of our people," Análí said. "The Nítch'i Bee Hane'e has offered up some wondrous miracles, but none of this significance."

Kirby continued to pace, seemingly unaware of Análi's words.

But Hollis was listening. "She was dying when I saw her."

Kirby stopped in his tracks and looked back at his friend.

Análi shifted his eyes slowly toward Hollis. "What is it that you saw?"

The boy didn't move his gaze from the horizon. "Someone shot her. There were a bunch of people around and she was lying on the ground by the road."

"Did you see someone shoot her?" Análi asked.

Hollis shook his head. "No, she was just lying on the ground bleeding."

"So she was not dead?"

Hollis shrugged his shoulders. "I guess not. I mean she was still alive, but it didn't seem like she was going to be for long."

"Who else was there, anyone you recognized?"

"No. There were some guys in suits and an old lady and some lights set up on the road, like it was a checkpoint or something... They were looking for something."

With a nod, Análi confirmed what Hollis had already suspected. "They were searching for the Nítch'i and they thought this woman had it."

"Yeah, but this was just a dream, right?" Kirby interrupted. "Unless this thing made Hollis into some sort of time traveler... seer guy."

"The Nítch'i Bee Hane'e has never been fully understood. It allows its bearer many capabilities that would seem unnatural. I have no doubt—given that he recognizes this woman—that Hollis indeed experienced something very important."

Kirby cocked his head. "So how can she be here and all good and everything if she's been shot?"

The question hung in the air for a moment before Análi spoke. "It may be that it was just a vision, an interpretation meant to be deciphered by your young friend here." He nodded toward Hollis. "Then again, perhaps her future still lies in our past."

It took a second for Kirby to understand what Análi meant.

"Whoa!" the boy shouted. "You mean this lady..."

Análí motioned for him to keep his voice down.

"You mean this lady," Kirby continued in a more hushed tone, "is still going to get killed in the future... I mean in the past... or whatever?"

Análí threw up his hands, casting an uncertain look toward the young man.

"This is nuts!"

"What I can tell you is that she is here for a reason. Whether she stays in our time or returns to her own, I cannot know.

Cha'Risa popped her head out the screen door. "She's all set." She stepped toward her grandfather and helped him stand up off the ground, speaking to him alone as the boys headed back inside. "So, what's the plan?"

He paused. "Hollis will need to be hidden for the rest of his life." Then he continued toward the screen door.

Cha'Risa pulled at his arm, halting him. "That's not a plan," she said as the screen door inched back open. Hollis had overheard their conversation.

"I want to see my parents," said the boy.

"I do not know if that is wise," Análí responded.

"I don't care if it's wise." Hollis' voice had risen. "I'm ten years old. I need to see my parents again."

The old man and Cha'Risa made their way into the office, where Eleanor was examining the computer screen on the desk and Kirby was studying Eleanor. Hollis was awaiting a reply with his arms folded in front of his chest. The blue tarp in which Eleanor had been wrapped was folded and draped over a set of boxes.

"I do not want you to be unhappy," Análí finally said. He reached for a chair and, with Cha'Risa's help, sat down. "I will need counsel. The government has long arms and sensitive ears and I have seen enough movies to know that I don't know enough. There is a man who may be able to help. We will go see him."

Mary Nez sprang in from out front, closing the door firmly behind her. She spied Eleanor with her hands all over the store's computer. It was only displaying the day's weather, but the stranger seemed spellbound. "Who's this?"

"This is a woman who came to us from a research facility in 1945," Análí answered.

Mary nodded her head. "I see. I'm sure that's not what it sounds like, but whatever. I think I found one, an oxygen tank."

"It's good to have connections," said Análí.

"Do you want me to have them bring it here?"

"No. We will need to get going. Can you provide an address? We will pick it up."

"I have her address right here." Mary held out a scrap of paper and Cha'Risa accepted it.

"Eleanor," Cha'Risa said. But the woman was focused on the computer's keyboard. "Eleanor!"

The woman spun around, aware once again of her surroundings.

"We need to get going and we think you should come with us."

XXIX

The agents had been following the grandfather's truck for more than an hour and Agent Grey was drumming her fingers on her knee, subconsciously expending some of her pent-up energy. Things never worked out well when she ignored her instincts and something definitely felt off. "I don't like this."

"I don't either," Breiner replied, one hand on the steering wheel. They'd been keeping their distance, but they couldn't even see the old man's truck; instead they were following the federal agents who were tailing the grandfather. "Where the hell are we going?"

They had left civilization, such as it was.

Breiner placed his second hand on the steering wheel and tightened his grip, the leather crinkling. "What if this isn't the grandfather?"

"What are you thinking?"

"What if the grandfather changed clothes with his son?"

"And took off in the other car."

Breiner wanted his partner to come to the same conclusion he had.

"But if this is the grandfather, this is our best chance to find the woman and the kid," she said.

"Yep."

Grey pulled a phone out of her jacket. "I'm going to check the satellite." But the phone buzzed in her hand with a no-nonsense ring. "Grey," she said into the phone. She listened, then conveyed the message to Breiner. "The grandfather is descended from the original owner of the medallion."

"You're shitting me," Breiner replied.

"Son." Grey was back on the phone. "Where's the other car? Mmm hmm." Grey looked at Breiner again. "Satellite tracked it to a store."

"Maybe we should go check the grandfather's place. What do you think?"

"Hold on," Grey said, raising up a finger. "Hold on! Five people just got in the other car."

Breiner slammed on the brakes and whipped the car into a u-turn, speeding back toward Navan.

~ ~ ~ ~ ~ ~ ~ ~ ~ ~

The always-stolid Análí, in the front passenger seat of the Toyota Camry, seemed like he might well have just been heading out for a cup of coffee. Cha'Risa was driving, eyes alert.

From behind Cha'Risa, Eleanor gawked out the window, each passing car quiet and streamlined. She studied the Camry's interior, so compact and such a smooth ride. There was no bouncing around like in her father's truck, the bumps on the road ticking by, barely noticeable. She'd never been out west. The land was flat for miles and miles until it wasn't. And then there were hills... mountains, even. It was so desolate.

She considered her parents. If these people were telling her the truth, her parents were long dead, all of her friends as well. Everything was different. She wondered how the world had changed. Had Japan rebuilt after the bombs on Nagasaki and Hiroshima? It had only been a few weeks to her, but this was decades later, the majority of a century. What had happened to the Nazi leaders?

The outfit she'd picked out this morning was gone. What had happened to it? One moment, she was pulling paper out of her desk, preparing for Colonel Clay's latest crisis and the next she was lying naked on the freezing dusty ground halfway across the country in the future.

Was Clay experimenting on her? Maybe he needed unwitting guinea pigs and had introduced some sort of mind control substance into her system. That would make the most sense. It was impossible to travel into the future. But this wasn't like a dream or any run-of-the-mill hallucination. She felt the car heating up, she could smell stale cigarette smoke seeping out of the upholstery. The boy next to her kept knocking into her arm as he fidgeted. No, this felt too real.

More than seven decades had passed? Was it possible that some of the people she'd known were still alive, maybe some children? They'd be old fogies now. How could she find out? She needed to get back to Virginia.

She examined the clothing she'd been given. It looked to be a man's exercise outfit. The top was printed with something, although she was too distracted to try to read it. It was a comfortable set of clothes, but she wondered what people would think of her when she stepped out of the car dressed like a man out for a jog. She wasn't about to complain, but weren't there any women's clothes in the store they'd just left?

The two other adults in the front seats looked to be Indians. And one of the boys said he had recognized her. She'd certainly never seen him before. So, where were they all going and why did they want her to come along? She had heard the medallion was an Indian artifact, and knew it was extremely important to the Defense Department. Colonel Clay had been put in charge of researching it and he wore it just like the boy did, like a necklace under his shirt. He had tried to impress her with it on several occasions; Clay had been chosen for his military acumen, he said, his intellect. There was no shortage of narcissistic embellishments he'd used to describe himself, but men of true brilliance rarely needed to bloviate. And despite all of his talk, she'd never seen the artifact glow like it did on the boy.

Then she caught a profile view of Análí, and he met eyes with her for a second. "I think I've seen you before," she said.

Análí spun his head around to face her. "Interesting. Was this in a dream?"

"No," she replied. "It was a picture. I just saw it this morning. You were just a child, but your eyes are the same. If it's really been this long... I don't know, I guess you'd be the age you are now."

"Where would you have seen a picture of me?"

"The man I work for had the picture in a folder. It looked like you were with your parents, or some other adults."

"That is indeed peculiar," he said turning his attention out the windshield again.

The car made a left turn onto a smaller road, which weaved around several curves, passing an auto body shop and a couple houses. Cha'Risa stopped the Camry at the third house, a drab single-level southwest brick structure. There was a long open porch and two rocking chairs facing the road. "This should be it," she said, checking the scrap of paper Mary had given her. She threw the driver's door open and made for the house. Disappearing inside for a moment, she returned wheeling a small oxygen tank to the passenger side of the Camry. She opened the door and hoisted the brushed aluminum and green tank in between her grandfather's legs.

"Did you pay these people for this?" Análí asked.

"We have more important things to worry about," Cha'Risa snapped back. "They know it's for you. They're okay with it." She slammed the door and returned to the driver's seat. After a quick u-turn, she gunned the car back to the main road. "Which way?"

Análí had fitted the oxygen mask over his nose and mouth and started the flow. He pointed to the right with a crooked finger and the Camry's tires spit out sand as it took off.

"You should keep it slow," Análí said, his voice muffled through the mask.

Cha'Risa eased off the gas. "I know. I'm under a little pressure here."

"No argument about that."

"Who is this guy we're going to see?"

"He is a little insecure. He has theories about the government that I cannot follow."

"So he's paranoid."

"I have no doubt he has been described that way."

"So what's he going to do for us?"

"I feel we are in a situation when a little paranoia could be helpful. He is very knowledgeable about computers and he has told me on several occasions that if I ever needed to disappear, I should come see him."

Cha'Risa sounded incredulous. "If you ever needed to disappear?"

"You know, get off the grid, avoid detection."

"Yeah, I got the point. When were you ever *on* the grid?"

"Do you remember the credit bureau data breach, where millions of people's identities were hacked? I was one of the millions. We are all on the grid, make no mistake."

"And this guy can, what, get Hollis off of it?"

"I know that he has studied this idea far more than I have."

Análí instructed Cha'Risa to head toward the reservoir, fifty miles from Dobie's. After passing through several small towns that were little more than a handful of buildings, he leaned closer to the windshield. "Turn up at that next road." Cha'Risa spun the car onto a glorified dirt path, the bumps and potholes becoming more evident on the suspension.

Eleanor craned her neck to look out the rear window and watched the road they'd been on disappear in a cloud of dust.

It was desert out here, dried patches of grass and an occasional spindly cactus. Every half mile or so, the car passed a home, caked in dust with a red tin roof and southwestern tile decorations. But after fifteen minutes, there were no more signs of life.

"Turn here," said Análí.

"Where?" Cha'Risa asked.

"Past the turpentine-brush." He signaled with his bent, wrinkled finger, tapping the window.

It was evident that a vehicle had driven where Análí had directed Cha'Risa, but it didn't even qualify as a dirt path. The Camry followed the tracks, which disappeared after a few dozen yards. They seemed to be in the open desert. "Is this the right way?"

"Head for that peak on the right," Análí replied, pointing to the distance.

Cha'Risa found she had to navigate around boulders and shrubs, always turning back toward the clay mountain dozens of miles away.

The car's suspension squeaked as the weight of five passengers pushed down against the uneven terrain. Ten miles per hour seemed about the top speed for the car. Occasionally, they'd hit a particularly big bump and everyone would bounce off their seats.

Eleanor leaned over Kirby, who was in the middle of the back seat, and she spoke to Hollis. "You saw me in a dream. No fooling?"

Hollis didn't face her. He stared out the side window and confirmed it. "I saw you in a dream."

"And what happened in the dream?"

Hollis held his tongue for a moment. "Nothing... there was just you and a bunch of other people hanging around."

"Does anyone know how I got here? Does it have something to do with the tom-tom?"

With those words, heads spun.

"The *what*?" Kirby asked.

"The tom-tom, the thing he's wearing." She motioned toward Hollis.

Análí spoke though the oxygen mask. "Is that what they call it at the research facility?"

"Yes."

"It has everything to do with it," Análí replied. "But it is the Nítch'i Bee Hane'e. The military killed my father and took it from him. That is why your boss had a picture of my family."

Eleanor squirmed. "Oh my lord. I'm so sorry."

"Hey Cha'Risa," said Kirby. "Let me use your phone."

"Why?"

"I just want to show her how awesome it is, you know, compared to the telegraph or whatever they had back then."

"I told you I turned it off so they can't follow us," she replied. "Remember?"

"Crud!"

Análí pointed to something in the distance, little more than a speck on the horizon. "That's it."

It was ten minutes at their ambling pace before the house became apparent, and another ten on top of that until they reached it. The small adobe structure melted into the landscape, a peculiar design with soft curves and awkward angles as if it had eroded through the millennia. There was an array of solar panels atop the roof and a satellite dish springing from the side wall, as well as an off-road motorcycle and dirt-encrusted Jeep.

Split and stacked wood lined the lower half of the front walls, and the chimney puffed out a steady billow of smoke along with the unmistakeable smell of burning mesquite. Análí placed the oxygen tank on the ground outside the passenger door and stood beside it. He removed the mask and breathed in deeply the smoky mesquite as a content smile lit on his face. The rest of the crew exited and stayed near the car. If there was a middle of nowhere, this house sat smack dab at the center of it.

"Come," the old man said. He placed his mask back on and wheeled the oxygen around the car. A few haphazard paving stones led to the structure's door, which was losing aged cyan paint in large chips. He rang the doorbell. It didn't *dong* as most would, but rather sounded the opening theme of Star Wars, its horns muted through the door.

"Cool," Kirby said, elbowing Hollis.

A voice shouted from inside. "Come in!"

Análí stepped in through the door, followed by the others, and moved toward the sound of a television in an adjacent room. A man sat on a sofa with his back to them, machine gun sounds blaring from the TV. He was playing a video game.

"How's it going, Análí?" the man squawked in a nasally tone, without turning or waiting for a reply. "Who're your friends?"

The old man laughed through his oxygen mask, then removed it. "He is fond of security cameras," he explained to Cha'Risa. Then he spoke to the man on the couch a little louder. "This is my granddaughter and her friends."

The video game paused and the man rose and faced them. His arms dangled out of his tee-shirt like a couple of noodles, six foot two and a hundred-twenty pounds sopping wet. His haircut seemed to be an afterthought, dark curly hair, cropped tight, but not neat. His most prominent features were a mouth that seemed to stretch to either side of his head, and his ears, which were two sizes too large. He grinned an enthusiastic welcome. "What a great surprise! You should have told me you were coming. I don't have anything here. What do you want, a tea or a pop?"

"Nothing, thank you," Análí responded. "Biggs, this is my granddaughter Cha'Risa." He motioned around the room. "And this is Eleanor, Kirby and Hollis."

Biggs bobbed his head as each name was called, raising his hand and waving. "You know, I'd advise keeping your oxygen tank a little farther away from the fireplace," he said to the old man just before shooting his eyes back to the boys. He lowered his hand as the smile dropped from his face. "Análí, man, what's going on?" He glanced back at Cha'Risa. "Shit! Are you kidding me, man? These people are hot right now, I mean really seriously hot!"

"All is not what it seems," the old man replied.

"This is the wunderkind and half the country's looking for your granddaughter for kidnapping him."

"You know as well as anyone that things are rarely as simple as they are made out to be."

"Geez! Were you followed? Aww, man! Why'd you come here? Why'd you have to come here?" Biggs shot to the front window and scanned the horizon before snatching the drapes closed.

"We weren't followed."

"Yeah, right." Biggs spun around in a panic. "Holy crap, what were you thinking, lady?"

"We need your help," Análí said.

"Boy, you spend your life staying off the grid and then someone you thought was your buddy brings over the target of every government agency in the world." He started to wheeze and stuck his hand into a tray of coins and rubber bands on a shelf and retrieved an inhaler, taking two puffs.

"Maybe you should sit," Análí told him. "We are the good guys."

"Yeah," he agreed, plodding back to the sofa, looking glum. "I got no doubt you're the good guys, but the good guys aren't the ones that crash through windows and erase people."

XXX

Biggs stiff-armed a door and led the party into a windowless room in the rear of his house, for "covert operations," he explained. He flicked the switch on the wall and a couple of desk lamps shot to life. They lit up a tempered glass workstation in the center of the room, on top of which were laid a trio of powered down laptops. There were a series of nondescript boxes with red, green and yellow flashing lights under the computers, all connected with a jumble of cables. There was a back door on the far wall that separated Biggs' control center from the desert outside and a humidifier ran noisily in the corner of the otherwise sparse room, which was a good 10 degrees warmer than the rest of the house.

The walls were bare except for a framed black BBC miniseries poster titled "The Code," featuring glyphs and indigo hexagons. With the lighting all centered around the glass desk and computers, the poster would have been easy to miss. The group followed Biggs into the room with Eleanor straggling at the rear. It was clear she was having a hard time taking in everything that had changed in more than seventy years. Her attention was being diverted every few seconds to something she'd never imagined.

"Can you shut that Eleanor?" Biggs asked, pointing to the door they'd all just past through.

Eleanor, catching her name amid a cloud of thoughts, turned and clicked the door shut. Everyone else gathered around Biggs' control center.

"There's all sorts of rumors about your granddaughter and her friends," Biggs said as he ensconced himself on the lone chair and woke the computers. "But I discounted most of them. Some guys just let their imagination run wild and posit whatever they want.

Scuttlebutt turns into accepted theory. Usual horseshit, you know what I mean? There's only a few people you need to give credence to. They have good sources and don't pretend to know stuff they don't. They just want the truth."

"They have good track records," Análí said.

"Exactly," Biggs replied, pleased that the old man was on his page.

Cha'Risa folded her arms in front of her chest. "So what are they saying?"

"Okay, well first of all, most of them are on your side. Those other quote, unquote agents, you know, the ones that were barely mentioned in the stories. No doubt, they were definitely military."

Biggs tapped away at the keyboard, windows popping up and closing on each of the three computer screens. "What do we have here? Does this look like your friends."

Cha'Risa leaned in for a better glimpse. "That's pretty damned close," she said. "Yeah, I'd say that's them."

The middle laptop was displaying sketches of the two agents who had tried to kill Hollis.

"Police released these a couple hours ago. Let's see..." Biggs was reading some text on one of the other monitors. "It looks like they're based on descriptions from your friends' parents. Cops are saying they're looking for the subjects for questioning."

"I'll tell you what I'd like to do to them," Cha'Risa replied.

"My guess is that these two characters want your young friend here to help with weapons research."

"They don't want me," said Hollis. "They want the Nítch'i."

Biggs spun around in his seat. "The what now?"

Hollis pulled out the medallion and displayed it for the lanky nerd.

"Geez," said Biggs, scrutinizing the object. "Look at that thing glow. What the heck is it made of? Looks like something out of Lord..." He was silent for a moment as his jaw slowly dropped. "No way! No way!" He grabbed the Nítch'i and yanked it closer, pulling in Hollis as well, who was still connected via the necklace. "Are you kidding me? Are you kidding me?" he said, his voice rising an octave. "The tom-tom! This is the freakin' tom-tom!"

"The Nítch'i Bee Hane'e," Análí corrected.

"Wow! This is a totally new ballgame. I had no idea you guys were toting this thing around." He relinquished control of the medallion as Hollis regained his balance. "That explains everything. Holy crap!"

"You've seen this before?" Cha'Risa asked.

Biggs' speech had become frenetic. He shifted again toward the computers and started typing. "You bet I have. It's supposed to be an old Native-American artifact, which makes sense given the company in the room, right? They say the government ripped it off back in the '40s to use for military research. It was stolen a few years before the A-bombs, you get me? A scientist named Robert Cox was put in charge of it. You never heard of him, have you? Well neither has anyone else. You know Oppenheimer and Manley and Serber. But Cox, he was the guy. They kept him under wraps, all right."

"So what are you saying," Cha'Risa asked. "That this guy Cox invented the atomic bomb?"

"That's what I'm saying. Don't get me wrong. The other scientists were geniuses, all the way. But Cox, he was head and shoulders above. And they say it was because of that medallion, the tom-tom."

"Níłch'i Bee Hane'e," Análí said.

"Whatever. The piece of metal tied around this guy's neck." Biggs took to the computers like a fish to water, his fingers flying along the keys and rough illustrations of the Níłch'i popped up on the laptop screens. "But you see, some people say Cox was a pacifist and he ended up dying of natural causes at the age of 46. Natural causes, my ass. He realized what he'd unleashed on the world and decided he was all done with it and some people were none too happy about that."

Análí interrupted. "So how did he die?"

"All I'm saying is it wasn't natural causes. My guess: the feds wanted someone a little more military-oriented. So that's when the tom-tom found its way out east to some facility in Virginia where it went missing."

Eleanor straightened herself up and the eyes of everyone but Biggs fell upon her.

"Eleanor," Cha'Risa said in earnest. "How did that scientist die?"

"I don't know," Eleanor replied. "Honestly, I don't know."

"So how do you know about the Níłch'i?"

Eleanor stood in the shabby sweats she'd been given. She bit her lower lip before answering. "The man I work for is in charge of it."

"Colonel Emory Clay," said a melodramatic Biggs as he spun in his seat, revealing a proud grin.

"Yes."

Biggs looked as if he'd caught the murderer in an Agatha Christie novel before his face melted into utter bewilderment. "Wait a minute, what do you mean the man you work for?"

"Miss Eleanor is from 1945," Análí explained.

As the conversation continued around him, Biggs couldn't have been more still if he were meditating. His face had gone empty.

Cha'Risa started. "Well, this doesn't really tell us anything new."

"I am not sure we need to know anything more than how to keep Hollis safe," Análí replied.

"What about me?" asked Kirby.

Cha'Risa and Análí eyed each other.

Biggs' hadn't budged. "She's from 1945." His words distracted the group for a second, but that was all.

"We will find a way to return you to your parents," Análí said to Kirby.

"What about me?" Hollis asked.

Neither Análí nor Cha'Risa had an answer.

"I don't get it," Biggs said, shaking off the momentary head fog. "I don't get it. What do you mean she's from 1945? You're not telling me that this woman is from 1945. Because that is just *spectacular.*"

"Biggs," Análí began, "what we need to know is how we can protect Hollis. Can you help us with that? It is very important that Hollis remains with the Nílch'i Bee Hane'e and is free to grow with it."

"Help me out here," Biggs said. "So you're saying she's *actually* from 1945. You're saying she's from 1945, that this woman was born in like 1920 or whatever and that now she's here and the tom... the nil-whatever is responsible for her traveling through actual time? That I'm looking at a time traveler?"

There was a moment of silence before Análí nodded. "We do not have an explanation yet. She appeared at the door as we were all meeting for the first time. It undoubtedly has something to do with the Nílch'i Bee Hane'e, but I have nothing to guide me here. There are no stories in our history of someone traveling through time. What I can say is that if Hollis had not recognized her from a dream, we would never have trusted her and brought her along. She seems certain that she was in 1945 before she appeared before us. More than that, I cannot say. I am as confused as anyone."

Cha'Risa was focused on Biggs. "Can you help Hollis?"

Biggs shook his head as if he were fending off a night of bad drinking. "I think I need a minute here. This is just nuts."

"Biggs." Análí's tone had grown serious. "You need to concentrate. Please. We do not have the privilege of time."

His lips tightened as Biggs nodded. "I can think about that later, right? I need to set some priorities. All right, what are we looking at? Hollis. Yes." His voice lowered as if he'd realized something troubling. "Oh boy."

"What is it?" Cha'Risa snapped.

"The thing is, I don't live this far away from everything for no reason. I picked this spot because I wanted bug out options. It's just that I can't believe I'm actually going to need them."

"Where would these options be?" Análí asked.

"A few miles away, at the base of the mountains. I lugged a bunch of junk out there so I could make it, you know, in the event of the apocalypse or whatever. There's enough there to keep you going for awhile so we can figure out some sort of plan to get you down to Central America. There aren't enough supplies to keep you going forever. It was only supposed to be me, you know. I wasn't planning on hosting a convention."

"All right," Kirby said. "What are we waiting for?"

Análí, Cha'Risa and Biggs eyed each other, silently acknowledging that the boy was right. Then Biggs turned to his computer one more time, logging himself out and shutting the system down. He hopped out of his chair and the group spun toward the door, stopping in their tracks.

Eleanor was gone.

In her absence, a pile of crumpled clothes lay on the floor.

Biggs was the first to speak. "What the heck?"

Cha'Risa threw the door open and shouted into the rest of the house. "Eleanor! Eleanor, what's going on?"

"I don't know that I would waste my breath," Análi said. "She was here for a reason and it seems she has left our realm in the same way she entered, having fulfilled the task."

"Whoa!" Kirby exclaimed.

Biggs held in both sides of his cranium with his stick arms. "Geez! You can't tell me she just went back to 1945!"

"I don't know where she went," Análi replied. "But she isn't here anymore. Come, let's find this bug out spot before anyone finds us."

They trampled over Eleanor's garments and made their way through the house for the vehicles, Biggs grabbing a backpack by the front door on his way out.

"It would appear we have an extra spot in the car," Análi said to Biggs as he climbed into the front seat of the Camry.

But Biggs was heading toward his motorcycle. "No thanks," he said. "Always good to have a backup. This baby was made for terrain like this." He threw on the backpack, fired up the bike with his thumb and revved it several times, the engine spewing out a cloud of black smoke. He pulled in front of the car and punched it toward the set of mountains in the distance.

XXXI

12:51 p.m., Wednesday, August 22, 1945

The first couple of seconds were utterly disorienting. One moment, Eleanor was tagging along with a group of people in a foreign world and the next second everything had gone blank, sheer white. Her vision needed to reset before it could even process what she was seeing, some sort of reference point. It was a ceiling. She was lying on her back at the front of her desk, having apparently returned to 1945. Her visit to the future had begun the same way, which somewhat prepared her for the jolt back. What on earth was happening to her?

She sat up, only then realizing she had returned in the same way she'd gone out—naked. The pounding in her chest doubled, fast and heavy. She shot her eyes to the office front door. It was closed. Then to Col. Clay's door, also closed. Thank god.

She heard his voice. He was on the phone in his office. And she was lying naked. There was simply no way this would end well if he strode out of his office. He'd take it as a sexual advance. How could he not? He believed himself to be irresistible and any protests by her would be seen as part of a game. Furthermore, he wasn't the kind of man who would stop, even if she fought.

She shot to her feet and darted around the desk, trying to stay silent, the floor cold on her bare feet. There they were, her clothes, lying in a heap on her chair. Without her body to support them, everything had just fallen. She reached for her blouse, which was on top, buttoned up. Her bra was still inside it. She shook the blouse and it fell out. Get the top on first, she thought; she could always hide her lower half beneath the desk.

She had never felt so exposed. With no clothes for cover, every movement created a breath of air across her skin. It'd be better to be nude in Times Square than at work with that chauvinistic slimeball in the next room.

She didn't bother to unclasp the bra. Just throw the straps over your arms, she thought. It can be fixed after you're covered up. Then she lowered the buttoned blouse over her head, looking somewhat normal from the waist up.

She grabbed the remaining clump of clothes from the chair and lowered herself onto it, trying unsuccessfully to keep it from squeaking. Then she inadvertently kicked over her shoes, which lay right where she always placed her feet. The wooden seat had remained warm during her disappearance, but it felt wrong upon her naked rump.

Col. Clay slammed the phone down, and Eleanor felt her heart speed up even more. She kept a nervous watch on the opaque glass of his office door. There was no movement inside and the room was quiet. There was only the sound of the clock on the wall of the outer office, its motor slowly turning the second hand.

She unzipped the skirt and, clasping it and the slip between her fingers, shook out her nylon stockings and underwear, raising up her butt enough to pull on the skirt and slip at the same time. She was at least covered. The clock read 12:52. No time had passed during her journey into the future. How was that possible? She slipped on her underwear and stockings, making sure to stay in the chair in case Clay came barreling through the door.

Her feet found the shoes while she simultaneously reached up the front of her blouse with both hands and unclasped the bra, still bunched up uselessly on the front of her chest. She placed the straps on either of her sides and raised the rear of the blouse enough to stretch the bra back together.

The thoughts of the last several hours were a jumble in her mind. Clay had shown her the medallion several times over the past few months, trying to impress her, but she didn't know anything about it. Had the military actually stolen it from an Indian family, killing an innocent American in the process? Did they use it to create the atomic bomb? And were they now making more hugely destructive weapons? But the bomb had saved lives, hadn't it? The war could have stretched on for years if Truman hadn't obliterated Hiroshima and Nagasaki. There was too much to take in.

Her hands jolted to her desk as Clay's door sprang open. There wasn't a chance to tuck in the blouse or straighten out her clothes.

Her peripheral vision picked him up. His lips were wrapped around a stogie, his eyes ogling her. He leaned against the door jamb and sucked on the cigar, removing it with his right hand and blowing the stinky smoke toward her desk.

Eleanor had to make an effort to slow down her breathing, which only caused her heart to gain momentum. Would he pick up on the fact that she was sweating? Did she look flush? She acknowledged her boss with a calm glance and set her eyes back on some papers covering the desk. She was trying to stuff her feet back into her shoes without appearing distracted.

Clay stepped to the front of her desk and set the cigar down in an ashtray. "That was General Groves," he said. "He's flying up from D.C. tomorrow."

Eleanor didn't want to look at Clay. Eye contact only encouraged him. She wondered how unkempt she appeared. Her hair was probably all tousled, her blouse loose. She replied while keeping her attention on a binder of papers on the desk. "Should I do anything to prepare for the general's arrival?"

"You know, General Groves is losing his secretary of thirty years."

Eleanor's mind was having a hard time focusing and this new information only added to the disarray. Maybe she could be reassigned to Washington, live in the big city, work for a professional. She could sense the possibility of a weight being lifted, a light at the end of the tunnel.

"I could put in a good word for you," said Clay.

And that flipped her back to reality. He wouldn't put in a good word; Clay would never let her go; he was too much of a dog. He was dangling a better job in front of her to grease the wheels, to use her own ambition against her. This was his latest maneuver to bed her. Her eyes met the ashy end of Clay's cigar, smoldering at the end of her desk and she swallowed her anger. "Thank you, sir."

Clay?"

"Stop it!" she shouted. She grabbed at his hands struggling to pull them free of her hips, but his arms were branches, and her own like twigs.

"Promotion or reprimand? You can decide that right here."

"I quit! Now let me go!" Eleanor's words floated right through him.

"Squirming is good," he said, before kissing her neck.

Eleanor couldn't see below the top of his skull, but he had moved a hand from her hip to his waist. He was unbuckling his belt. She reached up to the bookshelf, grasping for a book to hit him with. They were just out of reach. Then she felt something solid at her fingertips. Bending her arm back farther than it was intended to go, she clutched the object and whipped it around toward his head, the edge of it hitting with a satisfying thud. Clay stumbled back a foot and fell to the floor, reaching instinctively for the wound she'd just inflicted on the back of his skull. He lay on his side, his belt unbuckled.

She straddled the man and walloped him again three more times before straightening herself out. Clay had stopped moving and a small streak of blood was oozing out of a cut next to his eyebrow. The object in her hand was a cast iron replica of a cannon, with a solid square base, three or four pounds worth of metal. Placing it back on the bookshelf, she stared at Col. Clay, unconscious on the floor. Was he seriously hurt? She didn't mean to permanently damage him, but she didn't have a choice. Surely people would see that.

She pulled her skirt down off her hips. No. She didn't have a choice.

Too much had happened in the last few hours. Her life, whatever the consequences of assaulting Col. Clay, was about to take a drastic turn. The question now was what to do. Who would she even notify? Clay was the commanding officer at the base. Should she reach out to General Groves? How had this all happened? All she wanted to do this morning was try out a new look. Now she wondered if anyone would believe her. Certainly the other women on the base would, but what about the military officials? It would be her word against his.

The insufferable bastard lying at her feet had caused this whole thing. What was wrong with him? Why would he try to take her in the middle of their office? As far as she was concerned, he was no better than a common criminal. It's just that he had power to dangle over his victims. She thought of the old Indian she'd met just a few hours earlier, and his granddaughter. Then she considered the sweet little boy who would eventually wield the tom-tom. He was so much more deserving of the artifact than the sleazy hulk on the floor.

Inching toward Clay, she leaned over his chest and noticed the medallion pushing against the inside of his shirt. She ripped open a few buttons, and there it was, lying over his tank top, dangling from a ribbon around his neck, the tom-tom, the object that had uprooted her life. Was this her purpose? The medallion was supposed to go missing and it hadn't dawned on her until this very second that perhaps she was intended to liberate it from such an immoral man, to return it to the people from whom it had been stolen.

It wasn't glowing like it was in the future. It seemed a mix of stone and silver, a slick unnatural material. Seizing hold of the item, she lifted Clay's head and removed the necklace. The blood streaming down his forehead looked worse than it had even a few seconds ago. It was now or never. This was obviously an issue of national security. If she took it, that would be the end of her life as she'd known it. She would most certainly be sent to jail, or worse. At this moment, her loathing for Col. Clay was as much a determining factor as any. He would face harsh penalties for letting the item be stolen. That was good enough for her.

Eleanor straightened out her clothing, tucking in her blouse fully and pulling her nylon stockings tightly up her legs. Checking out her reflection in a picture frame on the wall, she did her best to make her hair presentable. She gave one last glance at Col. Clay, who lay motionless on the ground, then she stowed the tom-tom in the waistline of her skirt. She opened the office door and stepped through, closing it on the way out.

XXXII

Present Day

The mouth of the cave was slim, set into the side of the desert mountains. Everyone but Kirby needed to shuffle sideways to get through it. Up close it seemed that the rocks had split, like a tear in fabric. From a hundred yards away, the casual eye wouldn't even notice the opening. It appeared as another wrinkle on a range of crimson, clay mountains, resembling Análí's skin as much as anything else, like the old man was a part of them.

"It's not much, but I wasn't trying to set up the Waldorf-Astoria," said Biggs, his voice echoing as he began the nickel tour of his apocalyptic safety zone. Inside the fissure, Biggs' cave had opened up, his LED lantern casting a blue glow across the sandstone floor. The power of the light couldn't match the expansive cave. Its light faded overhead as the ceiling vaulted into the ether, and deeper into the mountain, several rounded passages gave way to desolate blackness like the eyes of a spider.

The air was dry and cold, the mountain providing unsurpassed insulation from the sun. Several black and yellow industrial storage containers lined one of the walls, next to a generator and a collection of five-gallon gas canisters. Along the other wall, a couple cords of wood were stacked neatly, and in the center of the area, the remains of past fires. Biggs had spent many nights camped out in the cave.

"There's a small stream a couple hundred yards to the west coming off the mountain. It isn't always flowing, so you need to store water for the leaner times," Biggs said. "The way I figure it, even at nighttime, a small fire inside here can't be seen from the air. We're going to have to hide your car somewhere. That's an obvious giveaway."

"What about heat tracking?" Cha'Risa asked.

"Nothing's going to be seeing through a mountain, but if you're outside... Hey, if they know where to look and have heat detection, what can I say? It isn't perfect, but it's available without a background check or a deposit."

"We'll take it," said Análí.

"I guess I should have thought to bring some blankets from the house. I can run back and get some."

Cha'Risa had the blanket she'd been using while camping with the boys, plus one from Dr. Deschene's car, but she knew they'd need more, especially at night in the desert. "That would be great. And we need to figure out what to do about Análí's oxygen as well. Buy a few tanks and bring them out here, I guess." She pointed to the dark passages deeper in the cave. "Where do those lead?"

"Most of what I've found have been dead ends," Biggs replied. "But there are some tunnels that keep going. I usually end up following them a few hundred yards before I turn around."

"So if anyone finds us, running deeper into the cave isn't our best option then."

"No way. All they'd have to do is stake out the entrance and wait for you to walk into their arms."

"Are there, like, rattlesnakes or something in here?" Kirby asked.

"Not at this time of year," Cha'Risa answered. "If we stay here for longer than a few weeks though, we'll start seeing them."

"I'd like to get you out of here sooner rather than later," said Biggs.

"Agreed," said Cha'Risa.

Análí's eyes lowered, his head shaking from side to side. "I have great misgivings of starting this child down a path where he is always looking over his shoulder."

"Me, too," said Hollis.

"What were you expecting, Análí?" Cha'Risa's voice was agitated. "You sent me out to get him and there wasn't ever a plan on what to do afterwards? That's just insane. You had your whole life to come up with something."

"I have spent many sleepless nights pondering this moment. How it would eventually play out, I could not know. It always seemed that I would have more time to formulate something which I hadn't considered, but I was never able to conjure up anything more than running. I am certainly open to suggestions." He noticed the boy at the center of it all, a fifth grader who was as lost as anyone, gazing blankly at the stone walls. "I am sorry, Hollis, that it has fallen to someone as young as you. For all of our history it has been handed down to someone much farther along life's road because of the immense responsibility. Only one person in each generation had the liberty of representing humanity to the gods."

"That's not what it is," said Hollis, still focused on the cave.

Silence fell as the boy took a seat on the ground by the industrial containers, his knees scrunched up in front of him, his head hung down.

"Hollis," said Análí. "What do you mean?"

"I'm not talking to the gods."

"You told Cha'Risa that you felt someone. Is that still right?"

"I said I sensed someone, but I didn't know who."

"So who is it?" asked Cha'Risa.

Hollis lifted a stone off the ground and tossed it into the darkness of the cave, its sound echoing off the walls.

"Hollis?" Análí prodded.

The boy wouldn't raise his head. "Alien."

"It's an alien?" Cha'Risa exclaimed.

He nodded.

A smile from ear to ear grew across Biggs' visage, his voice like a child's. "Whoa!"

"Are you sure? That would mean the whole mythology behind this thing has been all wrong," said Cha'Risa.

"I disagree," said Análí.

Cha'Risa sat next to the boy. "Hollis just said he's communicating with an alien, not a god."

Biggs' voice grew fevered. "This is *awesome!*"

The boy genius rose and left the cave, Kirby running after him.

"An alien," Biggs said, folding his arms in front of his chest, the lantern casting shadows as it swayed in his hand.

Análí cast a glance toward the cave entrance. "It makes sense when you think about it. I do not know that our ancestors would have seen a difference. It was someone not of this world, with knowledge far different from our own. Why would that seem like anything other than a god? It's just a matter of interpretation."

Biggs said, "Weapon-making aside, I doubt the government would want a kid being the sole voice to some super-advanced alien civilization."

The thought hung in the air for a moment before Cha'Risa spoke. "I'm going to check on him." She strode toward the entrance, sidling by to get out through the tight entrance. The outside temperature was a good ten degrees warmer than inside the cave. Cha'Risa made her way to the two boys, who had climbed on top of a couple large rocks, the sun beating down on them. "You two okay?" she asked.

Hollis and Kirby nodded and Cha'Risa hopped up on the rocks next to them. "We're going to find a way for both of you to see your parents again. And we'll keep you safe."

"How are you going to do that?" Hollis asked.

"I don't know, but we'll figure a way."

Kirby was rolling stones on his pant leg and tossing them down on the ground. "So where does this alien dude live anyway?"

Hollis pointed back toward the cave.

"Are you serious? The thing is living in there?" Kirby asked.

"Not in the cave. On a planet in that direction."

"What do you mean?"

"It's on a planet about twelve-thousand light years in that direction."

"So you know where it is," Cha'Risa offered.

Hollis nodded. "It's in our galaxy."

Kirby's face had bent out of shape. "I thought the stars were up there." He pointed to the sky.

"They're over there, too," said Hollis. "And under our feet. They're everywhere around us. In space, there is no up or down, east or west. In fact time is more flexible than most people think, too."

"Is that how come that lady could visit us from 1945?" Kirby asked.

"That's why."

"What's his planet like?" Cha'Risa asked. "Do you know?"

"It's smaller than earth," Hollis replied. "And warmer. It's a lighter atmosphere with liquid water. Two moons. The days are shorter than ours, too. They have a different kind of sun. The sky is yellowish during the day and red when the night starts. And depending on the moons, it can be calm or absolutely crazy."

"Wow," said Kirby.

Hollis continued. "And it's not a he. They don't have males and females."

"So can you see the planet?" Kirby asked.

"No. It's more like I can sense what it sees sometimes."

"What does it want with us?"

"It's curious. It loves to experience other places and beings. It gets a sense of what it's like here, what I'm like. It can feel what I feel."

Hollis stood up and gazed into the distance, back toward Biggs' house.

"What is it?" Cha'Risa asked.

"I think..." He squinted. "We're not expecting anyone, are we?"

Cha'Risa and Kirby shot to their feet and studied the horizon. In the distance, a tiny speck of dust was rising off the desert floor.

"Is that the wind?" Kirby asked.

Cha'Risa's skin turned a shade paler and her mouth dropped. She remained silent for a few seconds before speaking. "That's not the wind. Someone's coming this way."

~ ~ ~ ~ ~ ~ ~ ~ ~

"We need to get out of here now," Cha'Risa shouted, bolting into the cave. Análi and Biggs were in the middle of a conversation. They stared at her expectantly. Had she witnessed something outside? Was Hollis in need of medical help again?

Grabbing a liter of water off the cave floor, Cha'Risa barked at them again. "Now, goddamnit!"

"What is it?" Análi asked.

"Someone's coming."

Análi was as calm as they come, but Biggs was a horrible poker player and the look of horror drained all the blood from his face. He seemed as if he was about to collapse in a twitching bundle of nerves.

Análí, who had been seated on a flat rock, struggled to his feet. "How far out?"

"I don't know... ten, fifteen minutes, depends on what they're driving."

Análí rolled his oxygen tank toward the cave entrance, walking in baby steps as Biggs remained static. The old man spun around and raised his voice. "Biggs, you need to shake out of it. You cannot stay here."

It was enough to wake the man from his paralytic stupor. "Yeah," he said, rising to his feet. "Gotta go. Can't stay."

Outside the cave, Hollis and Kirby were in the Camry's back seat awaiting the crew. Cha'Risa shot to the driver's door and climbed in as Análí and Biggs made their way over. But Biggs stopped unexpectedly, and sensing the lack of motion in his friend, Análí turned again to face him. "Biggs, what is it?" Análí wondered if Biggs was frozen with fear. "Biggs, we need to go."

Biggs was staring at the cloud of dust in the distance as it drew nearer. He had once again lost all focus. "How did they know?"

Cha'Risa cranked the engine and poked her head out of the car door. "Biggs, let's go! We're not waiting!"

Análí edged back toward the man to encourage him to keep moving, but Biggs' voice grew more confident. "How did they know where you were?"

"What do you mean?" Análí asked.

"I mean, it's been an hour, probably more. There was no one coming when we left my house. How did they know where you were?"

"It doesn't matter, Biggs," Cha'Risa shouted. "What matters is getting out of here."

Biggs moved toward the car with no intention of climbing in. "Don't you see? They've got a tracking device on your car, or a satellite or something. They knew you were here."

For a moment, there was silence, just the idle of the Camry's engine. Then Cha'Risa stepped out of the car. "So what, they're watching us by satellite?"

"What, you don't think the government would stoop to using a satellite? That medallion is probably the number one military priority."

The boys climbed out of the back seat and turned their attention to Biggs.

"What do you suggest?" Análí asked.

"Cha'Risa, you can take my bike with the kids and head up the side of this mountain. They won't be able to follow you in a car. Head down the other side and there's a maze of rocks almost immediately— miles of hiding spots. It's at the edge of a state park. Wait until it gets dark, and if you keep your lights off, their satellites might not be able to track you."

"What about you two?"

Análí answered. "We'll take the car. Maybe they'll follow us."

"Not if they're watching us on a satellite," Cha'Risa replied.

"There's no cell phone reception out here. They won't be able to communicate with anyone," said Análí.

"Unless they have a satellite phone," Biggs offered.

"Just go!" Análí commanded, his brow showing signs of distress for the first time.

Without any hesitation, Cha'Risa opened the Camry's trunk and removed a backpack and her rifle. She threw the bag at Kirby and strapped the rifle across her back, climbing on the motorcycle. "Let's go!" She looked at Hollis. "You're in front."

Biggs helped to lift Hollis onto the front of the bike. The boy grabbed hold of the handlebars, his knuckles turning white as he gripped tightly. Kirby got a hold of Cha'Risa's backpack and pulled himself onto the rear of the bike as she sparked the engine to life, spitting sand out from the rear wheel as she steered toward a gentle incline up the mountain.

Análí and Biggs watched their three companions ascending as the sound of the motorbike gradually faded. But the serenity of the desert was their enemy now. As long as the bike could be heard at ground level, the trio were in danger. Análí eyed the incoming cloud of dust. "You'd better drive."

"Yeah," said Biggs, darting for the driver's seat. Análí's frailty slowed their exit considerably, his feet shuffling toward the passenger side of the Camry with the oxygen tank in tow. Biggs hit the gas, slamming

Análí's door closed.

"Take it easy," the old man said.

"Yeah, right." Biggs spun the car east, riding along the base of the mountain, the gravel crunching under the car's balding tires, a cloud of dust billowing behind it. Occasionally both riders would jump out of their seats as the loose, uneven ground tore up the Camry's suspension. Biggs glanced over at the vehicle barreling toward the mountain. "Are they following us?"

"I cannot tell," said Análí, who hadn't moved his eyes from the speck in the distance.

It was another minute before Análí could answer with any certainty. "They are not."

Biggs eased his foot from the gas and shot his eye toward the visitors. "So, what do we do?"

"I think we need to turn around."

Biggs slammed on the brakes and spun the car in the opposite direction, redlining the engine and losing a hubcap in the process. He couldn't tell whether he was hitting every rock in the desert or if the car was falling apart from the moonlike terrain. They were closing fast on a silver SUV, which was dangerously close to Biggs' cave.

As the SUV drew to a stop in front of the cave, two figures stepped from its interior. They were clad in sunglasses, dark pants and white shirts.

"Shit," said Biggs. "That is definitely government issued trouble. What should I do?"

Análí didn't answer.

"Should I ram them? I should ram them," Biggs said. "I can't ram them. What am I crazy?"

The figures raised their arms toward the Camry.

"Are they motioning me to stop?" Biggs asked. Years in front of a computer hadn't done the man's eyes any good.

Análí scrunched into his seat. "Get down!"

The agents began firing gunshots toward the car.

Biggs put his head down just in time as the windshield cracked, spiderwebbing. It didn't even sound like much, like he'd hit a small rock, but there was a hole in the center of the web and the driver's side headrest had its stuffing blown out. Three more bullets hit the windshield in succession, making it all but impossible to see through. Biggs was driving blind as the sound of more bullets pierced the car's body, barely discernible thuds over the roar of the engine. He felt the car suddenly jerk to the left. They'd shot out a tire.

As Biggs hit the brakes, the right side of the car jolted upwards and in a second the car had flipped onto its side, Análí falling down onto Biggs, along with his oxygen tank. The car skidded to a halt in the gravel.

XXXIII

Cha'Risa no longer had a clear view of the mountain's base. She skirted the motorcycle along a precipice, Kirby's arms wrapped around her waist, his fingers clawing into her stomach. He was cursing under his breath. Clinging onto the handlebars in front of her, Hollis had gone silent. The path Cha'Risa had chosen seemed like the only viable route up the mountain. It would have been a difficult climb on her own, but with two young boys strapped onto the motorcycle as well, it had proven a slog. To her left, the red clay rose sharply and to her right, the ground fell away to a hundred foot drop. There was only a narrow edge on which to navigate.

Hundreds of feet below, the SUV that had been approaching from across the desert was obscured from view. She hoped that Análí and Biggs had been able to divert whoever was following them, or at least had reached safety somewhere, but she didn't have high hopes. In all likelihood, there were government agents already ascending the mountain, closing in on her and the boys.

The hillside soared steep and treacherous in front of her. She inched forward a few feet, but knew the motorcycle would not be able to make it up such an incline. She turned the wheel toward the adjacent walls and spun the motorcycle around, the front tire rolling up the stone and forcing the bike half-vertical in the process. Kirby's added weight on the rear nearly caused her to lose balance, a disaster that would have brought the motorcycle crashing down on top of them all. The boys clung on as she revved the bike on again, ever upwards.

The ground opened up for a few hundred feet, a gentle incline with room to spare on either side. It was the fastest she'd been able to push the machine in awhile, but the path once again narrowed and her options ceased. By the time she realized the motorcycle wouldn't be making it up the mountain on their current route, it was too late to turn back. The only other viable options were close to the base of the mountain. They'd be walking right into the arms of their pursuers.

She shut down the engine.

"What's going on?" Kirby asked.

"Come on," she replied. "We need to walk from here on."

Kirby held on to her backpack and unloaded himself. "Are you serious?"

Cha'Risa pried Hollis' fingers from the handlebars and helped him find his footing on the ground again. "It's too steep," she said, dropping the bike on the incline.

The air was biting at this height, the sun strong. Against the hillside, the sky burned a rich cobalt blue. They all squinted up at the summit, still a precipitous journey ahead of them. She led the way up, clutching at bits of rock to steady herself, the rifle strapped across her back. Hollis followed and Kirby took up the rear. There was rarely room for two across as they made their way skyward. Hollis stopped, leaning an arm on his knee, his face as red as the clay, but Kirby urged him onward. This was no time to be taking it easy.

Occasionally, Cha'Risa glanced down, trying not to alarm either of the fifth graders. She couldn't catch sight of anyone tailing them, but she knew they were there, tightening the screws with every passing minute. At a steady pace, anyone following them would eventually catch up, but the question was whether or not Cha'Risa and her troop could make it over the mountain to the maze of rocks Biggs had promised. Every second in haste brought them that much closer to being caught. Cha'Risa knew it, as did the boys. But there was only so much Hollis could physically undertake. Climbing a mountain was hard work for anyone. For someone with heart disease however, it might not be manageable. She could hear the boy wheezing behind her.

Hollis threw up a hand. "I need a second." His chubby face was coursing with blood, the sweat beading off his forehead, his hair wet and matted down despite the chill in the air. They were near a plateau, but he was having trouble catching a full breath.

"Okay," said Cha'Risa, her own heart pounding from the ordeal.

"Rest a second. I'm going to take a look from up there."

She climbed another ten feet and stretched to her tiptoes for a better view. The rocks had flattened out and in any other situation, it would have been a good place to make camp for the night. But that wasn't an option. She peered over the edge of the slope simultaneously rummaging around in the backpack. Her hand settled on something cold and solid, one of the pistols she had taken from the agents in the Whittaker house. She removed it from the bag and checked the magazine. It was fully loaded. Shifting the stock of the rifle which was strapped across her shoulders, she tucked the handgun into the back of her jeans. Then she zipped up the backpack and flung it over her shoulder.

For nearly a minute there were no other signs of life, just a vast desert stretching out below her. But then she saw it... a movement. It was someone's head, just visible over a rock for a half second. Unmistakeable.

She took a few steps down the hill and offered her hand to Hollis, trying not to let the panic pulsing through her brain become evident. "Come on. We need to keep moving."

The boy accepted her help, his arm almost wrenching off as she yanked him up to the plateau, his friend on his tail, apparently no worse for the wear.

"We can't stop," Cha'Risa said. "I'm sorry."

Hollis nodded and followed her to the next incline, where the grunting and heavy breathing continued. The boy thought back to the races he held in his back yard, races with only himself. He was always victorious, the fastest kid on the field. But this was reality. He couldn't outrun anyone younger than a hundred. His predicament was finally settling in. He was going to die. He'd never see his parents again. The thugs who tried to kill him before would win, the one who beat up his father. If he'd had any strength, Hollis would have been raging, but he was running on fumes, his heart pounding at a mile a minute. Every once in awhile Cha'Risa glanced behind him down the hill. She didn't think he noticed, but he did. "Come on," she said. "Gotta hurry."

He knew what was happening. Someone was closing in.

For over an hour, every time they thought they'd reached the top of the mountain, it was just another bit of flat ground, a summit mirage. But their next plateau proved the last. There was nothing more above them. The sky spread out vast in every direction. Cha'Risa pulled Hollis up and started speed walking across the expansive mountaintop, not even pausing for a breather. Hollis knew they were in trouble. Kirby overtook him as they both jogged to keep up with her, but Hollis' legs were finalizing their transformation into rubber. His brain was pounding in his skull, his heart in his chest. He began to trip over his own feet. Then he fell to the ground. He let out an involuntary yelp as he hit the ground, which caught his comrades' attention. They raced back for him and helped him up, then urged him to keep moving.

And so he did. But his strides were no longer sufficient. He was chugging along like an underpowered train struggling up a hill. A small indentation in the rocks was all it took. He went down a second time. Cha'Risa stepped back to the boy, who was now face down on the rock. "Here we go, pal," she said, reaching out and grabbing his hand.

It was limp.

She heaved him onto his back, his cold sweat tacky through his shirt. His eyes were rolled back into his head.

"No," she said. "No. Not now, oh god, not now." She slapped his face a couple times, kneeling beside him. "Come on buddy, don't do this now." She felt the pulse on his neck. It was racing.

"Oh Jesus," said Kirby. "What do we do?"

Cha'Risa unstrapped the rifle from her back and handed it to Kirby, who took it without flinching. Then with all of her strength, she yanked Hollis up over her shoulder and slowly straightened herself up. She turned for the far edge of the mountains and started jogging.

A sudden loud crack from behind her stopped Cha'Risa in her tracks, a rock at her feet disintegrating into dust. There was nowhere to go. The far edge of the mountain was still fifty yards away. Whoever was following them had caught up and fired a warning shot.

"I missed on purpose," came a deep voice from behind.

Cha'Risa and Kirby turned to face the two agents they'd escaped when their journey together had begun, a man and a woman looking for trouble. They were forty feet away and marching toward their prey.

The woman clutched her firearm by her side, but the man had his arm fully extended, aimed directly at Cha'Risa.

"Put the boy down," said Agent Breiner. He pointed his gun at Kirby.

Cha'Risa considered the weapons she'd taken off the agents back in Virginia. They didn't know that she had one tucked into the back of her pants.

Out of breath and wide eyed, she did as she was instructed, laying the boy on the red clay mountaintop, his breath coming in quick bursts. "You don't have to kill him," she said. "We know a way to break the connection with him. You can have the damned thing and leave him alone." She was lying, but the agents wouldn't know that.

Breiner and Grey closed the gap. "Put the rifle down," Agent Grey ordered Kirby. The boy didn't budge.

"You heard the lady," Breiner said, cocking the firearm, which by now was clearly aimed at Kirby's head. The boy stood firm.

Cha'Risa placed her hands on her hips, closer to the pistol in the back of her jeans, but she couldn't take a chance with Kirby's life.

The agents stopped a few steps away, both of them red with exertion and breathing through wide nostrils.

"You don't have to do this," Cha'Risa said. "I told you there's a way to disconnect him from it. I can show you how."

"You really fucked up our assignment," Breiner replied, without moving the gun from Kirby's head. He glanced at Cha'Risa. "Move your hands off your hips. I want them out in the air."

There just wasn't an opportunity to grab the weapon from her jeans. She hesitated, but Breiner's cold eyes squinted and she did as she was told, moving her hands out from her body, palms toward the agents.

"How'd you know we were coming?" Breiner asked. "Back at the house?"

Cha'Risa was under no illusions that she, Kirby or Hollis would be making it off the mountain alive. They would be left here for the buzzards and the insects. As far as she was concerned, the fewer facts her interrogators had, the better. She wouldn't mention her grandfather or the Nítch'i's role in their family. "It was part of our folklore."

"Folklore, huh? So a housekeeper drove across the country and stopped me from completing my duty because of her *folklore*, right? You buy that Agent Grey?"

"I do not," Grey replied, her cold eyes staring directly into Cha'Risa's.

"Do you know what happens to people who disrupt our assignments?"

Cha'Risa was silent.

"You do, don't you?" Breiner snarled, basking in the vulnerability of the target. The mountaintop fell silent for several seconds. There was no wind, no motion before Breiner finally spoke again. "We kill them."

He moved his arm two inches to the right, aiming at the center of Cha'Risa's chest. She gasped in anticipation, but at that moment Kirby whipped the muzzle of the rifle up in Breiner's direction. The trained killer had no trouble moving the two inches back to Kirby's head before the boy could complete his maneuver. The agent's finger squeezed on the trigger.

And then Breiner's gun dropped to the stone with a sharp clack, along with his clothes and sunglasses. He had vanished.

Kirby froze with the rifle at half mast.

Agent Grey's eyes went wild. She saw Breiner's clothes in a heap on the rocks and was momentarily stunned.

Hollis sat up, bent ninety degrees at his midsection. He was calm and studying Agent Grey.

In a split second, Grey realized that Hollis was responsible for whatever happened to Breiner. She jerked her handgun toward his torso, her eyes wide, obscured behind shades, her mouth open in panic.

And then she disappeared. Her gun fell to the ground, as did her clothing, her glasses landing silently on top of her shirt.

XXXIV

Hollis' bedroom had been cleaned, the clothing and toys picked up off the floor, the books neatly stacked and his bed made. The curtains were open and a ray of bright sunlight illuminated half of his room. Kaos, King of the Orcs reared his menacing mug from the poster on the wall.

The boy grinned, resting his hands on his hips. The room was still indelibly his. He stomped to the bureau, floorboards creaking, and was buoyed to see his stack of *Lurkin's Realm* comics, still wrapped in cellophane, held its place of honor inside the top drawer. He pulled out a pair of underwear and socks. There was no sense in reintroducing himself into his parents' lives clad in nothing.

The Niłch'i was in his fist, a permanent blue glowing through his fingers. He inspected the next few drawers. All of his clothes had been washed and folded. It bugged him when everything was creased, but it was also comforting that his parents had prepared for his ultimate return. He slipped on a pair of jeans and a T-shirt, placing the medallion in his front pocket before dropping to his knees at the end of his bed to search for sneakers. There they were, two pair lined up neatly under the bed. He grabbed the blue ones and hopped on the bed to tie them on.

A subtle noise caught his attention. It was his bedroom door handle slowly twisting. His parents had heard the commotion he'd been making and were cautiously inspecting.

"You can come in," he said.

It was a second before the door burst open. His parents stood in the jamb, their faces pale as ghosts. His mother nearly knocked over his father as she barreled past him into the room, her arms extended. Her emotions clamored to get out of her—fear, relief, exhilaration, anger, joy—the color flowing back into her cheeks. She rushed to the other side of the bed and wrapped her arms around the boy, lifting him off the bed and holding him tightly. His father ran over and embraced them both.

Hollis heard his mother whimper, her warm breath next to his ear, "Oh my god," as she began sniffling. "We missed you so much. Are you okay? Oh, my god, you're back."

"You can put me down, I'm fine," Hollis said. She was holding his head into her shoulder. "This is actually a little uncomfortable."

But she continued to hold him, his feet dangling a foot off the floor, the laces of one sneaker untied and the other foot still shoeless.

"Mom," he said.

She lowered him back onto the bed, and his parents just stood and stared at him.

"What happened to you, buddy?" his father asked. "Are you hurt?"

"Never better," the boy replied, as he continued to tie on his sneakers.

His mother took a seat next to him, close enough that you couldn't slip a piece of paper between them. "Honey, where have you been? How did you get in here?"

"New Mexico," Hollis answered. "We drove out to New Mexico."

"New Mexico?" his father parroted. "Did that lady drive you back here? What did she want?"

"Cha'Risa's still in New Mexico."

"What about Kirby, is he okay?"

"Kirby's home, too."

"We were so worried," his mother said, putting her arm around the boy's shoulders. "After that man tried to kill you... And then we figured maybe that woman who took you was going to do the same thing."

Hollis finished tying his shoes. He glanced at his mother, deep into her eyes. He had missed his parents like he'd never imagined he could. And it was good to be back. "Cha'Risa saved me. And the two agents..." He eyed his bookshelf, and in particular, a picture book on ancient Egyptian history. "We're not going to be seeing them again."

"Why not? Were they arrested?" His mother seemed unconvinced.

"Let's just say I hope they like sand."

"Well, we're going to have to call the police," his father said.

"You can't call them, Dad."

"What do you mean? They need to know you're back. There are a lot of people looking for you right now and somebody's gotta be held accountable for whatever happened to you and Kirby."

"Cha'Risa's one of the good guys. There's nobody to arrest."

"You don't know what you're talking about Hollis. This is one of those times that adults know better." His father turned for the door, but Hollis grabbed his arm.

"I'm serious, Dad. The people that tried to kill me were with the government. If you tell the police I'm here, they'll find out and they'll try to kill me again."

"Honey," his mother said. "That woman filled your head up with lies. She might have seemed nice, but she needs help."

"We're going to have to agree to disagree on that one," Hollis said.

"Buddy," his father began. "You know we only want what's best for you, right? Whatever that woman told you was just made up. I don't know who those supposed agents were, but the government doesn't kill innocent American kids."

"Not usually," Hollis replied. "Look, this is going to be embarrassing for me, but you need to know that this is all real." With that, his clothes fell silently onto the bed, his sneakers dropping with thumps onto the floor, socks still in them. With no body to hold it up anymore, his mother's arm fell before her muscles instinctually stopped it midair. A look of horror shot across their faces. They'd lost him once before and now he had up and vanished right before their eyes. But a noise from his bureau drew their attention. Hollis was standing naked, the medallion in his grasp, pulling out a set of underwear from the top drawer. "Don't look," he said, pulling them on. "I said this would be embarrassing."

The boy grabbed a pair of slacks from the bureau and slid one leg into them. "I think I'm going to name the new planet Fern."

His parents were having a hard time processing the boy's apparently magical transportation.

Hollis pulled the other leg through the pants and buttoned them up. "Look, I have a lot to tell you about what happened after I left, but there are bigger fish to fry."

His father plumped down on the bed next to his mother, both of their jaws agape.

"Cha'Risa's already waiting for us. How do you guys feel about living in Central America?"

~ ~ ~ ~ ~ ~ ~ ~ ~ ~

Wednesday, August 22, 1945

"Where is it?" Margaret snarled.

Eleanor's eyes didn't move.

"I thought I shot her in the side," said the man.

Margaret grabbed Eleanor's shoulder and pulled, exposing a back caked in dried leaves and a bullet hole directly in its center spurting out blood. Then she let go and the injured woman flopped back onto the ground. Margaret shot the man an angry scowl. "Well, you missed."

They glared at Eleanor. "Double check," Margaret said.

The man bent over Eleanor and ripped open her blouse, buttons popping off with the force. Enraged, he reached down to the bottom of her skirt and yanked it up. Eleanor let out moans of pain as he pulled her torso off the ground and continued jerking at the garment until it was bunched up around her waist. "Look for yourself!" he bawled.

Margaret kicked Eleanor's leg, which didn't even get a reaction from the incapacitated woman. "What did you do with it?"

Eleanor's breathing was short; her eyes had begun to glaze over. Margaret hovered over her for a few seconds, then leaned over and slapped Eleanor's face, knocking it to the side. It didn't rouse her. "Where is it?" Margaret seethed.

Nothing.

Margaret stood up straight, eyes widening, reached her arm out and took hold of the pistol the lead man had in his holster. The man relinquished the weapon without a word.

Margaret placed her foot in the center of Eleanor's bra and shifted her weight onto it, causing groans of pain and increased gurgling.

Eleanor rolled her head toward Margaret. The added weight on her chest made it impossible to breath.

"Goddammit!" Margaret screamed, her eyes wild and piercing, dragging Eleanor out of her listlessness. The two women glared at each other. Margaret pointed the gun at Eleanor's head, and put more of her weight on the dying woman's chest. The pain was unbearable for Eleanor. Her eyes rolled up in her skull. And Margaret pulled the trigger.

Eleanor's clothes dropped, her body having vanished. Margaret's bullet shot straight into the earth.

She straightened herself out in shock. "What the hell happened to her? Where did she go?"

"Jesus," the man said. He moved in, kicking at the clothes lying crumpled on the ground.

"She was here. She was right goddamned here!" Margaret cried. She emptied the gun into Eleanor's now discarded clothing, cursing all the while. "Goddammit! Somebody's head is going to roll for this and it isn't goddamned going to be mine."

The lead man glanced back and met eyes with one of the other agents closer to the road.

CPSIA information can be obtained
at www.ICGtesting.com
Printed in the USA
LVHW040809260720
661549LV00001B/97